THE
AGENT

OTHER TITLES BY MARK DAWSON

MARK **DAWSON**

THE AGENT

AN ISABELLA ROSE THRILLER

THOMAS & MERCER

Text copyright © 2017 Mark Dawson
All rights reserved.

Published by Thomas & Mercer, Seattle

www.apub.com

Amazon, the Amazon logo, and Thomas & Mercer are trademarks of Amazon.com, Inc., or its affiliates.

ISBN-13: 9781477818022
ISBN-10: 1477818022

Cover design by Stuart Bache

Printed in the United States of America

Prologue

C ome on,' Michael Pope urged. 'We have to get out.'

Isabella Rose carefully peeled back the edge of the dressing on Pope's arm. 'When I've finished this,' she said.

'Be quick.'

She pulled the dressing away and inspected the wound on the underside of Pope's right arm. He had been stabbed, the blade of a kitchen knife sliding into his triceps. It had been nineteen days since the fight in the apartment. He had been unwell on the flight from Rome to Mumbai, but it had been on the train south to Palolem that the infection had really taken hold. They had disembarked at Kankavli and Isabella had found a hospital for him. The doctors had treated him for a week and they had continued south again just as soon as he was able to travel.

They had been in Palolem for eleven days.

And now they were moving again.

Pope flinched as she prodded the wound. 'What did they look like?'

'I told you,' Isabella said as she soaked a wad of gauze in saline solution and wiped the skin with it.

'Tell me again.'

'Two white males. First one was in his forties, the second was younger. The first one had ginger hair and a sunburn; he can't have been in the country for long.'

'And?'

'They were driving a hired car. There was a sticker in the window.'

'You're sure?'

'I watched them for five minutes, Pope. They were going up and down and asking questions. Showing people photographs. They were looking for someone.'

Pope rapped his fist against the table with the same irritation that he had evinced earlier.

'Hold still,' Isabella chided.

She inspected the wound. It was healing. The infection had gone and the physical damage from the stabbing was slowly being repaired. It was still badly bruised, and she noticed how he winced when he moved his arm without thinking, but it was improving. She patted the area dry with a pad of tissues, applied a fresh dressing and wrapped a bandage around it to hold it in place.

'Finished?'

'You're very impatient,' she said.

Pope took his shirt and put it on. 'I know, and I'm sorry about that, but we need to go. We don't have a weapon. They will. And it'll be easy enough for them to find us if they ask the right questions.'

They had concocted a story on the journey south: Pope would be Isabella's father. Her real father had died over a decade ago, shot in the head while she watched. Isabella had been abducted after that, her mother fleeing before she shared the same fate as her husband. Beatrix was dead now, too. Isabella had no one. Pope was the nearest thing she had to family.

He took a bag and stuffed in the things that they would need: their money, travel documents, the sheaf of papers that Isabella had printed in Palolem's Internet cafe. There were news stories and grabs from conspiracy sites. There were emails, too. One of Pope's contacts had confirmed that his wife and children were alive. They had been taken from the apartment not long before Pope and Isabella had been attacked.

Isabella looked around the simple hut that had been their home for the last eleven days. It was basic, but they had made it more than comfortable enough to serve their purposes. They only really used it to sleep and cook, spending most of their time outside. The door opened directly on to the beach, a glorious stretch of sand that curved away in both directions in the shape of a broad sickle. The hut was three miles from town, and Isabella had made it her morning routine to run there and back. The sea was clear and warm, and Isabella finished her exercise by swimming to the uninhabited island that lay three hundred yards out from the beach.

Pope went outside and checked that they were not being observed. He led the way along the path. Isabella had left the scooter on the coast road, above the steps that led down to the beach. Pope put a hand on her shoulder and ascended first, waiting at the top to check again before getting on to the vehicle and sliding forward so that there was space for her behind him.

'Ready?' he said.

Pope started the engine. Isabella glanced back to the beach and saw the ospreys and kites drifting on the thermals above the water. She had known that she and Pope would have to move on eventually, if only to try to draw together the scraps of evidence that might give a clue as to where his family had been taken, but it was peaceful here and she would have liked to stay for longer. However, Pope had warned her that the people looking for them would be relentless, as had been proved.

She put her arms around his waist and held on.

PART ONE:

Washington, DC

Chapter One

Senator Jack Coogan opened his mail and looked at the message he had received yesterday afternoon at 5.43 p.m. It sat there, in its own private folder, a single line of text displayed in the preview pane with a paper clip icon next to it denoting an attachment. The email had been sent to his private account.

> LINUS GOSLING
> To: Jack Coogan
> Senator,
> Be at the Greene Turtle tomorrow at 2200.
> Let's talk about Katie.

Coogan had never heard of Linus Gosling. He had been drilled on the importance of not opening attachments sent from accounts that he didn't recognise, but those final four words had hit him like a sledgehammer. He had stared at the email for five minutes, his finger hovering over the zipped file, before he had succumbed and opened it.

It wasn't a virus.

It was much worse than that.

The attachment contained photographs and pictures of scanned documents. The photographs were of the intern that he had once been seeing. It had been so long ago – and there were so many women with whom Coogan had had relationships – that he'd almost forgotten about her. Her name was Katie, and, as he recalled, she'd been fun until he'd lost interest.

The photos of her face showed bruises around her eyes, a purple contusion on her right cheekbone and blood around her nostrils. The ones of her body showed bruises down her ribs and on her arms and nasty welts on her back. There was a written statement from the girl, where she described in detail what Coogan had done. It was the same statement that she had sent to him with the threatening note a week after he had broken up with her. She said she wanted paying or else she would take everything to the police department's sexual assault unit.

Coogan was a young and ambitious senator from Massachusetts. He had enjoyed a stratospheric rise through the party. He was beloved in Boston. He had a big place in Hyannis Port, just like the one Teddy Kennedy had owned. The girl could have taken it all away from him. Paying her off was not an option. Coogan couldn't be sure that she wouldn't shake him down again.

Plan B.

She had brought it on herself.

Coogan had an old army friend from his time in the 1st Cavalry Division who'd got himself into debt with the East Cleveland dealers who serviced his meth habit. Coogan had paid the man fifty grand in return for shutting her mouth.

Katie had been found dead in her apartment, suffocated while she slept. The police investigated, but there was no connection between her and her killer, and he had been careful enough to leave no evidence behind.

The case went cold.

That should have been the end of it.

But it wasn't.

Another email had arrived ten minutes after the first.

LINUS GOSLING
To: Jack Coogan
Senator,
In case you doubt my bona fides.

This one had an attachment, too.

A video file.

Coogan's friend talked to the camera and laid out what the senator had asked him to do and how he had gone about doing it.

Coogan opened the emails again and again. It was like a scab that he couldn't resist picking. It was as if opening them might exorcise them and turn the clock back, make it all how it was before.

It didn't.

He thought about ignoring the invitation.

He knew that he couldn't.

Chapter Two

The Greene Turtle was a dive right by the Verizon Center. The Caps had been at home tonight, so it was busy with fans looking for a drink to drown their sorrows after they had gone down 3–2 to the Hurricanes. Highlights of the game played on screens above the bar, soundtracked by jeers and boos as Jeff Skinner slapped home the winning goal.

Coogan wasn't watching the game. He was sitting on a stool at the bar, turned around so that he could face the room.

He looked at his watch: a minute after ten.

He only noticed the man as he sat down next to him. He had come from the direction of the men's room and was dressed scruffily in a military jacket, ripped jeans and with a frayed cap pulled down low on his head.

'Good evening, Senator.'

Coogan stared at the man. He was unshaven and his thick, black-framed glasses were held together by a twist of duct tape. The cap looked as if it was an eighties original; Coogan recognised the logo of Atari on the front.

'No pleasantries,' Coogan snapped. 'Let's not pretend this is something it isn't. You're blackmailing me.'

The man held his hands apart and gave a shrug. 'True enough. But we had to get your attention. Would you have come tonight if you had a choice?'

'Of course not. I don't even know who you are.'

'There's a group of us. I'm just the representative. We're all very keen to work with you. I'd much rather we cooperated out of a mutual love for our country, but you shouldn't be in any doubt: if you don't cooperate, we'll ruin you.'

'How did you do it?'

'Get the evidence?' The man waved his hand dismissively. 'Simple enough. Katie put everything into Dropbox before you had her killed. And your friend just can't help himself where money is concerned. He's got into trouble again. We bought the debt from the man he owed. Moved him out of Cleveland in case you had any ideas that you might be able to shut him up, too. You won't be able to find him now.'

'I'll deny it,' Coogan said.

The man's eyes glittered darkly in the shadow cast by the peak of his cap. 'Good luck with that.'

Coogan found that he was clenching the sides of his stool. 'How much do you want?'

'Money? We don't want money. Couldn't be further from the truth.'

'So what do you want?'

The man leaned forward. 'I've got good news for you, Senator. You are to be appointed as the new chairman of the Emerging Threats and Capabilities Subcommittee of the Armed Forces Committee.'

'What? Bullshit.'

'I know, crazy, isn't it? A man like you. But it's going down. Gonna happen tomorrow.'

'How could you possibly know that?'

'Because Senator Lennox is going to step down. He's going to say that he's unwell. That's not the real reason, of course. He's been schtupping a junior lobbyist. He used taxpayer money to take her on trips, including an official visit to India and paying for her as a member of "staff", when in fact everyone knows she was no such thing. He knows what would happen if we put that information out there. We could really fuck him up. He decided to do the right thing. Get out with what's left of his honour still intact.'

The man caught the eye of the bartender and ordered a rum and Coke. Coogan sat on the stool next to him. He felt the pounding of the blood thundering around his head and the heat in his cheeks. He wanted to be anywhere else but here, although he knew that he had to stay; he was trapped.

The bartender delivered the drink and the man took a sip.

He rested the glass on the bar and looked at the scratched digital watch on his wrist. 'Ten past ten. The senator is going to call you within twenty minutes to explain that he is stepping down. And he's going to tell you that he's arranged for the Democratic caucus to recommend you as his replacement.'

'I can't—'

'I know, Senator Coogan, you'd rather be out on your boat than doing the work that you've been elected to do, but you're going to take this very seriously from now on.'

He tried to see the man's face under the shadow of his cap. 'What? What do you want?'

'Senator Lennox has been abusing his position. He's been in the pay of the industry that he agreed to oversee. He's been keeping the focus off areas of defence funding that we believe require close forensic oversight. Spending on research that we think the American public deserves to know about. All we want is to provoke a debate. That's your job. That's how you're going to help us.'

'How?'

'The military's black budget this year is nearly sixty billion dollars. Your committee is responsible for the allocation of four billion dollars to the Defense Advanced Research Projects Agency. Some of that money is funnelled to classified projects.'

'That's public knowledge.'

'Yes, but this isn't.' The man reached into the inside pocket of his scruffy jacket and took out a folded piece of paper. He left it on the bar. 'There's a company headquartered in Delaware. Daedalus Genetics. They say they're developing genetic therapies to fight a host of diseases: cancer, AIDS, cystic fibrosis, Parkinson's and Alzheimer's diseases, amyotrophic lateral sclerosis, cardiovascular disease and arthritis. Very laudable. And some of it is true. But it's not all they do. Look at the paper, Senator.'

Coogan unfolded the paper. It was a copy of a bank transfer. The names of the remitting and receiving companies were unknown to him, although the reference – TRACTOR NAIL – was the kind of meaningless designation that he was used to seeing when the Pentagon wished to play hide-and-seek with its budgets.

The amount that had been transferred was large: just short of a billion dollars.

Coogan was still looking down at the paper when his cell phone rang in his pocket.

'That'll be Senator Lennox.'

Coogan glanced at the screen.

'Better take it.'

Coogan accepted the call and put the phone to his ear.

'*Jack?*' the voice on the other end of the line said.

'Who's this?'

'*It's Jim Lennox. How you doing?*'

Coogan found that his mouth was dry. 'I'm fine,' he managed to say. 'It's late. What's going on?'

'*Look, I don't want to drop this on you like this, but I've got some news I wanted to get to you before you hear it from anyone else. I'm stepping down from the subcommittee. Between you and me, I had a heart attack a month*' ago. *Not a big one, but enough for me to decide that I want to take things a little easier from now on. That means there's going to be a vacancy in the chair, and I can't think of anyone better qualified to take it up than you.'*

The senator didn't like Coogan. He'd always made that very plain.

'*I've recommended you to the party,'* Lennox went on. '*They agreed. I'm going to make the announcement tomorrow. I'd like you to be on the Hill so we can make the announcement together. Sound good?'*

'Yes,' he said. 'I can do that.'

'*Great. Swing by my office at midday. We'll do it then.'*

The call ended.

Coogan looked across at the man in the cap.

'Believe me now?' the man said.

'Why are you doing this?'

He waved the question away. 'Your first act as chair of the subcommittee will be to establish an emergency oversight hearing into the work that Daedalus is doing. We're going to provide you with evidence that will demonstrate that elements within the US government are responsible for providing significant funding to private projects of absolutely fundamental importance to what it means to be human.'

'What are they doing?'

'They're building monsters, Senator. And we are going to stop them.'

PART TWO:
Skopje

Chapter Three

Vivian Bloom had taken a room in the Marriott at Plostad Makedonija in the middle of Skopje.

Bloom had been to Macedonia before, back when he was based at Moscow Station. He had visited the city under the pretext of negotiating the import of agricultural equipment. Western businesses had not been as prevalent in the city in the eighties as they were now, and he remembered that the building that now housed the hotel had once been a dowdy department store that had been notable only for the paucity of goods on its shelves. Times changed.

It was nine in the morning. He looked down from the window of his room on the fifth floor. Rain poured down from iron skies, and the men and women on the pavements of the main square hurried about their business, sheltering beneath umbrellas. The Old Bazaar was within easy walking distance and, just visible through the sheets of rain, the bulk of Mount Vodno loomed over everything. Bloom had hiked to the top of the mountain the last time he had visited. He was in his forties then, fit and hale, but he was older now and clambering up the path to the top was something he knew would be beyond him.

It had been a difficult couple of days. Bloom had been in New York to attend a debriefing on the Italian operation.

The senior participants in the project wanted answers to explain why events had not proceeded as they had intended. 'Help me understand why this went so badly wrong,' was Jamie King's typically passive-aggressive instruction at the end of the conference. There had been impatient references to loose ends and balls that had been dropped. Bloom had requested the assignment of a Daedalus asset to eliminate the surviving members of Group Fifteen, but that request had been parked while they worked out what had gone wrong in Montepulciano.

This all meant that they had lost a rogue agent and a fifteen-year-old girl somewhere in the Indian subcontinent and that he had a handful of dangerous men and women in a stood-down programme who might start to ask difficult questions.

So, yes. It had been a very difficult few days.

He had flown from JFK into Alexander the Great Airport the previous afternoon and had been picked up there and driven to the hotel in a bulletproof SUV by a driver who made no attempt to hide the pistol that was secured in a shoulder holster beneath his jacket. Bloom had looked out of the window as they had made their way into the city and, to his eye, not much had changed. The government's recent construction spree had provided new museums and other municipal buildings, but no amount of extravagant fountains and statuary could hide the poverty that was always just below the surface.

The staff spoke excellent English and the room, utilitarian and businesslike, could have been found in a similar chain in any other city of the world. The familiarity should have alleviated some of Bloom's trepidation, but, as he stared at the cars sluicing through the surface water on the road below, he found that it did not.

He was nervous.

He had slept badly and had had just a cup of black coffee for breakfast.

He looked at his watch.

Nine fifteen. He was due to be collected at nine thirty.

He went and sat on the edge of the bed and switched on the television. The hotel subscribed to CNN, the BBC and Sky News, and Bloom flicked between them. The same story was being covered on all three channels: the shooting down of the British Airways passenger jet bound for New York as it took off from Heathrow. Sources within the investigation were reporting that it was now confirmed that the incident was being treated as Islamic terrorism, a brutal coda to the attack on Westminster that had left hundreds of dead and wounded.

The anchors spoke over the footage that had initially been uploaded to YouTube by a member of the public who had unwittingly recorded the moment of the attack on the dashcam of his car. The surface-to-air missile could be seen streaking from the ground on a straight diagonal that intercepted the jet as it climbed from the runway. The explosion of the missile and the breaking up of the jet were all recorded; subsequent footage from Heathrow's observation lounge showed the separate pieces of the jet plummeting to the ground.

Bloom watched the footage with dispassion. He had seen it many times before – it was constantly being replayed, after all – and it had quickly lost any shock value that it might once have held. He regretted that it, and the Westminster assault, had been necessary, but he was certain that they were.

Bloom had become convinced. Something was required to disturb the public's numbing complacency so that they became aware of the threat that they faced. The failed British military campaign in Iraq was now seen as a terrible misadventure, a shameful moment in history that had wrecked the reputations of the politicians involved. It had created a parliament of craven isolationists and made it almost impossible to entertain a situation where they might sanction a similar expedition. Pacifists decried those who were calling for further intervention in Middle Eastern affairs as murdering crusaders, even as ISIS rampaged across borders and committed genocide in the name of Islam. Thousands marched on the streets in opposition to war, even as the death cult threatened to export its poisonous dogma to Europe and beyond. Bloom was privy to the classified governmental reports that set out the threat in apocalyptic terms.

Chemical weapons released in subways, killing thousands.

Dirty bombs spreading radiation across whole cities, rendering them uninhabitable for decades.

Bloom did not enjoy the success of the operations he had overseen. He regretted the men and women who had lost their lives. But they had been sacrificed for the greater good. Far better a few hundred deaths than the tens of thousands that would be lost if they did nothing.

His conscience was clear. The motives of some of the other players in their illicit coalition were less pure, but he had no trouble sleeping at night.

He collected the jacket of his tweed suit and his overcoat and, folding both garments over the crook of his elbow, he left the room and made his way to the elevator.

Chapter Four

Bloom waited in the reception. The rain hammered down, rivulets churning along the gutters and overflowing the drains so that sheets of water spread out across the street.

A car pulled up outside and flashed its lights. It was the same SUV that had delivered him to the hotel and, as Bloom hurried through the downpour beneath the umbrella that the doorman had offered him, he saw that the driver who opened the door for him was the same man as before. He was a blandly anonymous American who, Bloom suspected, most likely worked for Manage Risk, the private military contractor that provided the local security for the project.

There was another man waiting for him in the back of the car.

Jamie King.

'Morning, Vivian.'

'Good morning, Jamie.'

King was the CEO of Manage Risk, the largest private military contractor in the world. He was an ex-military man, still wore his hair close to his scalp, and he kept himself in good shape. He had the leonine cocksureness of a man worth several billion dollars.

'I didn't know you were coming,' Bloom said.

'Last-minute change of plan. I want to know what really happened in Italy.'

'I'm more than a little curious about that,' Bloom said.

The botched operation to eliminate Pope and Isabella in Italy had been on Bloom's mind since he had received the report. Pope and the girl had served their purpose. They had successfully planted the evidence that implicated Salim al-Khawari in the London bombings, allowing them to draw a line of responsibility that led back to ISIS. But al-Khawari had kidnapped the girl before the Americans could take him and had fled with her and his family to Lebanon. They had been forced to land in Turkey and then had been abducted themselves by an ISIS snatch squad. The family and the girl had been taken to Syria. Pope had found them again and that, in turn, allowed for Bloom and his co-conspirators to conclude the job. That was the end of Pope's usefulness. He should never have been allowed to leave the country. That he and Isabella had escaped was of concern to Bloom. They knew too much.

'What about Pope?' he asked. 'Any news?'

'Like we said, we lost them when they got to Mumbai.'

'It's a mess.'

'I know, Vivian. It's a fuck-up. A complete fuck-up. And it's concerning. But we'll get to the bottom of it. On the plus side, we have your man's family. He's not going to do anything as long as they're in play.'

'Where are they?'

King waved his hand. 'Riga. An old CIA black site. Place like this. We'll keep them on the move. There's no need to worry. And we'll flush him and the girl out. It's been almost three weeks. They can't stay hidden forever.' He shone Bloom one of his dazzlingly white pop star grins. 'Now, then. You said that you were concerned. You were worried with how the short-term projections were looking. You want to tell me why?'

'My intelligence is suggesting that the prime minister's appeal for assistance won't be answered. There was a CNN poll today. Did you see it? Seventy per cent of Americans are against getting involved.'

'None of this is a surprise. Once bitten, twice shy. No rational person would support sending troops back into that hellhole. It took long enough to get them out the first time. But we anticipated that, Vivian. Like I said in New York, we have a contingency.'

The subject had come up at the conference. 'You said it would be tomorrow.'

'We're pushing it back.'

'Why?'

'Timing's not right.'

Bloom didn't reply and looked glumly out of the window as they raced into the countryside on the eastern fringe of the city. The operation should have taken place today – that was what he had been promised – and now it was being delayed. He had thought that they had a grip on the narrative, but with the loose ends left in Syria and now this, it seemed that their grip was slackening. Without a corresponding American operation, he risked being left out in the cold.

'Cheer up, you miserable bastard,' King said. He took out a tablet and scrolled through his emails. 'You mentioned polls,' he said, passing the tablet to Bloom. 'You seen this one?'

Bloom looked down at the tablet. The document being displayed was the top-line summary of polling that had been carried out in London over the course of the last twenty-four hours. The conclusions were heartening. Public opinion was now reported to be heavily in favour of direct military action in Syria, Iraq and Libya. Non-intervention was no longer seen as defensible. The events of the last few weeks had made it impossible to argue for pacifism.

'This is good,' Bloom said. 'But we need the same thing to be happening in Washington.'

'Will you please take it easy? It's coming. We just got to do it right. It's not something you can rush. And the Islamists aren't going anywhere.'

Bloom thought of what was happening back home. He knew that pressure was being exerted on ministers for a debate to now take place. A vote would be taken to decide whether intervention should be scaled up from the present tokenist gestures that had never been satisfactory to him and the others within the project.

'We've got a thirty-minute drive,' King said. 'Read it all. It'll cheer you up.'

Chapter Five

The Daedalus campus comprised a series of buildings, low slung and sleekly futuristic, surrounded by a neatly planted line of trees that obscured the electrified fence that was just within their curtilage. There were armed Manage Risk guards within the grounds, and the signs that had been fastened to the mesh warned that this was private property and that lethal force was authorised to be used against intruders.

There was nothing to suggest the provenance of the facility; it had been provided to the CIA by Ion Eliade, the former President of Romania, as a goodwill gesture intended to smooth the way to the country's eventual accession to NATO. There were sister sites in the Ukraine, Latvia, Azerbaijan and Kazakhstan. Black projects like Prometheus required the discretion and latitude that could be provided in countries that were outside US territory and legal jurisdiction.

The driver stopped the SUV at the guardhouse while their credentials were checked. Bloom found himself staring ahead at the building behind the fence, at its windows with their smoked glass that reflected the bleak landscape and the gunmetal grey clouds.

The driver parked, stepped out and opened the doors. Bloom and King went through into the reception area. It was sleek, with a metallic desk that sat before a wall of smoked glass. They sat in the plush leather chairs that had been arranged on the other side of the room.

'Relax, old man,' King said. 'You're going to enjoy this. It's going to blow you away, I guarantee it.'

They did not have to wait long. A door in the glass wall opened, sliding aside with a gentle hiss to reveal a bright white room beyond. The man who emerged was wearing a white laboratory coat. He was tall and slender, with a shaven head and glasses that would not have looked out of place in the office of a San Francisco tech start-up. His name was Professor Nikita Valeryevich Ivanosky, and he was one of the senior staff responsible for Prometheus.

He went straight to King. 'Good morning,' he said.

'Nikita. You remember Vivian Bloom from the conference?'

'Of course. I'm pleased you could come, Mr Bloom. Welcome to Macedonia.' The professor's voice bore the subtle Russian accent that had not been rubbed away by the years that he had spent in the United States.

Bloom had studied the man's résumé on the flight. He had graduated from St Petersburg State Pavlov Medical University in 1968 and had then been a resident doctor at the maternity hospital in Norilsk. He had returned to his alma mater, where he became Professor of Obstetrics and Gynaecology before taking up a similar position at the University Hospital in Addis Ababa, Ethiopia. He'd made contact with the US embassy and claimed asylum after a year in Africa; Bloom had seen his name and those of his family on the passenger list of the CIA flight that had taken him to Mozambique and then on to the United States.

His history became a little more opaque after his defection. Everything was confidential, but the documents that had been provided to Bloom touched on the high points. Ivanosky had been responsible for the classified research that had cloned a sheep from an adult somatic cell. He had gone further, abandoning somatic cell nuclear transfer in favour of a new technique that he had pioneered that allowed him to derive pluripotent stem cells from differentiated adult skin cells, avoiding the need to generate embryonic stem cells. This had accelerated the speed of his research into genome editing and the genetic modification of human embryos and other tissues. That was his focus now.

The professor's pleasantries were perfunctory and he quickly disregarded Bloom in favour of King. He had a keen understanding of who was responsible for the funding of his work.

'How was your flight?' he asked.

'Awful,' King said.

'And your hotel?'

'Distinctly average. Still haven't found one here that I like.'

'Macedonia would like you to think that it is a civilised country, but it is a backwater. It is not the most comfortable of venues for our work, but there is a certain amount of discretion that can be bought. It is worth the inconvenience.'

King waved that away. 'Shall we get on with it?'

'Yes, of course. I hope I can make your visit worthwhile.'

'Vivian hasn't been here before,' King said. 'Let's show him the highlights.'

'Indeed. It would be a pleasure. I think you'll be impressed, Mr Bloom. This way, please.'

King and Bloom followed Ivanosky as he went back into the bright white room behind the glass wall. There was another door with a palm reader, and they waited as the professor placed his hand flat against it. The backlit display changed from red to green, and the door slid open to reveal an elevator car.

The three men went inside. There were five buttons on the elevator, each floor described by a brief legend.

The professor pressed a button. The notation beside it read 'Level One: Zoology'.

The elevator started to descend.

Ivanosky turned to Bloom. 'This might not be the most pleasant venue, but it has its advantages,' he said. 'Progress has been much faster without having to concern ourselves with the burdens of regulatory oversight.'

'Or ethics.'

'Ethics have a place, of course, but they can have the unfortunate consequence of acting as a brake on progress. We still have a distance to go, but I am confident that we are making very significant progress. This is the frontier, in many ways. The cutting edge. The work that has already been done in this building will change how we look at many things. And we are at the very edge of what will eventually be possible.'

Ivanosky stepped out of the elevator.

'Shall we?'

Chapter Six

Level one was about five yards underground and off-limits to all except those with the highest clearance. The corridor ahead was all white – floor, walls and ceiling – with hidden lights running in recessed strips where the walls met the ceiling. It was impressive, just as everything in the complex was impressive. Bloom had heard estimates of how much the operation had cost. It was certainly in the billions, the money funnelled from black budgets and hidden from political oversight beneath layers and layers of obfuscation and subterfuge.

'I'm going to show you our baboons,' the professor said as he led the way along the corridor.

They came to an airlock that the professor unlocked using another palm reader. The air hissed out of the vents and the door slid aside. They stepped inside and waited in the chamber as the door closed behind them. Bloom heard the buzz of the scrubbers that cleaned the air and, after a minute, the interior door opened.

The change was immediate and striking. The sterile, white walls on the other side of the airlock were replaced by a rough concrete finish. The cool, sanitised atmosphere was immediately polluted by a heavy, pervasive smell of musk. Bloom could smell urine and excrement, too, so striking that he almost found himself gagging. Ivanosky made no mention of it and led the way along the corridor. He reached an opening and stopped. King and Bloom caught up with him and looked out. The level was cavernous, with a walkway encircling a series of walled spaces that must have enclosed an acre. Natural light was provided by a light well in the middle of the vaulted ceiling, the illumination augmented by powerful arc lamps that were positioned around the room. The walkway continued around the periphery of the space, offering a series of lookout points where staff could observe the activity in the spaces beneath them.

Ivanosky led them down a flight of stairs to an open passageway that bisected the circular floor space. A second passageway met theirs in the centre of the room, dividing the circle into four equally sized quadrants. The walls were open at the top and punctuated at regular intervals by large windows. The thick panes of glass were clean on this side, but smudged and dirty on the other. Bloom saw tracks that had been scored into the material by sharp objects, and smears of excrement that had been rubbed across the panels.

'We have four pens,' the professor explained as he led the way along the passageway. 'Each pen can accommodate a troop of baboons.'

'How many do you have?'

'Just over a hundred in two troops.'

Ivanosky stopped and turned to the right. Bloom looked into the pen. There was a collection of rocks that had been arranged into a steep pile, tree stumps, and a rope that had been erected six feet above the muck and dirt with tyres strung along it. He saw baboons, the big monkeys arranged throughout the space. The baboons shared certain characteristics: long, canine muzzles and, beneath them, prominent jaws that were lined with sharp teeth. They had thick fur except for at their muzzles and short tails. Their buttocks protruded, with rough, hairless pads of skin that provided comfortable seats when they rested. Bloom watched, fascinated, as they interacted with one another. One of them loped over to one of the suspended tyres and heaved itself aloft with an easy tug of its long arms. Others lounged on the rocks, picking at food that had been left for them: baskets of fruit and vegetables and sides of rotting meat.

'These are chacma baboons,' Ivanosky said. 'Old World monkeys, part of the subfamily Cercopithecidae. *Papio ursinus ursinus.* Native to Africa and Asia and adaptable with regards to their environment: they can be found in rainforest, on the savannah, in shrub land and on mountain terrain. They are omnivorous, with a preference for meat if they can get it. Our baboons are from South Africa. They were raiding villages, taking lambs and goats. There were reports that small children had been taken, too. The locals were shooting them. Save lions and crocodiles, they have no other natural predators.'

The baboon that had been swinging on the tyre noticed them and dismounted. It came close to the glass and pressed both hands against it. It had small, close-set eyes, glassy black orbs beneath a lowered brow, and obscenely pink lips that were pursed as if in an expression of contemplation. The fur was a little thinner on the baboon's arms and chest, and Bloom could see the bulges of well-developed musculature beneath it. Bloom locked eyes with it for a moment before the baboon drew back its hands and slammed its palms repeatedly against the window. The glass looked thick, but it quivered with each blow. The baboon flashed its eyelids and displayed its ugly teeth with exaggerated yawns. It screeched, a high-pitched clamour that filled the holding area. The other baboons joined in, too, and the screeching and barking very quickly became almost unbearable.

Ivanosky tolerated it for a moment and then held up his hand. The baboon stopped shrieking at once, and, within seconds, the others also stopped. Ivanosky lowered his hand, the baboon following it with his eyes. The animal looked up, found Bloom again, and pulled back its pink lips to reveal a jagged upthrusting of sharp teeth. It put them together in a gruesome smile. Bloom felt a moment of unease.

It was as if the baboon were speaking to him.

If you were on the other side of this cage, I could rend you limb from limb.

'Baboons are ideal for our purposes,' Ivanosky explained. 'The scientific community has been using them for years. They are ideal research models for the study of common complex diseases: dyslipidaemia, hypertension, osteoporosis, obesity. And species with similar phylogenetic relationships to humans like this not only share biological characteristics, but also have many of the same genes influencing relevant phenotypes operating on a similar genetic background. Biologic processes associated with reproduction, growth, development, maturation and senescence in baboons differ very little from those in humans. The baboon heart is so similar to a human's in function and size that it was used in early xenotransplantations. Lipid, lipoprotein and carbohydrate metabolism and disorders associated with their disruption are very similar in the two species.'

'In English, Professor?'

'The genetic similarities make them ideal for perfecting the new techniques that we are developing. They are also extremely aggressive.'

'I can see that,' Bloom said.

Ivanosky was so engaged with his explanation that he was seemingly unaware of Bloom's discomfort. 'We have found that to be particularly interesting. We have been able to identify the baboon gene connected to aggressive behaviour.'

'All right,' King said. 'Enough of the zoo. Let's go and see what it means in practice.'

Chapter Seven

Ivanosky led the way back to the stairs. The baboons started to bark and whoop as they retreated, and as they reached the top, Bloom turned to look back. The animals had drawn together, gazing in their direction. They hopped and jumped and slapped their palms against their barrel chests. He felt fresh unease and was glad when he heard the hiss of the airlock. He turned away and hurried after the other two men.

'The infirmary is on level four,' Ivanosky said, pressing the requisite button.

The elevator descended again, smooth and silent.

Bloom couldn't stop thinking about the monkeys.

'The baboons are test subjects?' he asked.

'Partly. Like I said, their genome is very similar. It's the reason I've been working with them for so long. Once we remapped it, we realised that there were enough points of similarity that they would be well suited to that purpose.'

The doors parted and the automated concierge relayed a warning that Bloom found unsettling.

'*Warning. Authorised personnel only. Biological hazards present.*'

The white-walled corridor led to the left and right. Ivanosky went right.

He continued to speak. 'Let me try to explain it as best I can. Baboons have forty-two chromosomes arranged into twenty-one pairs. What we've been able to do is add a forty-third. It's possible to modify the genetics of an organism without that forty-third, but having it there makes it easier. Think of it as a scaffold. We can add new genetic modules to the scaffold and remove old ones when they are obsolete. We have been able to significantly adapt the genome and then either switch on or switch off the modifications with a simple injection.'

They passed several doors before they reached one that was stencilled with the legend 'Infirmary Number One'. The professor put his eye to the retinal scanner next to the door, held it there until his eye was successfully scanned and then stepped back. The door unlocked and opened.

'Messing around with monkeys is one thing,' King said.

'Of course,' Ivanosky agreed. 'It was our starting point. But we've managed to do the same thing with the human genome.'

Ivanosky pulled the door all the way back and held it open for King and Bloom.

Bloom went inside. The door accessed an observation suite that looked down upon an infirmary. He stepped up to the curved window and looked inside. There was a bed flanked by rows of medical equipment. A woman was sitting on the edge of the bed.

'Is that her?' Bloom asked.

'That's Maia,' Ivanosky said.

Bloom had never seen the woman before. She was a little taller than average. Five foot nine or ten, he guessed. She was slender with long hair that was woven into a French braid. She was wearing a hospital gown that was fastened at the back by two ties. The ties had not been pulled tight, and Bloom could see her naked shoulders, back and coccyx. There was another person in the room with Maia. She was wearing a white smock and was inspecting Maia's shoulder. She loosened the ties and pulled the gown down so that she could examine her back more carefully.

The asset turned her head and stared straight at him. Bloom would not have described her as pretty, but there was an attractiveness to her rounded face. Her nose was very slightly flattened, but it was her eyes that detained him. He could see that they were brown, but instead of holding soulfulness, they were blank. She stared up at the window, her face inexpressive. Bloom felt a twist of nervousness in his gut.

'She can't see me, can she?'

'No, Mr Bloom. The glass is one-way.'

Maia was the asset that they had relied upon to tidy away the evidence of extra-governmental involvement in the recent events in London. The man called Mohammed had been the cut-out, the stooge that they would have relied upon had anything gone wrong, but his downing of Flight 117 had also signalled the end of his usefulness. His loyalty had been bought; a million dollars had been his price to kill hundreds of people. What would he do for two million? What would he say? He could ask for more, any request backed by the implicit threat that he knew far too much to be allowed to bear a grudge.

Maia had followed him throughout the first and second phases of the operation and, when his usefulness was at an end, she had eliminated him.

That task, at least, had been performed satisfactorily.

King was looking down at Maia and the woman treating her. 'Tell him about her.'

Ivanosky needed little encouragement; it was clear that he was inordinately proud of what he had achieved and what the asset represented. 'Maia was the first of the thirteenth iteration to show promise. We had seen levels of success before, even in the early days, but we were unable to maintain healthy and stable development. The hazards of germ line transmission of DNA modification are well known by now. The literature on transgenic animals contains numerous examples. The biology of each individual embryo is fundamentally altered by the genetic manipulation. We saw extensive perturbation of development. The disruption of normal gene development by the insertion of foreign DNA caused lack of eye development, lack of development of the semi-circular canals of the inner ear and anomalies of the olfactory epithelium, the tissue that mediates the sense of smell. We might have been able to find ways around those problems, but germ line introduction of improperly regulated genes also resulted in progeny with increased incidence of paediatric tumours.'

'They all died,' King added unnecessarily.

'Correct. From very nasty cancers. But the "M" cohort, on the other hand . . .' – Ivanosky paused and smiled – 'that has been very different. So far as we can ascertain, they have adapted to the improvements that we have made to their genome with no serious side effects.'

The woman in the smock went to collect a syringe from a small chrome table fixed to the end of the bed. She returned to Maia's side and gently rolled up her sleeve.

'Who is that?' Bloom asked.

'Aleksandra Litivenko. She's a doctor of experimental molecular embryology. She works exclusively with our female assets. Because we've made changes to the germ line, the women are particularly valuable. The genetic enhancements are already present in their eggs.'

'And what's she doing? What's she injecting?'

'One of the changes to the genome was to introduce genetic material from the monkeys. Their muscle twitch responses are faster than our own, for example. They are also more naturally aggressive, as you saw. We discovered that they have a mutation in a gene that makes an enzyme called monoamine oxidase A, or MAOA. The function of the enzyme is to break down norepinephrine and dopamine. A deficiency causes elevated levels of those neurotransmitters, and that stimulates the brain circuitry that encourages aggressive behaviour. There was a study twenty years ago in Holland. Twenty males within a large family unit were all discovered to have MAOA deficiencies. Affected males differed from unaffected males by increased impulsive and aggressive behaviours.'

'So what does that mean? You made sociopaths?'

King interceded: 'It means we can breed soldiers who are temperamentally well suited for the kinds of work they are asked to do.'

'Correct,' Ivanosky said. 'Some people might call it a side effect. We think of it as a benefit.'

'And the injection?'

'A very large dose of citalopram. It's a selective serotonin reuptake inhibitor.'

'For depression.'

'That's the usual use. But, in this case, it increases levels of serotonin and balances out the dopamine and norepinephrine. They have it every week. It keeps them level.'

'When we want them a little bit more dangerous, we just decrease the dose,' King said. 'It's like an on-off switch.'

Ivanosky crossed the observation lounge to a two-way intercom. 'Let's see how she is,' he said, toggling the switch. 'Good morning, Doctor. It's Ivanosky. I'm here with Mr King and Mr Bloom, from London.'

The doctor looked up to the window and nodded her greeting. 'Good morning, gentlemen.'

'How is she?'

'The knife wound? She's healing as we would expect.'

Bloom had read the report. Isabella Rose had stabbed Maia in the shoulder and then the asset had jumped out of a third-floor window when it was clear that she needed to retreat. He could see her back as the doctor examined it; the wound had almost completely healed.

'When was she stabbed?'

'Nineteen days ago. Can you see? Can you see how fast she heals?'

'It's remarkable,' Bloom admitted.

Ivanosky spoke into the microphone. 'Thank you, Doctor. We'll leave you to it.'

Litivenko raised her hand in acknowledgement.

Ivanosky toggled the intercom off.

He turned to Bloom. 'What do you think?'

'Vivian thinks that you're creating monsters,' King suggested.

Ivanosky snorted. 'Monsters?'

Bloom shrugged.

'No,' Ivanosky said. 'Not monsters. We're making angels.'

Chapter Eight

D r Aleksandra Litivenko leaned closer and touched the wound with gentle fingers. 'How does it feel?'

'It feels normal,' Maia said.

The doctor wore a small voice recorder on her lapel. She activated it with a press of her thumb.

'This is Dr Aleksandra Litivenko with subject M-18273, referenced Maia. I'm conducting an examination of the subject's recent wound. To recap, subject was stabbed in the right shoulder. The blade pierced the skin over the deltoid muscle and was dragged down all the way to the triceps of the right arm. The incision was deepest at the shoulder, the blade withdrawing all the while as the subject twisted away from her attacker. The wound was inflicted nineteen days ago, yet cicatrisation is almost complete. The incision was shallower on the back of the subject's arm, and the wound there has healed. The deepest point of the incision was at the deltoid and that is healing, too. The subject reports that haemostasis clotted the blood within minutes. The inflammatory phase was completed fifteen days ago. White blood cells, growth factors, enzymes and nutrients have all diverted to the area in extraordinary amounts.'

Maia sat quietly on the side of the bed while Litivenko continued to record her observations.

'Exudate levels have receded. The signs of early-stage healing – erythema, heat, oedema, pain and functional disturbance – they are already gone. Proliferation is advanced. The wound is already being rebuilt. New granulation tissue is already being generated. Angiogenesis is progressing normally. The fibroblasts are receiving far more oxygen and nutrients than would be the case for a normal person, and much faster, too.'

She took a scalpel from the table. 'This might sting a little,' she warned.

'It's all right, Doctor.'

Aleksandra pressed the edge of the blade into the healthy new tissue. She had to push down a little before there was any sign of blood.

'I'm trying to draw blood with my scalpel. It shouldn't bleed easily, and it doesn't. The tissue is the right colour, no sign of poor perfusion, ischaemia or infection. The epithelial cells have almost resurfaced the wound.'

Maia turned her head. 'What does that mean, Aleksandra? Is it as it should be?'

'It means it's healing well. As we would expect.'

'That's good.'

'It certainly is. I understand the science, but I still find it remarkable what your body can do.'

She placed the scalpel back on the table and gently pushed Maia's head down so that she could look at the back of her neck. She ran her fingers over the skin and felt the small bump of the nano-transmitter between the C6 and C7 vertebrae. She had never grown used to the idea of it nestled there half a centimetre beneath the skin. Maia didn't seem to mind it being there – why should she, since it had first been implanted when she was a little girl? – but Litivenko hated what it signified. It made her think of slave collars or tattooed numbers, signifying both ownership and servitude. She found it obscene.

She took a breath and switched off the recorder.

'How long will I have to stay here?' Maia asked.

'Not long. How's your ankle?'

Maia held her leg aloft and flexed it. 'Fine. I have full range of movement.'

Litivenko swabbed antiseptic cream over the small wound she had made with her scalpel and then refreshed the dressing. Maia waited patiently, the muscles in her back and shoulders flexing occasionally. Her physique was remarkable. There was barely an ounce of fat on her and, despite the fact that she was only a little heavier than Litivenko, the doctor had seen how prodigiously strong she was. Skeletal muscle, the muscle that was targeted in strength and conditioning exercises, typically made up around 45 per cent of the average person's body weight. Maia – and the other subjects in the cohort – had levels of around 55 per cent, and that muscle was served by much more efficient blood vessels that supplied hugely increased levels of nutrients and energy. It made them stronger, faster and more resilient than any subject Litivenko had ever studied before.

She taped the dressing around Maia's shoulder.

'Comfortable?'

'Yes. Thank you.'

Litivenko glanced self-consciously around the sterile laboratory. She knew that there were microphones and cameras everywhere, and she was acutely aware that Ivanosky might still be in the observation suite. Privacy was not a luxury that Maia had ever been accorded, and it meant that Litivenko would have to choose her words carefully.

'What happened out there?' she said.

'What do you mean, Aleksandra?'

The use of her first name still occasionally caught her by surprise. Maia was so dispassionate that any familiarity stood out. Litivenko found it unsettling, even though it was she who had told Maia that she should use it. Maia was excessively formal with everyone else: the doctors at Daedalus were all accorded their formal titles whenever she spoke to them or even referred to them in conversation with others. Litivenko had worked with Maia for ten years. Her main function was to address her from the standpoint of embryology, but she had effectively become her personal physician. Maia had been an eleven-year-old girl when their relationship had commenced. Litivenko remembered it very well: the girl had been quiet, preternaturally intense, and she never smiled. Conversation had been difficult. Litivenko had found the situation uncomfortable and, despite very clear warnings from Ivanosky that it would be dangerous to form an attachment, she had insisted that Maia call her by her first name.

It was a small thing, but it helped. Despite early discomfort, the girl had quickly adapted to the suggestion. Litivenko had been pleased, but, after the first few operations when she had learned exactly what Maia was capable of doing, she had wondered if a strictly professional relationship might have been better, after all. Perhaps she would have been better with a buffer between them. Perhaps Ivanosky had been right.

But Maia had no one else. She was just a girl, albeit a very unusual one, and Litivenko couldn't withdraw from her.

She looked up at the blank eye of the observation camera on the wall above them. She guided Maia across to the room's table and two chairs and indicated that they should sit. 'The operation. What happened?'

'I explained it when I was debriefed.'

The camera's motor whirred as it adjusted so that they could continue to be filmed. 'I know,' Litivenko said. 'I read the report. But they're saying it doesn't make sense, and I have to say, Maia, I know what they mean. It was Michael Pope and a teenage girl. Just two of them. And you had the advantage of surprise. It should have been easy. Was there anything else?'

'She had a gun,' Maia said, repeating the line that she had used again and again with the analysts who had debriefed her.

'But you let her get it.'

'Yes, Aleksandra. I made a mistake.'

'You don't make mistakes.'

'This time, I did.'

'There was nothing else? No other reason for what happened?'

Maia paused, her jawline bulging almost imperceptibly as she bit down. 'No, Aleksandra,' she said. 'I made a mistake. That was it. There's no other reason.'

Litivenko didn't believe her. She lowered her voice even more. 'If there *was* something else to explain what happened, you have to keep it to yourself. If they think you're flawed in some way, if they think you can't be relied upon to complete your orders, they'll have no further use for you. You understand what that means, don't you, Maia?'

Litivenko wondered whether Maia was about to tell her something new, but instead she turned her head a fraction to look up at the camera and then looked back down to face her again. Maia held her gaze for a moment, long enough for Litivenko to recognise that she would have said more but for the fact that they were being observed.

'It was a mistake,' she said.

'All right, Maia. I understand. I just want you to be careful.'

She rose from the chair; Maia did, too.

'Why are you talking like this, Aleksandra?' she said. 'I don't understand.'

'There's no reason.' Litivenko collected the clipboard with her notes from the table.

'Is everything all right?'

She swallowed, finding that her throat was suddenly dry. 'I have to go now.'

'You seem concerned about something. Is it something I've done?'

'No, Maia. Nothing at all. You should rest. Try to get some sleep.'

'When will I be sent out again?'

'A week, maybe two.'

'Will I see you tomorrow?'

'Of course you will.'

'That's good.'

'Why do you say that?'

She smiled shyly; the grin came awkwardly to her lips, as if it were something she was trying out for the first time. 'I only have you to talk to, don't I?'

'You can talk to the other doctors.'

'It isn't the same.'

Litivenko tried to swallow. 'Get some rest,' she said. 'It'll help finish your recovery. I'll see you later.'

Maia nodded and watched as Litivenko made her way to the airlock. The doctor stooped to the retinal scanner and waited as the light played across her eye, leaving a tracer of blue that only went away when she blinked.

Despite everything – despite all the evidence of Maia's murderous potential – Litivenko still found herself harbouring tender thoughts towards her patient. Maternal thoughts. Maia was just a rat in a cage. She did as she was told. She followed orders without question, unthinkingly loyal. But, sometimes, when they were together and Litivenko could steer their conversations towards topics that were not connected to Maia's physiology or the things that she was tasked to do, she saw flashes of vulnerability. Maia was just twenty-one years old. She had been in the programme from the moment of her conception. She had been taught that she did not own her body or her mind. She was chattel, practically stamped with a barcode. She had no independence. No life.

That might all be true, but Litivenko doubted that even the programme that had moulded Maia into the weapon that she had become could completely erase the things that still made her human.

She cast her mind back to the Snapchat conversation she'd had with William, her husband, when he had made the suggestion that they betray Daedalus and leave. He had explained that the encryption was unbreakable and that they were safe to talk, but seeing the words on the screen still felt reckless. It also made the idea real.

William had worked hard to persuade her.

She knew that he was right, but still she had said no.

There were two reasons for her reluctance.

The first?

She was the only person in the facility who cared for Maia.

The second?

It was fear.

Chapter Nine

Litivenko took the elevator up to the third floor and emerged into the corridor with the offices that served the senior research staff. Her office was at the end of the corridor. One wall of the room was taken up with a picture window that offered a view of the countryside and, in the distance, the lights of Skopje. The skies were grey, veined with regular crackles of lightning. The storm had arrived first thing this morning and it showed no signs of moving on. Rain lashed down, smearing the glass, and rumbles of thunder boomed across the bleak hills. It was inauspicious weather, but, she thought, particularly appropriate for her mood. The course of events that she was about to instigate was serious and wrapped up in a sense of foreboding that she had found impossible to shift.

She went over to the door and looked back into the corridor.

It was quiet.

Aleksandra closed the door, went back to her desk and woke up her computer. She had a potted plant on the desk and, hidden just beneath the soil, there was a small SanDisk memory stick in a plastic seal. Everyone at the facility was subjected to full searches when they arrived and left the campus. Random escalations could mean full strip searches, and no one was exempt. Aleksandra had smuggled the stick into the building by swallowing it and then waiting for it to pass through her system. With the waterproof seal, the stick had been undamaged. She took it out and laid it on the desk, tapping her finger against it as she contemplated, for one final time, the audacity and danger of what she and her husband were proposing to do.

Aleksandra knew that she would be able to access the data. Their plan was ironclad. She had a Common Access Card, a smart card that was preloaded with the cryptographic keys and digital certificates that authenticated her identity and allowed her access to the data systems that she needed for her work. She had been assigned level three clearance, a significant level of responsibility, but not enough for her to access everything that she needed. But that was where William had come in. Her husband was a senior systems administrator at Daedalus's data storage facility in Michigan and he had fabricated additional keys and certificates that would allow greater access. William had used his status to persuade forty other project employees to provide him with their login credentials. That allowed him to scale up Aleksandra's reach and reduce the time she would need to gather the files they needed.

She picked up the memory stick and tapped the end against the side of her computer. William had uploaded a set of macros that would automate the collection process and cloak the downloads from discovery.

All she had to do was put the stick in the drive and tell it to get to work.

She paused. That would be the point of no return. William was confident that their theft would not be noticed immediately. He had been thorough in his preparation, and the macros would be surgical in taking just the files that were absolutely necessary. The process of downloading the data would be quick and precise enough so as to avoid setting off any alarms. But Aleksandra and William were planning on disappearing, and as soon as their absence was noted, they knew that there would be a full security audit. They had seen it before when the procedure was activated before Christmas. A molecular biologist working on adjusting the abilities of mitochondria so that biochemical processes could be optimised had gone missing. The facility had been put into lockdown, and the resident asset – at that time it was Morpheus – had been dispatched to find the man.

He had been discovered a day later, floating face down in the Vardar, his throat opened from ear to ear. The local police were underfunded, inept and corrupt. There had been no surprise when the death had been characterised as a robbery that had gone wrong. No one said anything, but they all knew: Morpheus had murdered the man and left him in plain sight as a warning to everyone else.

Once you started work on the project, you couldn't leave.

The incident had disquieted Aleksandra. She had known the geneticist a little. His name was Franks. He had been a professor at Caltech before he came to work for Daedalus, a quiet man with a nervous laugh. They had shared dinner together in the canteen on more than one occasion.

She had woken up several times with the image of him floating in the river still fresh in her dreams.

She closed her eyes. There was no going back now. She aligned the memory stick with the port and pressed it home. She opened up the command menu and typed in the sequence of instructions that William had taught her. Information immediately sped across the screen, and the download bar began to fill.

Aleksandra held her nerve, even though everything was telling her that she should take out the stick, discard it and forget the whole foolish enterprise. She bolstered her resolve with thoughts of William and the future together that they were planning.

The computer buzzed: the download was complete. It had taken ten minutes. Aleksandra took the stick, wrapped it in a fresh plastic seal and put it in her mouth. It was as difficult to swallow as it had been the first time that she had tried, and she needed a glass of water to help aid the process along. She felt it scratch its way down her oesophagus until she couldn't feel it any more.

She switched off the computer, collected her coat and briefcase and left her office for the final time.

Chapter Ten

Aleksandra took the elevator down to the reception and waited in line to pass through security. There was a body scanner and then a team of guards who picked members of staff at random for frisking. She waited for her turn to pass through the scanner, watching the vigilance of the guards, and convinced herself that she was about to give herself away. These were not locals, they were imports from abroad with Manage Risk training. They were civil to the staff, but they were hardwired to be cautious, and Aleksandra had heard the stories of strip searches – and worse – for those who aroused their suspicions.

She tried to look normal, but couldn't decide what normality looked like. Impatience? Boredom? And concentrating on being normal just meant that she was sure that she was overplaying it. Her palms grew slick with perspiration, her gut was knotted with tension and her heart was beating quickly in her chest.

Surely they could see how nervous she was?

'Step forward, please, Doctor.'

She did as she was told and passed through the scanner.

It remained silent.

No lights.

No alarms.

Nothing happened.

She paused before the guard, still convinced that her guilt was plain on her face, but the man nodded his acknowledgement and then stepped aside. 'Thank you, Doctor. We'll see you tomorrow.'

Aleksandra fought a moment of dizziness and continued on. There was an underground garage beneath the building. She took the elevator from the reception, stepped out and crossed the dark space to her Mercedes-Benz. She sat inside the gloomy cabin for five minutes, willing herself to be calm.

The dizziness and nausea passed.

She started the car and pulled out.

The campus was just outside the hamlet of Petrovec, six miles to the southeast of Skopje and a five-minute drive to the airport. Aleksandra passed through Ognjanci and, as she left the tiny village, she saw the tail car. They had been following her for the past month. The agents drove a Cadillac Escalade with blacked-out windows. They didn't try to be subtle. They *wanted* her to know that she was being followed.

Aleksandra was many things, but she was no one's fool. She had known that there were doubts about her dedication. It had started with a summons to attend a session with the campus shrink, where she had been asked questions about how she thought she was performing, whether she was enjoying her work and how she saw her role developing over the next few months. There had been a second session that had focused on whether she had any ethical concerns about their work, and then a third where she was politely informed that the director was concerned and had approved a programme of special measures that would include a much more thorough assessment.

It had been the impetus that she and William had needed.

They started to plan how they would leave.

She glanced up in the mirror and watched the Escalade. The driver was holding back, leaving a quarter of a mile between their two vehicles. She continued northeast and merged on to the westbound A1, heading towards the city. It was a four-lane motorway and it was never particularly busy. The rain slammed down on to the windshield, the wipers sluicing it off and providing a moment of clarity before the view ahead was obscured once again. Aleksandra kept to sixty in the slow lane, following the blurred red tail lights of the lorry that was two hundred yards ahead of her.

She looked up into the mirror again and saw the headlights of the Escalade behind her, a little closer now.

The lights of the city glowed through the murk as she turned on to Boulevard Alexander the Great. The Escalade turned off with her. She drove under the overpass with hoardings for Telekabel, UniBank and Neocom, the road overlooked by tall electricity pylons and old-style Soviet architecture. She turned on to Boulevard Goce Delchev, crossed the Vardar and saw the familiar majestic arches of the Daut Pasha bathhouse at the end of the road ahead of her. She loved the building, especially the romance of how its interior had once been lit by fireflies that were caught in silk nets. But time had moved on, and the hammam had not been spared; it was lit by electricity now and had been turned into a gallery.

Progress. It was not always to be welcomed. She could attest to that.

She drove into the underground garage beneath her apartment block, stopped at the gate, took a moment to retrieve her key card from her pocket and pressed it to the reader. As the gate opened and she pulled forward, she saw the Escalade crawl by the ramp.

She parked in her usual space, locked the car and took the elevator to the third floor. Her apartment had been provided by Daedalus. She slid the key card into the reader, waited for the lock to slide back and then very gently opened the door. She had made it her practice to leave a small marble behind the door before she left every morning, and she was always careful when she came back into the flat at night. She couldn't feel the marble today and, as she pushed the door all the way back and stepped inside, she saw that it had been moved.

It was the fifth time in the last week. She knew campus security retained spare keys so that they could covertly search staff accommodation. The marble was more than enough evidence for her to know that she was under formal investigation, even before the interviews with the shrink.

She glanced around. The apartment was pleasant enough: bedroom, sitting room, kitchen, small bathroom. Men like Ivanosky had places outside of the city. The professor had a big villa nestled on the slopes of the mountain. This place was blandly utilitarian, somewhere for her to sleep when she wasn't sleeping at the lab. Daedalus wanted the staff to work. Luxury might give them a reason to go home, and they didn't want to encourage that.

She went to the window, parted the blinds and looked down into the street. She saw the thirteen domes of the bathhouse and the fine old Ottoman buildings that stood at the edge of the Old Bazaar.

She couldn't see the Escalade.

She went into the bedroom. She had deliberately not packed a case. She had no interest in leaving anything in the apartment that might suggest that she was looking to leave. William was in charge of finding the things that they would need.

She changed into a pair of jeans and a sweatshirt, swapped her wet mackintosh for a leather jacket, collected her umbrella from the wardrobe and, after taking a final look at the apartment, went back outside into the corridor, closed and locked the door and made her way back to the elevator.

Chapter Eleven

Aleksandra paused in the lobby of the building, looking out through the window and into the street. She looked left and right, but couldn't see the Escalade. She nodded to the door-man, thanked him as she went through the opened door and stepped out into the rain.

She went south, into the Old Bazaar. The streets were narrow and winding, with shops pressed in close on either side. The cobbles were slick from the rain and Aleksandra trod carefully as she negotiated a path through the tangled thoroughfares. The tables outside the cafes had been abandoned; the wizened old men who stationed themselves at them had taken up residence inside, smoking cheap cigarettes, drinking strong black coffee and glaring out through rain-smeared windows. She passed into the area that was given over to stallholders. She saw the stalls offering leather slippers, traditional crafts, then rows of fruit and vegetables. She saw watermelons stacked into pyramids, racks of oranges and limes, women in burkas heaving bags full of produce that would last them all week.

She was next to the tiny St Spas church when she paused and turned back and saw the man. He was wearing a smart black overcoat and polished black shoes, and a black umbrella shielded him from the downpour.

The man paused as Aleksandra paused, and stared right at her.

He was not even attempting to hide.

He wanted her to know that she was being tailed.

She hurried on, her footsteps splashing through the puddles that had gathered on the waterlogged cobbles, turning away from the church and the Kale fortress and climbing the hill to the rose garden of the Mustafa Pasha Mosque. She was out of breath, a combination of the exertion of the climb and a sudden, irrational fear that William might not be waiting for her. How much did they know?

Aleksandra turned back and saw that a second man had joined the tail. He had a phone to his ear.

The two men were walking quickly, closing in.

She turned away from them and walked faster, trying to match their pace.

They knew.

They *had* to know.

The rain was hammering down on to the street, with fierce little rivulets running along the gutter and slurping into the drains. Aleksandra reached Opincharska and the narrow road that offered a view of the mosque's soaring minaret, and she saw the car that William had described. It was a blue Volkswagen Golf, the engine running and fumes spilling out of the exhaust. The red tail lights were blurred by the droplets that she tried to blink from her eyes.

She risked another glance back: the two men were fifty yards away from her and walking fast, almost on the verge of a trot.

Aleksandra reached the car, opened the passenger door and slipped inside the cabin.

'Go!'

William didn't need to be told twice. He lowered the handbrake, put the car into gear and started to pull away. Aleksandra swivelled in the seat and watched as the two men broke into a run. William negotiated a sharp turn, slowing as he edged between two parked cars, and one of the men reached the car and slapped his palm on the rear window.

Aleksandra felt sick. 'Go, *go!*'

The road widened beyond the turn and William was able to accelerate away. Aleksandra watched in the mirror as the men fell back into the distance, their black coats merging into the gloom until she couldn't see them any more.

There was a moment of silence. Aleksandra felt an almost staggering sense of relief that she had managed to get this far.

It didn't last long. Her tail would report that she had gone missing and her superiors would be contacted.

She thought of Franks and his lifeless body in the Vardar.

She blinked the vision away. They had passed the point of no return now. There was no going back. No point in torturing herself.

William glanced across the cabin. 'Did you get it?'

Aleksandra nodded.

'All of it?'

'Don't worry. It worked. I got everything we need. Are you ready?'

'Yes. The suitcases are in the trunk. And I have the passports.'

Aleksandra nodded to the satnav accommodated by a holder that was stuck to the windshield. 'How long?'

'About three hours if we go through Kyustendil. Four hours if we go north through Vranje.'

'Go north. It's quieter. Less chance that we'll be seen. Do you have the money for the tickets?'

William nodded. 'You're still happy with Shanghai?'

They had given plenty of thought to their destination today. William had explained that there would be very few places in the world where they would be safe. Their employers had a long reach. They had settled on China. The communists were investing huge amounts into genetics, even more than the Americans, and she knew that they would leap at the chance of benefitting from the research that she could deliver.

But handing themselves over was not their aim. Asylum in exchange for information was the fallback. The option would only be considered if the main plan fell through. She and William had negotiated a transaction that would make them rich enough to disappear.

'Aleks?' William prompted.

'Yes. I'm happy. Do you have the phone? There's no point in waiting.'

'In the glovebox.'

Aleksandra reached forward, opened the glovebox and took out the pay-as-you-go phone that William had bought. She removed it from the box, pushed in the SIM, switched it on and, after it had fired up and found a signal, she dialled the number that she had memorised.

The call connected.

'*Dr Litivenko?*'

'Yes.'

'*How are you?*'

The voice was distorted. She had no idea whether the person with whom she had been talking was male or female. She had no idea where he or she was. She had first been contacted six months ago and, with great skill and tact, her trust had been cultivated and nurtured until she was confident that the contact could be trusted, at least inasmuch as Aleksandra was prepared to trust anyone.

'We're on our way out.'

'*The data?*'

'We have it.'

'*Very good. I needn't remind you to be careful.*'

'I know that better than anyone.'

'*Your absence has already been reported. They are in contact with the local police.*'

'Do you have the money?'

'*It's ready. You just need to tell me where you'd like to meet. We will send a courier to make the transaction.*'

'Stand by. I'll call you with the location tomorrow.'

Aleksandra ended the call, took the case off the phone and prised out the battery.

'We're here,' William said.

He turned the wheel. They were at the entrance to the garage near the old flower market. The car bumped down on to the ramp and William pulled up at the machine to take a ticket. The bar rose and he drove forward, slotting the Golf next to a Lexus. He switched off the engine and got out.

Aleksandra got out, too. William unlocked the Lexus and opened the door. Aleksandra paused.

'Aleksandra?' William said after a moment had passed. 'Are you all right?'

'I'm frightened.'

'I know. I am, too. But this is the right thing to do.'

'Doesn't make me feel better.'

'They don't know where we are—'

'They will,' she cut in. 'And I know who they'll send after us.'

PART THREE:

Mumbai

Chapter Twelve

Isabella Rose opened the window and looked all the way down. Their apartment block was on the edge of Dharavi, Mumbai's most populous slum. The district took up barely more than a square mile, yet a million people were crammed inside it. It had originally formed around a water pipe within the bounds of an old garbage dump, but since then it had spread like a fungus. Isabella gazed out at the slum and the random streets and alleys that served the ramshackle habitations. The structures became more rigid and permanent as they drew closer to the middle. The buildings on the edges were little more than wooden shacks and lean-tos that were periodically swept away by the municipal government.

She had ventured into the slum after they had settled into their apartment upon arriving yesterday. There were rats everywhere, large ones that were the size of cats and small dogs, and she watched them as they gorged on the garbage that was tipped outside front doors and allowed to fester and congeal. The sewers were non-existent, and there were roads where the sludge of excrement trailed down the middle into overflowing drains. There were beggars slumped against the sides of buildings, men dragging rickshaws out of storage so that they might go out and start the search for passengers in more affluent areas, women bearing ewers of water from the standpipes that were only switched on for two hours every day.

Pope had decided they would be more anonymous in the bustle of the city, and Mumbai was the apogee of that. It was also the location of a Group Fifteen arms cache, and they had planned to recce it and, if it was safe, resupply themselves.

The apartment was tiny, found within a large block six floors tall, and wrapped around in bamboo scaffolding for a refurbishment project that never seemed to begin. Each flat was furnished with a balcony that was accessed by opening a metal grille that was secured to the wall of the building. The other tenants used the outside space to store their junk and to dry their washing on lines that hung low from the weight of the clothes that had been loaded on to them. The rent cost just short of thirteen thousand rupees a month.

The place was composed of a single room with a kitchen fitted into a tiny adjoining cupboard and a separate space for the bathroom. They had passed their first night on bedrolls next to each other, folding the rolls away when they awoke to be used as seating. Pope had stayed awake longer than her, festooning one of the walls with everything he had been able to discover about the disappearance of his family. He had trawled missing persons websites and forums and had called in favours from the intelligence contacts that he still believed he could trust. Isabella had printed out their emails in Palolem and he had stuck them to the wall next to a map of the world that Isabella had bought for him. He had scrawled a ragged red circle around Montepulciano, the Tuscan town from which his wife and daughters had been taken by the conspiracy that was now searching for them. He had marked the nearby airports and ports, drawing lines across the country to indicate potential routes that might have been used to ghost them away. There had been no leads, nothing to suggest that any one route was more likely than another.

The map, with all of its desperate scribbling, was a reminder that Pope had no idea where his family had been taken.

The other wall was dedicated to news reports concerned with the attacks in London. There were stories dealing with the bombing at Westminster and the attack on the Houses of Parliament. Isabella had been on a train as the bombers in the station had detonated their belts, killing dozens along with themselves. Other reports concerned the shooting down of British Airways Flight 117 and the deaths of all 347 men, women and children aboard it. The reports all traced the attacks back to Syria and then to Raqqa and the Islamic State. They drew a line from London through the Swiss accounts of Salim al-Khawari, now publicly confirmed as the financier of the operation.

Pope and Isabella knew that the attribution of the attacks to al-Khawari was wrong. They knew that the evidence that was being used to prove his guilt had been planted. Al-Khawari had been framed. They knew that because it was they who had framed him. Pope had been manipulated by Vivian Bloom for an end that he could only speculate upon. The most obvious motive – that Bloom had framed al-Khawari to demonstrate a link between the attacks and ISIS – was almost too outrageous to believe credible. If one assumed that to be true, it was not so great a leap from there to the assumption that the attacks themselves had been staged.

Isabella had read the conspiracy websites that Pope studied so obsessively. She read about false-flag attacks: events that were staged to impugn others and further agendas. She would have told him that he was being paranoid, but she couldn't say for sure that he was.

Could it be possible?

Really?

Was everything different from the way it had at first appeared to be?

She had seen what had happened in the desert with her own eyes. She had helped Pope fight off the attackers who had descended upon them in an unmarked Black Hawk, and then she had watched from the shelter of a cave as a Warthog had screamed overhead and obliterated the wrecked helicopter and all the evidence that they might otherwise have scavenged from it.

How had they been found in the desert? They were miles from anywhere. It should have been impossible. Pope was convinced that they had been betrayed by the GPS tracker in the radio that he had been provided with.

It seemed incredible, yet they had no other ideas.

They had hurried to his Tuscan apartment only to find that they were too late. Rachel, Clementine and Flora were gone, and an assassin capable of extraordinary things was lying in wait for them.

They had barely escaped with their lives.

Isabella turned away from the window and looked over at Pope. He was sorting through a pile of papers, grouping them into those documents that warranted closer inspection and those that could be dumped. He looked older than he had when he had come to Marrakech to visit her. Worry ate away at him. Lack of sleep consolidated the damage, as had the wound to his arm. His face was more lined than she remembered, his hair a little more grey.

'I'm going out,' she said.

Pope didn't look up. 'Fine,' he said.

'Do you want anything?'

He took a printout of a map and fixed it to the thin plywood wall with a drawing pin.

'Pope?'

'Sorry,' he said. 'What?'

'Do you want anything?'

'Oh,' he said. 'A bottle of water? We're low. Get a big one.'

'Okay.' She pointed to his arm. 'What about your painkillers?'

He flexed. 'Probably. I think I'm out.'

She made for the door.

'Be careful.'

'I always am.'

Chapter Thirteen

I t was 7.30 a.m.

Their apartment block was large for the area, but dwarfed by the glittering new skyscrapers that had been erected in the city's more prosperous quarters. They were not so distant from here, yet they might as well have been a million miles away for all the similarities that they shared. They were sleek and elegant, reaching up into the early-morning sky that was stained by a red that promised another hot day. Their block, in contrast, looked ready for demolition.

Men, women and children spilled out of the main street that led into the heart of the slum. The time was irrelevant; the streets were always busy. There were so many inhabitants inside the slum that it felt like a city within the city. Residents were sucked in from the outlying rural regions of Maharashtra and beyond, lured by the promise of prosperity and given something very different instead. There were separate areas for Muslims, Christians and Hindus. It was a vibrant place that was more than just a collection of habitations; Isabella had read that it housed industry that brought in more than a billion dollars a year, the constant flow of commercial vehicles heading into and out of the area bearing testimony to that. Columns of smoke piled up into the air from industrial furnaces and the thousands of open fires over which water would be boiled and food prepared.

Isabella put the block to her back and set off towards the old fish market. She had walked there yesterday evening while she searched for a pharmacy. It was a mile away from the block, but she could smell it as soon as she turned on to the main road. The trawlers had been landing at Ferry Wharf to the southeast of the market all night, and now the catch was being brought here to be sold. Isabella strolled by open lorries and pickups that were loaded with baskets of fish: limp Bombay duck and rawas, pomfret with bulging eyes and protruding lips, leathery skate, proud king mackerel and curled shrimp. Women were queuing to get inside, their baskets empty, ready to be filled with whatever produce the women could afford. The fishermen spoke with the dialect of the Kolis, an indigenous tribe once resident on the swamp marshland of Mumbai, but their language was subsumed within the clamour of shouted Gujarati, Telugu, Hindi and countless dialects.

Isabella went by, ducking as a basket of red snapper was propelled from the back of a lorry up to a first-floor window, where it was deftly snagged by a trader. Big specimens were pulled up by their tails and inspected; children laid out fish on tarpaulin sheets and gutted them with tiny knives held in deft hands. Prices were argued over, rupees exchanged, the shoppers dispersing with their prizes.

The New Raj Chemist and General Stores was opposite the market. The dusty white sign above the window bore the name of the business in both Marathi and English. Isabella went in through the open door and waited in line to be served. The queue shuffled forward slowly as the languorous clerk went to and fro between the desk and the store at the back of the shop, bringing back medicine in tatty white bags.

Finally, it was Isabella's turn. 'Yes, miss,' the man said, in awkward English. 'How can I help you?'

Pope had arranged a prescription from a doctor that he seemed to know from a previous visit to the city. The man was crooked and, for the sake of a few rupees, he had been prepared to refill the prescription as many times as they wanted. Isabella took it out of her pocket and handed it over. The man straightened his glasses and squinted down at it.

'Do you have any ID?'

She took out the passport that she had been travelling on. It was the one that belonged to Pope's eldest daughter. They shared the same colour of hair, but that was about it. The border guards had not given the document much attention, as Pope had anticipated; that had been fortunate.

The clerk gave it a similar cursory glance and slid it back across the counter.

'Wait.'

Isabella turned away from the counter and glanced out of the dirty window on to the street outside. It was busy, with a traffic jam slowly edging forward, the drivers of the cars providing an angry symphony as they leaned on their horns. Men and women went about their business, slumped forward as if bent that way by the weight of the mounting heat. The shop was ventilated by a fan, the streamers fixed to the aluminium cage snapping straight out in the stiff breeze that the blades provided. There was a queue of twelve men and women waiting for their turns. The man behind her was younger, his limbs thin and the insides of his wrists ruined by unmistakeable needle marks. He was jittery, his hands trembling and his jaw bulging as he ground his teeth together.

The man came back with a paper bag. 'Here, miss,' he said, putting the bag on the counter.

Isabella took out the bottle that she found inside. She recognised the white plastic and the blue lid of the Percocet. Pope had been relying on it to dull the edge of his pain.

'Three thousand rupees,' the clerk said, putting out his hand.

It was extortion. He knew that the prescription was bogus, he knew she wasn't eighteen, and he was charging three times what he should

have charged because he had come to the conclusion – correctly, as it
happened – that Isabella was not in a position to shop around. She was
paying him to look the other way.

She took out the notes, laid them on the counter and made off with
the prescription before anything else could be said about it.

She was on the stoop, blinking into the brightness and already buf-
feted by the wave of heat that washed over her, when she felt a vibration
in the pocket of her jeans. They each had burner cell phones that they
had purchased from the Raghuleela Mega Mall. Isabella took hers out.
It was ringing. She looked at the display, covering it with her hand so
that she could read it in the glare of the sun. It was Pope.

'I'm here,' she said.

'*Hello, Isabella.*'

It wasn't Pope.

'Who are you?'

'*Listen carefully. I'm here to help you. But you need to move quickly.
You and Mr Pope are in great danger.*'

The voice sounded artificial, with robotic distortion around the
edges, as if it had been run through a piece of software to render it
anonymous.

She heard the sound of a siren. It was an angry up-and-down yowl
and it instinctively set her nerves on edge. She felt an immediate thrill
of anxiety. There was no logic to her reaction; Mumbai was a vast city
of twelve million people, and the slums attracted the worst of society
with the promise of anonymity, just as they had attracted Pope and
Isabella. But sirens signified authority, and Isabella knew that they were
being hunted.

She put the phone back to her ear.

'Why are we in danger?'

'*You have been compromised.*'

Three vehicles came into view: two lorries and a large car behind
them. The two lorries were painted blue and had 'Mumbai Police'

stencilled along the flanks. They travelled fast under blue and white lights, their sirens wailing and engines roaring as they sped by on Isabella's right, racing by the Dharavi Sports Club and on to the main road. The third vehicle was different to the lorries that had preceded it, a black Ford SUV with tinted windows and red and blue lights mounted into its grille.

'*Did you see them?*'

'Yes.'

'*They're on their way to your apartment now. Mr Pope is not answering his phone. You need to warn him. And then you need to leave.*'

She started to walk: slowly at first, then faster. 'Who are you?'

'*A friend. More than that is irrelevant now. Be quick, Isabella.*'

Chapter Fourteen

Isabella ran.

The snarl of traffic at the entrance to the slum had slowed the convoy, despite their sirens and lights. She caught up with them as the apartment block came into sight and, rather than walk right by, she turned left and then right and approached the building along a side street.

She reached the block as the first lorry drew up. It parked outside the entrance to the building and was joined by the second lorry. The doors opened and armed police jumped out. Isabella shrank back and watched. She counted twenty men. They wore body armour and were toting a mixture of MP5 submachine guns and combat shotguns. The third vehicle – the black SUV with the tinted windows – pulled up. One of the armed officers jogged over to the window of the SUV and conversed briefly with the occupants. The policeman gave a stiff nod, turned back and pointed to the building. The men nearest to the door opened it and led the way inside. Most of the others followed.

Isabella took out her cell phone. She dialled Pope's number. There was no response.

They had agreed on a fallback. There was a landline in the apartment, too, and Pope had said that it was never to be answered. They would listen instead: four rings would signify that they had been compromised. They would evacuate the area and rendezvous at Chhatrapati Shivaji Terminus. The railway station was one of the busiest stations in India and offered both long-distance trains and the commuter shuttles of the Mumbai Suburban Railway. It would be easy to melt into the crowds and disappear.

She dialled. Nothing. The phone wasn't even ringing. Isabella looked at the display. The bars at the top of the screen said she had no signal.

'Are you having trouble, too?'

Isabella turned. A woman was leaning against the wall of the building next to her. She was holding up her own phone.

'Can't get a signal,' Isabella said.

'Neither can I.'

Isabella glanced out at the street. She saw others looking at their phones with confusion on their faces.

The local network had been blocked.

She looked back at the apartment block and up to the window of their flat.

Pope was inside. She had to warn him.

⌣

The convoy had blocked the road. A lorry from the fish market was unable to get through and a snarl of cars and other commercial vehicles quickly congealed behind it. The morning sun beat down, dust clouds eddied and the drivers of the trapped vehicles took out their frustrations by leaning on their horns. The lorry driver opened his door and stepped down, turning back to the angry queue behind his lorry, and proffered his raised middle finger. The malodorous stink from the fish in the back of his lorry filled the air.

The crush was a useful distraction, and Isabella took advantage of it. She knew that the police would have been given her description as well as Pope's and, in many ways, she stood out more than he did: fifteen-year-old white girls on their own were not common here. She did her best to stay out of the way. She jogged a hundred yards down the road and crossed, passing between a car and an autorickshaw. There was no way that she could use the main entrance. Four of the armed policemen had been posted there.

There was an alleyway between their building and its neighbour. Isabella slipped into it, the temperature dropping instantly as she moved into its dark shadow. The bamboo scaffolding started on the first floor, and there was a ladder halfway along the alleyway that offered access to the platform above. She clambered quickly up it, scrambling on to the rough boards and then regaining her feet. Another ladder offered a way up to the second floor and she took it, then taking the ladders that led to the fourth, fifth and sixth floors. The platform on the sixth floor was below the lip of the roof, which was too high for her to reach and so haul herself up. She hurried around the boards to the back of the building. An air-conditioning unit had been fixed to the side of the wall and, by clambering on to the rusted box, she was able to stretch up for the lip of the roof. She pulled herself up, found purchase for her feet and scrambled over the parapet so that she could roll on to the roof.

It was burning hot now, and there was no shade. She was sweating and out of breath, but there was no time to gather her strength. A raised brick structure in the middle of the roof had a door. She ran to it. The door was fastened with a rusted padlock. Isabella cursed, but looked for options. The builders had stacked a collection of bricks on the roof and Isabella took one. The clasp of the padlock was corroded, and it only took three hard strikes with the edge of the brick to snap it apart.

She discarded the broken lock and the chipped brick and opened the door. A flight of unlit stairs was directly ahead of her, leading down into the building.

She took them.

Chapter Fifteen

Isabella could hear the sound of boots on the stairs below. It appeared that the intelligence that had been given to the police was incomplete. They knew that Pope and Isabella were in the block, but they didn't know in which apartment to find them. They were going door to door. That gave her a limited window of opportunity.

She hurried. Somewhere below she heard the sound of hushed, urgent voices. Isabella tried to work out what floor the police were on. The first? They had two or three dozen apartments to check before they reached them.

She vaulted the last few steps, ran down the corridor to their door and fumbled the key from her pocket. She unlocked it and went inside.

Pope was on the bed. He had been asleep.

'We have to go,' she said.

Pope sat up. 'Why?'

'They know we're here.'

Pope slid off the bed. 'Who does?'

'Armed police. They're inside. They're on the way up.'

Pope knew to trust her judgement, but asked, 'You're sure they're for us?' as he quickly got to his feet.

'I had a call just before I saw them. A warning.'

'From who?'

'They didn't say.'

Pope frowned, but there was no time to pursue that now. He looked to the papers scattered on the floor and the bed, and the documents that he had tacked to the walls.

'How many?'

'I counted twenty. They've left four on the door.'

They both froze as they heard the clatter of booted feet in the corridor outside.

'*Police!*'

The voice came from farther down the corridor. They hadn't reached their door yet.

But they couldn't leave through the door.

'Get under the bed,' Pope said.

'What about your arm?'

'I'll have to manage. Get under the bed.'

Isabella did as he asked, dropping to her belly and sliding beneath the iron frame until she was out of sight.

She watched as Pope went to the door. He unlocked it and quietly pulled the handle, leaving it ajar. The door opened back into the space that was left between the side of the wardrobe and the wall, and Pope pressed himself into it. Isabella heard the sound of terse conversation from the apartment next to theirs and the sound of a baby crying. The men had gone inside to check.

Isabella steadied herself.

'Police!'

The voice was loud and close, right outside their open door.

Isabella breathed in and out. She could see Pope; he was still, his fists clenched.

Isabella overheard a quick, tense conversation between two men and then held herself stock-still as their door was gently pushed open.

She watched as the first man came into the apartment. He was dressed in a blue police uniform, bulked up with body armour and with a balaclava covering his head. He was toting a weapon in both hands, the muzzle pointed ahead. A shotgun. He had a can of pepper spray and a pistol in holsters clipped to his belt.

He stepped forward so that a second man could come into the room. He was similarly equipped to the first, except that he wasn't carrying a weapon. He had a holstered pistol. His hand rested on the butt.

Pope waited. The first man came into the room, right up against the edge of the bed. The second man edged forward, turned to the left and pushed the door that opened into the tiny kitchen. Pope crept out from behind the door. The holster's retaining strap was undone. He slipped the fingers of his right hand around the butt of the pistol and grabbed the back of the man's body armour with his left. He shoved the policeman into the door frame at the same time as he yanked the pistol out of its holster, drew it back and crashed it down against the policeman's head. The man's body went limp.

The first man turned, the shotgun lowered.

Pope pulled the dazed policeman closer to him, looping his arm around his chest to support his dead weight. He winced; the effort evidently caused him pain.

Pope aimed the pistol squarely at the man.

'Put it down,' he said.

The man stopped there, the gun levelled. If he pulled the trigger from this range, he would kill Pope and his unconscious colleague.

Isabella slid out from underneath the bed.

Pope kept his face blank as Isabella took a step forward.

'I said put it down,' Pope repeated, doing his best to distract the policeman as Isabella closed in.

She reached for the pepper spray.

Before the man realised what was happening, she had taken it from the holder and stepped to the side so that she could spray it into his face.

She was close and couldn't miss; the liquid splashed across his eyes and nose and mouth. The man staggered away, turning in Isabella's direction and blindly swinging the shotgun at her. She danced back out of range, and Pope took the opportunity to dump the body of the man he had knocked out so that he could close in. He grabbed the shotgun, prised it out of the policeman's hands, flipped it and drove the butt backwards into his face. The man dropped to his knees. Pope struck him again, the butt crashing off the man's chin, and he fell to the side and lay still.

'I told you to stay under the bed,' he said.

She shrugged. 'You were having trouble.'

Pope closed the door to the apartment and propped one of their wooden chairs against the handle. 'We need to be quick,' he said.

Chapter Sixteen

They had stripped one of the policemen of his uniform and now Pope was wearing it. The balaclava was pulled down tight over his head so that only his eyes and mouth could be seen. The body armour was a little small for him and the balaclava only partially hid his white skin.

'Well?' he asked.

Isabella shrugged. 'I think it'll be obvious if anyone takes a long look at you. What about your arm?'

'It's sore,' he admitted, 'but I can use it. We only need to get outside. The lights are off in the corridor and we're not going to hang around. We just need it to buy a little time.' He reached over to the dresser and picked up the can of pepper spray. He tossed it over to her. 'Just in case,' he said. 'Keep it out of sight.'

She wedged the can of pepper spray into the back of her trousers, the cylinder pressed into the small of her back, the aluminium cold against her hot skin.

He stooped down to collect the shotgun. 'You ready?'

She nodded.

Pope removed the chair from the door, opened it and stepped outside. He paused in the doorway, looked left and then right and then indicated that she should come out, too.

She did as he asked.

He held the combat shotgun in his left hand and rested his right hand on her shoulder.

All of the bulbs in the corridor had blown, and the only illumination was what penetrated the dusty windows at either side of the building. Pope impelled her forward, towards the stairs. They started down, Isabella going first with Pope close behind, his hand still on her shoulder.

They crossed the landing to the floor below and saw four police officers working the doors, knocking on one after the other, with the families who had already been disturbed watching them as they knocked on the other doors and searched the flats behind them. Pope and Isabella kept going down, following the stairs down through the fourth, third and second floors.

They reached the main entrance. Daylight blazed in through the open doorway and Isabella had to blink until her vision corrected itself. She could see the silhouettes of the men who had been left outside to guard the entrance. She had seen four of them before she had climbed the side of the building; she could see the shapes of two men now. Pope had seen them, too: she felt the tightening of his grip on her shoulder.

'Stay close,' he said quietly and, at her tiny nod of acknowledgement, he pushed her forward and through the door.

One of the guards was at the door and the other was talking to an elderly female resident, who was angry that she was being prevented from going inside.

The man at the door turned as Pope led Isabella out into the bright sunshine. Pope gave him a firm nod of his head and marched her ahead.

The blacked-out SUV was directly ahead. They had only taken a handful of steps when two men emerged from the car. They were dressed in jeans and shirts and they had black sunglasses pushed back on their heads. One had cropped blond hair and the other was bald. They stepped forward and put themselves between Pope and the street.

The bald man spoke first, in English. 'Is that her?'

Pope nodded.

'Where's the man?'

Pope angled his head in the direction of the building.

Isabella felt the buzz of adrenaline. Pope was trying not to speak; he knew that his accent would betray him. They had to get away from here. The longer they stayed, the harder it would be to maintain what was, even at its best, a rickety deception.

The blond man stepped up. 'Take it off,' he said, pointing to Pope's balaclava.

Pope shrugged.

The man laid his hand on the butt of the Glock that was in a holster on his belt. 'Take it off. Right now.'

Pope squeezed Isabella's shoulder.

That was the signal.

Pope took his hand away.

Isabella was young. It made little difference how well briefed these men were, how much they had been told of what she was capable of, the details that they had been given of her heritage and her training and the outrageous things that she had already done. She was fifteen years old, and she looked it. There was an instinctive response to that knowledge that distracted from the details in her file. Isabella knew that to be true and knew that it gave her a significant advantage.

Pope was slowly removing the balaclava, their attention on him. They didn't notice as Isabella reached around and slid the can out of her trousers.

Pope took off the balaclava.

They were both turned to face him as Isabella brought the can around and pressed down on the plunger. The bald man was closest to her, and it was easy to spray the aerosol into his face. The blond man noticed what was happening and raised his arm to block the spray when Isabella turned it on him.

It didn't matter.

Pope flipped the shotgun and clubbed the man in the side of the head with it. He sprawled over on his side.

The policemen at the door turned at the commotion.

Pope flipped the shotgun around and covered them both.

'Turn around.'

Pope brandished the shotgun to urge them along and they did as they were told.

'Put your hands on your head.'

They did as they were told.

'Kneel.'

Pope didn't take his eyes off the policemen.

Isabella took the pistol from Pope's belt and turned to the road.

'Check the car for the keys,' he said.

Isabella crossed to the big SUV. The door was still open and, as she climbed inside the cabin, she checked for the key fob that would need to be inside before the engine would start. There was no sign of it. She pressed down on the brake and pressed the starter button, but nothing happened; wherever it was, the fob was not close enough for the engine to start.

'It's not here.'

There came the clamour of angry voices.

Isabella looked back at the entrance: two more armed police officers were in the lobby. They saw their colleagues with their hands on their heads, kneeling on the pavement.

Pope sprang back, aimed the shotgun and fired a warning spread into the ceiling. Plaster tumbled down. The armed officers dropped beneath the line of the door, out of sight.

'Run,' Pope said.

Chapter Seventeen

They ran into the slum with two policemen following them. Isabella led the way. She was smaller and more agile than Pope, and she was an accomplished distance runner. She settled into a steady stride, ducking in and out of small spaces, gaps between the slow-moving vehicles and the men and women who swarmed around them. She turned back, saw that Pope was losing ground on her and slowed down so that he could catch up. The policemen were still following them, doggedly pursuing them into the sprawl. They were thirty feet behind Pope, but he was gasping for breath and they were gaining.

Isabella skirted a table and chairs that had been set up outside a cafe where grizzled men were drinking *chai* and darted around a small lorry that was unloading the ubiquitous blue drums in which the locals stored their water. She slowed to look back again and saw Pope and then the two policemen, the three blue uniforms easy to pick out amid the colour of the slum. Pope looked back, too, and missed the emaciated dog that scurried out from the open door of a nearby hut. He tripped and fell, crashing to the ground and sending up a cloud of dust.

He glanced up at her as he scrambled back to his feet. 'Go!'

The policemen had closed in. They were fifteen feet away now, close enough for Isabella to see the sweat on their faces and their open mouths as they gasped for breath.

She set off again with Pope behind her. They reached the narrow lane of Rajendra Prasad Chawl and forced their way through a scrum of people. It was barely two and a half yards across, and Isabella was almost able to touch the buildings on both sides by extending her arms. She ran on, deeper and deeper into the heart of the slum, the clamour of the voices around them changing as they rushed through districts that were populated by those who spoke Hindi, then Marathi, then Telugu and then Tamil. They passed a series of tiny businesses: a stall selling sizzling fried food, a small recycling plant with the sound of plastic being shredded within, the clatter of sewing machines and the tinkling of cutlery against pots and pans.

Isabella pulled away. She saw a junction up ahead and she darted to the left and turned into it. She was approaching a public toilet, a noisome stench crawling out of the open door. There was a pile of garbage pushed up in a drift at the side of the road and the walls were marked with obscene graffiti. She sprinted for the door, throwing herself inside and then pressing herself against the wall, able to look back into the road without giving herself away.

Pope came first. He was panting hard and, as he looked for her and realised that she was out of sight, his expression became heavy with concern.

He slowed.

The policemen came next, both of them rumbling around the sharp junction together.

Pope backed away from them.

They had abandoned their shotguns, but both men had sidearms.

Isabella held her nerve, waiting for them to clear the doorway of the toilet.

The area was quieter than it had any right to be. She heard the melodic sound of devotional singing and then the rush of water as a standpipe was opened. One of the residents had opened her hose to wash down the lane as her husband stood in the doorway to brush his teeth.

'Stop,' the leading policeman said.

Pope paused. He looked ready to give in. He was still weak, his recovery leaching all his strength from him, and he was bent over and gasping for air.

The first policeman went by the doorway.

Isabella drew the pistol that she had taken from Pope's belt.

The second policeman paused right in front of her.

She held the pistol in her right hand and the can of pepper spray in her left.

The first policeman drew his weapon and took aim at Pope's midriff. 'Put your hands up,' he called out.

The second policeman took another step, far enough to clear the doorway. Isabella could see the back of his head now. He wouldn't be able to see her.

'Where's the girl?'

She slid out of the doorway and took a step towards the man at the rear.

Pope saw her, but didn't react.

'Where is she?'

'I have no idea.'

Isabella extended her arm with the can of pepper spray in her hand.

'Hey!' she called.

The officer turned and Isabella doused him in the face. He exclaimed with the shock of sudden discomfort.

The first man turned and looked into the barrel of the pistol in Isabella's other hand.

'Drop it,' she said calmly.

The second man dropped to his knees, pawing at his streaming eyes.

'Drop it,' she said again, indicating the first man's pistol.

He didn't get a chance. Pope advanced on him, reached for the man's arm, pinned it back and took the gun from him. Isabella stepped back and covered the man she had incapacitated. Pope went to work quickly, taking the cuffs from the first policeman's belt and clipping one of the bracelets around the man's wrist. Pope dragged him so that he was next to his colleague and put the other bracelet around that man's ankle. He disarmed that man and put the gun into his own belt.

'Come on,' Pope said to Isabella. 'They won't be the only ones. We need to get out of here.'

Chapter Eighteen

They made their way through the slum.

Pope stripped off the body armour and dumped it into an overflowing trash can, then undid the first few buttons of the shirt. He was soaked through with sweat and there was a little patch of blood at the top of his right sleeve. The exertion had almost been too much for him. He had thought that he was almost recovered from his stabbing and the debilitating infection that had followed, but the chase had proven otherwise. He doubted that he would have been able to lose the two cops without Isabella's help.

They emerged from the western edge of the slum. There was no sign of the police, nor any indication that they were drawing attention amid the hundreds of other men and women going about their business on the busy street. They found a bus stop and took the first bus into the centre of the city. They transferred on to a second bus that was going to Chhatrapati railway station and got off two stops before the end. It was likely that their enemies would have people watching the train station and the airport. They would leave another way.

There was a large parking lot south of the station. Pope led the way to a quiet section, away from CCTV, and, as Isabella stood sentry, broke into a Nissan Altima and hot-wired the engine.

'Where are we going to go?' Isabella said as they pulled out of the parking lot.

'I'm not sure,' he admitted. 'We'll work it out on the way.'

He had given some thought to their destination as they had ridden the bus away from the slum. They couldn't go south again, back to Palolem or somewhere else in Goa. They had been discovered in Mumbai. He had no idea how, and he had no idea where they had been compromised. It wasn't safe to return to somewhere they had been before.

He wondered about following the coast north to Gujarat or perhaps east to Nagpur.

Nothing felt safe. Maybe the country was spoiled for them now.

It felt as if their options were limited.

The horizon was closing in.

'You said someone called you this morning with a warning.'

'Yes,' she said. 'I don't know who it was.'

'You didn't recognise them?'

'No. The voice was distorted – as if they were using something to disguise it.'

'The phone number?'

'That was weird. It was your number.'

Pope drummed his fingers on the wheel. Someone had spoofed his number? They had very deliberately kept that information between themselves. He had no idea how anyone else could have found out about it. It shouldn't have been possible.

'Give me your phone,' he said.

She reached into her pocket and handed it to him. He took out his own phone, opened the window and tossed them both outside. He didn't understand what had happened. Better safe than sorry.

Pope was anxious. They were already caught up in something far bigger than themselves. Fresh layers of confusion were being added. They were even deeper in the hole than he had anticipated.

Pope had picked the simplest route out of the city.

He merged on to the NH3 and headed northeast, towards Nashik. National Highway 3 started in Agra and ended in Mumbai. It had four lanes, two on each side of the central reservation, and it was in reasonable condition. Pope followed it until Nashik and then turned due east, on to NH160.

It would take eleven hours to reach Nagpur from here.

He drove carefully, maintaining a steady sixty miles an hour. The last thing that they needed was to be stopped for driving too fast. The car would have been reported as stolen by now, and even the simplest check of the registration would betray them.

The day drained away as they put more and more miles between themselves and Mumbai. They stopped at an Indian Oil gas station on the western approach into Aurangabad to fill the empty tank. Pope took the opportunity to stretch out his arm.

'Take off your shirt,' Isabella said.

He did as she told him and held out his arm for her to check. She peeled off the dressing. It was soaked with fresh blood.

'Does it hurt?'

It did, but he downplayed it. 'Not too bad.'

'Don't lie to me.'

'A little.'

'Wait here.'

She went into the store to pay for the fuel and buy supplies, returning with a litre bottle of Coke, bags of chips and a plastic box that had been filled with aloo gobi. She carried a green plastic box that contained a motorist's first-aid kit. She cleaned away the blood and redressed it.

Pope looked out at the vista as she worked. The forecourt offered a panoramic sunset, the brightness of the day dying in a cavalcade of oranges and reds and purples that stained the infinite horizon from the dusty plains to the peaks of a distant range. It was still stiflingly hot, the baked earth pulsing the heat back at them like the radiant warmth from an oven. Frequent traffic went by, tyres rushing across the asphalt.

'There,' she said. 'Done.'

She reached into her pocket and handed him a plastic bottle.

'You got the pills?'

'Got them before I got the phone call.'

He opened the bottle and tapped it until two of the painkillers fell into the palm of his hand. He put them in his mouth and swallowed them down with a mouthful of Coke.

They sat with their backs to the car, the metal warmed by the sun, and ate their food. They were both quiet. They were in shade, but even so, the air seemed to thrum with the heat.

Isabella dumped the garbage when they were done and they got back into the car.

'Are you okay to drive?' she asked as she turned the cap on the bottle of Coke.

'I'm fine.'

'I can do it,' she said.

'I know, but you need to be sixteen.'

'I can pass for that.'

'Maybe.' He put the car into drive and pulled out of the forecourt. 'But we don't want to take any chances. We can't afford to get pulled over. I feel fine. The pills will help. And I'll stop when I'm tired.'

He looked over at her; she said nothing and stared out of the windshield as he merged on to the 753A to Jalna. It would take them another two hours to get there and then another seven to Nagpur. They would get there at around eleven.

Chapter Nineteen

Dusk faded into night, and the road was illuminated by the street lights of the occasional hamlets that they skirted and the glow of the other cars. Traffic was light and, although Pope was fatigued and his arm hurt, he felt alert enough to continue.

They were going to Nagpur because Pope had been there before. He had been given a bodyguarding assignment at the start of his career with Group Fifteen, a stint babysitting the CEO of a UK multinational. The man had received death threats from a local criminal syndicate whose nose had been put out of joint after the man had refused to cut them into the profits of a hydroelectric power plant that was being built across the Krishna River. The corporation's Indian headquarters were in Nagpur, and Pope had been stationed there.

Mumbai had offered safety because of its teeming crowds. That safety had proven to be illusory, so he would try to find it in another city; smaller, perhaps, but one with which he had the benefit of familiarity.

He looked over at Isabella. She had taken off her jacket and bunched it up, shoving it into the crook of her neck so that she could use it as a pillow against the window. She was asleep, her legs drawn up to her chest. She was relaxed, inhaling and exhaling deeply. Her habitual expression was one of wariness, underpinned by a ready doubtfulness that was often expressed as scorn. She looked older than fifteen most of the time. The edge was gone now that she was sleeping. She looked younger now, more like her age.

And she had proven herself again. Pope knew that he underestimated her, that he was guilty of it all the time and that she interpreted his reluctance to involve her as a lack of trust. She clearly found that irritating, and he couldn't blame her. But it wasn't a lack of trust. It was because of an obligation that he had already abused, one that he had no intention of abusing again.

Pope had promised Beatrix, Isabella's mother, that he would do his best to keep her safe. He had done that. He had wiped her identity, scouring all traces of her from government records and turning her into a ghost. She had gone back to Morocco after Beatrix's death.

Pope could have left her there.

He *should* have left her there. She would never have been found.

Instead, he had visited her and offered her a chance to work for him. He knew that she would accept. He had only had to spend five minutes with her for it to be obvious that she was hungry to live up to her mother's reputation.

Beatrix had trained her in the year that they had spent together before she had died. Her daughter was prodigiously talented. That talent had seemed obscene to Pope when he compared it to the pastimes of his own daughters. Clem and Flora were older than Isabella, but that was artificial. Just numbers. They had been brought up in a household of loving care, wanting for little, cosseted from the sewage in the world through which Pope was paid to navigate.

Isabella had not had their good fortune. She had lived through so much already, and it had made her older than her years.

And Pope had gone to her and made his offer. Encouragement was unnecessary; the offer itself was more than enough.

And one thing had led to another had led to another.

She had volunteered to infiltrate the household of the man suspected of financing the London attacks. That had led to her abduction and her transport deep into ISIS territory in Syria.

The urgency of the situation was no excuse. Isabella was a fifteen-year-old girl. Her precocity was irrelevant. Her unique background and training were irrelevant, too. Pope bitterly regretted what he had done and, although he had defied orders and risked his own life to bring her out of Syria, he did not feel able to absolve himself. She was still in danger. Being with him made her a target. Yet he couldn't leave her now. Staying with her was better than abandoning her, but neither was better than what she would have had if he had left her to get on with her life.

The fuel gauge flashed its second warning. They were just approaching Amravati, the last city before Nagpur. Pope saw the sign for a gas station and turned off.

Pope filled the car, took his wallet from the dashboard and went to the store to pay.

The man greeted him in Hindi.

'I'm sorry,' Pope said. 'Do you speak English?'

'Yes indeed, sir.'

'The fuel on pump two, please.'

'That will be three thousand, six hundred rupees. Are you paying by card?'

'Cash.'

He took two jumbo bars of Amul dark chocolate and another bottle of Coke and put them on the counter. 'These as well, please.'

The man rang it all up.

Pope looked back at the display of the register. A moment ago, it had shown the amount due. In the time since he had stooped to collect the chocolate, the message had changed.

It was very different now.

>> MICHAEL POPE <<

'Sir?'

Pope did not take his eyes off the display.

>> WE NEED TO SPEAK <<

He knew he was staring at the reader, his hand with the banknotes hovering over the counter.

'Your cash, sir?'

>> CALL 011 202 879 3240 <<

'Are you all right?'

The clerk was staring at him.

'Sorry,' Pope said. 'I was a million miles away.'

'Your cash, please, sir.'

Pope found a smile that suggested embarrassment, nodded his acknowledgement and counted out the money.

'Thank you, sir.'

There was a stack of yesterday's papers on the counter and Pope took one off the top. It was a copy of the Hindustan *Times*. Pope took out five rupees and put the coins on the counter. 'Could I borrow one of those pens?' he asked.

The clerk had a collection of ballpoint pens in the breast pocket of his shirt.

'Of course.' He took one, put it on the counter and arranged Pope's notes in the till.

Pope noted down the telephone number in the margin of white space at the top of the front page and handed the pen back.

The display switched back to the amount that was due.

'Thank you,' he said.

Chapter Twenty

Pope pulled out on to the road and continued east. It was a hundred miles to Nagpur. They would be there at ten or eleven. Isabella was still asleep, curled up with her head resting against the window. He was tired, but adrenaline and the ache from his arm kept him awake.

He put the newspaper on the dashboard in front of the wheel. His eyes flicked down to the number that he had written there. Someone had been able to track the two of them, and that person, whoever they were, had been able to spoof their phones, and, when they had discarded their phones, that person had hacked the cash register so that they could pass a message to him.

It was twenty minutes later when he saw what he was looking for. They had just passed through the small town of Nandagon Peth with the highway continuing along the same route as a north–south railway line. He had just gone by the police station when he saw the telephone box. He indicated and pulled off the road, rolling to a stop next to it. It was a red box, similar to the design of the old-fashioned boxes back home, and for a moment it reminded him of what he had lost.

He opened the door of the car and stepped outside into the sticky evening heat. It was thick and damp, an almost physical presence that washed over him as soon as he was out of the air-conditioned oasis of the Altima's cabin. Overhead power lines loomed over the railway track, the electricity buzzing and popping. The police station was little more than a wooden hut; it was closed, all the windows dark. Pope thought he could hear the call of an owl in the darkness above it.

He crossed the dusty parking lot, opened the box and went inside. The heat was unbearable, and he had to prop the door open with his foot so that a little air could circulate inside. The ancient Bakelite handset was hot to the touch, and as he pressed it to his ear, Pope wondered whether it would still work. The dialling tone sounded. Pope folded the newspaper on the shelf, thumbed in two rupees and dialled.

He recognised the first three numbers as denoting a number in the United States and the next three as identifying a number in Washington, DC. He listened to the pattern of clicks as the call was placed and then the intermittent tone as it rang. The tone sounded once, then twice and then a third time.

And then the call connected.

No one spoke. All Pope could hear was the hiss of static on the line.

'Hello?' he said.

'*Mr Pope.*'

'Who is this?'

'*It doesn't matter. All that is important is that I am a friend.*'

The voice was distorted. Pope couldn't tell whether it was a man or a woman.

'How did you do that?' he asked.

'*Send you a message?*'

'Yes. The phones. The petrol station. How did you do it?'

'*Just a simple trick. Don't be distracted by it. The means are not relevant. We needed to speak to you.*'

'How did you find me?'

'*The same way that they will. You have been sloppy, Mr Pope. The Altima you stole is equipped with a monitoring device to record data from* hard-braking incidents. Motorists are bribed with lower insurance premiums if they use them. But the transponder transmits your location in real time. And the owner has reported the car is missing. Mumbai state police are reporting fifteen cars as stolen in the last twelve hours. We tracked all of them. Whenever each car stopped, we hijacked local CCTV and disregarded those cars that were driven by someone else. Eventually, we found you, and we've been able to hack your car. The passenger seat belt in the car is engaged – so Isabella Rose is still with you. We can see your route, your speed, how many more miles you could travel before you need to refuel. We could even tell you what radio station you've been listening to.'

Pope felt a trickle of irritation. The implicit criticism was not something he enjoyed. 'So I'll take the transponder out.'

'You could do that. But what about the electronic data recorder? The infotainment system? The transponder that allows you to use toll roads without stopping to pay? They are all transmitting. Your car will do everything it can to rat you out. Are you going to disable everything?'

Pope gritted his teeth.

'I'm not criticising you, Mr Pope. We're trying to keep you safe. It was easy enough for me to find you. Your enemies are not as good at this as we are, but they'll find you, too. They won't be interested in a telephone conversation. They could re-task a satellite to follow you. And then they might send a strike team. They could send a drone.'

'You didn't go to all this trouble to rub my nose in it. What do you want?'

'We want to help you.'

'Why?'

'Because our interests intersect. You want to find your family—'

Pope interrupted. 'What do you know about my family?'

'We know that they've been taken.'

'Where are they?'

'We don't know. We're looking. And when we find them, we'll tell you.'

Pope gripped the receiver tightly. 'Why? Why would you help?'

'It's not purely altruistic, of course. The people who took your wife and your daughters did so because you are a threat to them. They sent one of their agents to kill you in Montepulciano. You did well to survive the meeting, truth be told, but they took your family. We want to expose those agents. We want the world to know about them. They are dangerous, Mr Pope. Not because of what they can do, but because of what they are.'

'So?'

'You want your family. We want their lies to be revealed. We can help each other to achieve our goals.'

'How?'

'A man and a woman have gone on the run from the company responsible for the agent who attacked you. They have information that we can use against them.'

'Information?'

'Data. It doesn't matter what it is.'

'Where are they?'

'China. They will sell the data to us. We have been negotiating with them, and we have agreed to the parameters of a deal. We want you to make the exchange.'

'Why me?'

'You are an experienced operative. We don't have men of your talents in our organisation. And it might be dangerous.'

'Where in China?'

'They are in transit to Shanghai.'

'I'll need more than that.'

'Of course, Mr Pope. You have this number now. Go to Shanghai and call us. We will know where they are by the time you arrive.'

Pope shook his head. 'No. I'm going to need more than that. I don't know who you are and I don't know your agenda. You're good at surveillance. Well done. I'm impressed. But you haven't given me one good reason to believe that you can help me find my family.'

'*A demonstration, then? There is another gas station up the road from where you are, near Mojhri. Go there. They have a fax machine beneath the counter. We will leave something for you.*'

Pope heard the sound of a car and turned as lights blazed through the dirty glass of the telephone box. The car continued on, and Pope followed the red of its tail lights as it disappeared around a bend.

'All right,' he said. 'I'll do that. But what do I call you?'

There was no reply.

'Hello?'

Pope heard the hiss of static but nothing else. The line was dead.

Isabella was still asleep as he got back into the Altima and drove on. He quickly reached Mojhri and then saw the lights of the gas station on the eastern side of the tiny hamlet. He pulled into the parking lot and jogged inside.

'Excuse me,' he said. 'Have you had a fax this evening?'

'No,' the man said. 'We haven't had a fax for—'

He stopped. Pope could hear the chatter of a printer below the counter.

'That's strange,' the man said. 'We haven't had a fax for months.'

The printer chugged, the old unit whining a little from unaccustomed activity, and then it fell silent. The clerk reached down and collected a sheet of A4 paper. He looked at it, shook his head and then laid it out on the counter. Pope turned it around so that it was the right way for him to see it.

He felt a twist in his guts. He was looking at a photograph from a CCTV camera. It was up high, angled down on three people who were about to pass beneath it. A woman in the middle and two teenage girls on either side, all of them holding hands. The woman's face was angled up just a little, enough for the camera to be able to capture the anxiety on her face.

It was Rachel.

The two girls on either side of her were Clem and Flora.

'Why has that been sent here?' the clerk said.

Before he could answer, the phone started to ring. The clerk picked it up and put it to his ear. He listened for a moment and then proffered the receiver. 'Are you Mr Pope?'

Pope's mouth was dry. He nodded.

'It's for you.'

He put the receiver to his ear. 'Yes?'

'*That photograph was taken at Lielvārde Air Base in Latvia. Two days after your wife and children were taken. They boarded a Gulfstream V that we know has been used for CIA rendition flights and were taken here. They were put into a car registered to a corporation based in Bermuda and driven southeast, towards Riga. We lost them there, but we have leads that we are tracking. We will find them. We're good at what we do, Mr Pope. Our enemies are good, too, but this is our speciality. And, if you cooperate with us, when we find them, you will be the first to know. So – do you trust me now?*'

'No.'

'*But you will cooperate?*'

'What do I have to do?'

'*Go to the luggage lockers at New Jalpaiguri railway station. We will leave passports, tickets and money for you in locker 324.*'

'And the girl.'

'*For you and Miss Rose, then. The passcode is 7-6-7-3-P-O-P-E. Collect them.*'

'And then?'

'*China, Mr Pope. You have to go to Shanghai.*'

PART FOUR:

Skopje

Chapter Twenty-One

Vivian Bloom was standing at the rear of a small corridor. There were two rooms to the right, both served by a single door and with smoked-glass mirrors that enabled those outside to view the interior. The rooms were bare and functional and reminded him of the interrogation rooms in which he had interviewed Soviet defectors in Berlin during the Cold War. There were two guards at the other end of the corridor, both armed with holstered pistols and Tasers.

Maia was in the first room. Bloom could see her from where he was standing. She was sitting, her arms folded on the table in front of her. She seemed calm and relaxed. Her face was blank and expressionless and her hands were still.

Nikita Ivanosky and Jamie King were standing just ahead of Bloom.

'Are you ready?' Ivanosky asked.

'Let's get on with it,' King replied impatiently. 'The longer we sit here holding our dicks, the longer it's gonna take to start fixing the godawful *mess* that you've caused.'

Ivanosky glared back at King, but was wise enough not to retort. 'You stay here,' he said instead.

King looked incredulous. 'What?'

'I'll talk to her. She'll respond better to me.'

'Fuck that,' King said, pushing by the professor. 'I *own* her. She'll answer my questions or I'll have her taken outside and shot.'

King opened the door and went inside. Ivanosky turned to Bloom, as if ready to say something, but instead he held up his hand to tell him to wait and then followed King into the room.

Bloom did not need to be told twice. He had no interest in speaking to the asset. He was not ashamed to admit that she frightened him. Instead, he stepped up to the window and watched as King and then Ivanosky sat on the other side of the table to the woman.

There were microphones in the room, and they relayed the conversation to outside observers through discreet speakers in the wall.

Ivanosky began. 'How are you, Maia?'

'I am well, Professor.'

Bloom folded his arms and watched.

'How's your shoulder?'

Maia flexed it, rolling her arm in its socket. 'Very much better.'

'That's excellent news.'

Jamie King was palpably restless. He was sitting forward in the chair, his forearms resting on the edge of the table and his hands clasped together. His jaw was clenched, and Bloom could see the spasms of the muscles in his cheek.

Ivanosky ignored him. 'And your leg?'

'It was just a sprain. I'm very close to being—'

King slapped his palms on the table. 'What did that bitch say to you?'

Maia stopped. A moment of confusion passed over her otherwise expressionless face. 'I'm sorry, Mr King. I don't understand. Who are you talking about?'

'Dr Litivenko. The day before yesterday. What did she say to you?'

'I don't remember.'

'Try.'

'She was asking me about my shoulder. We spoke about the operation a little more – about what happened.'

King took his phablet from his pocket and set it on the table. He tapped the screen and an audio recording started to play. It was Aleksandra Litivenko's voice. '*If there was something else to explain what happened, you have to keep it to yourself. If they think you're flawed in some way, if they think you can't be relied upon to complete your orders, they'll have no further use for you. You understand what that means, don't you, Maia?*'

King tapped the screen. 'What did that mean?'

'I don't know,' she said.

'What about this?'

He tapped again. '*I just want you to be careful.*'

'Why was she warning you? What did she mean?'

'I'm sorry, sir. I don't know.'

'Something bothered you. You asked her.'

King tapped again and Bloom could hear Maia's voice.

'*You seem concerned about something. Is it something I've done?*'

'Why did you say that?'

Maia was thoughtful for a moment. 'She seemed distracted. Not herself. What's happened? I didn't see her yesterday. Is she okay?'

King slammed his fists down on to the table. The phablet bounced and slid over the edge, falling to the floor with a crack. 'What the fuck is going on? Stop pretending like you don't know. Where has she gone?'

Maia turned to Ivanosky. Bloom could see her face more clearly now that the angle between them had narrowed; there was worry amid the confusion now.

'Dr Litivenko has gone missing, Maia,' Ivanosky explained slowly, as if he were speaking to a child. 'She left the facility two days ago, after she saw you. She went back to her apartment in the city, and then she left. She was followed by some of our security staff, but she made an effort to lose them. We don't know where she is. I will be honest, Maia. We are very concerned.'

'Why would she do that?'

'We don't know,' he replied. 'We were hoping she might have said something to you. As Mr King says, your last conversation sounds unusual in the circumstances. You must *think*, Maia. We are worried about her. Anything you can tell us about what she might have said to you, or anything you might be able to surmise from the way she has been behaving – well, it would be very valuable.'

Maia gave a small, helpless shrug. 'I thought she was anxious, but she didn't say why. She doesn't talk to me about her private life. She is only interested in me.'

'Are you *sure*, Maia?'

'I wish I could help, but I cannot.' She turned to look at King. 'What will happen to her?'

'The doctor is a traitor. She's trying to sell information about this project, but they're not as clever as they think they are. We'll find them.'

'And bring her back?'

'Are you fucking naïve? What do you think we'll do? We'll send one of our monkeys to take care of them for us.' King stood and straightened his jacket. 'We're done here.'

⌣

King came out of the room. Ivanosky said that he wanted to spend more time with Maia.

King signalled that he wanted Bloom to come with him. They made for the elevator lobby.

'What did you make of that?' King asked him.

'Dead end.'

'You buy what she said?'

Bloom nodded. 'She looked confused. If she knew anything, she hid it well.'

'That's the thing,' King said. 'They don't lie very well when it's off the cuff. Give her a cover story and enough time to rehearse it, she could tell you she was Frank Sinatra and fool a polygraph while she did it. But you put them on the spot? Uh-uh. We would've been able to tell. I think you're right.'

'So what do we do?' Bloom asked. 'We can't have Litivenko out there pimping operational data.'

'Damn straight we can't, which I say makes it just as well we have a lead. We know where they are. They went over the border into Serbia, drove north and flew out of Belgrade.'

'To where?'

King grimaced. 'Amsterdam first, then they changed on to KLM to Shanghai. They arrived yesterday.'

'And?'

King chuckled at Bloom's anticipation. 'And Blaine and Curry are on a Gulfstream headed there right now. They're due to touch down in' – he checked his ostentatiously expensive watch – 'two hours.'

'That's that, then? They'll clean up – end of problem?'

'It will be. We're going to put them under surveillance. We've had intelligence that they've got a buyer for the data she took, and that they're going to make the exchange there in the next day or two. They're dead, one way or another, but I'd like to find out who's been stupid enough to try to buy our stuff. I think that could be enlightening.'

The elevator arrived and they got in.

'There's something else,' King said. 'You heard of Jack Coogan?'

'The senator? I know his name. From Boston? Not much beyond that.'

'He's the chairman of the Emerging Threats and Capabilities Subcommittee of the Armed Forces Committee. Jim Lennox was his predecessor. Lennox was our man – bought and paid for. The committee has oversight of the kind of work Daedalus is doing. Everything here is off the books, of course, we've never told them we've gone beyond the theoretical stage, certainly not that we have assets in the field. The climate's not there for that yet. Soon, but not yet.'

Bloom knew what King meant. Bloom was invested in their project for ideological reasons. He wasn't foolish enough to ascribe the same motivational purity to all of the others. Jamie King – and the other men and women from what Eisenhower rather foresightedly called the military-industrial complex – stood to benefit commercially. Put crudely, there would be a greater demand for missiles and bombs. And the ethics of any overseeing politicians would be flexible if Daedalus could produce metabolically dominant war fighters. That flexibility would be worth billions and billions of dollars.

King leaned back against the wall of the elevator as it surged upwards. 'Lennox was very useful. He gave us advance warning when we needed to know things, and he nudged the agenda away from us when it was too hot. He was expensive, but it was worth every last red cent. And then, without any warning, he resigned. Didn't tell us, just did it. He said it was because of a heart attack, but that was bullshit. He's as healthy as a horse. I flew out and had a talk with him myself. Turns out he was blackmailed. He'd been misusing federal funds. This guy emails him, threatens to go to the press unless he resigns, so he did. Coogan was his replacement.'

The doors opened and they walked through into an executive area.

'And that's where it gets unfortunate. Coogan has a hard-on for what Daedalus is doing, or at least he says he does. He's lined up a hearing for next month. "Civilian and Military Genetics: The Way Forward". It's not going to be even-handed. The word on the Beltway is that he's gonna bring the hammer down on everything we've been doing, choke off our DARPA funding, do everything he can to shut us down.'

'So deny it. You said it yourself: no one knows what's happened here.'

'That's the problem. We've been told Litivenko's data is being bought for the hearing. They're going to jump us with it. I'm not worried about Litivenko. She and her husband are dead. And we're going to deal with Coogan, too.'

'How?'

King put his hand on Bloom's arm. 'It's in hand. He won't be a problem for much longer. But I want to know who's moving the pieces in the background. We get rid of the senator, maybe they put someone else in his place and we go through it all again.'

'What are you going to do?'

'It's like my grandma used to say: you lance the boil, get rid of it before it can get worse.'

PART FIVE:
Tibet

Chapter Twenty-Two

They stole another car in Nagpur and then continued east. It took them another thirty hours to cover the thousand miles to New Jalpaiguri. By the time they arrived at the railway terminus, they had a better idea of the scale of the trip they were undertaking.

They arrived at midnight of the third day since they had fled Mumbai. Pope led the way to the luggage lockers at the garish, neon-soaked station, found locker number 324 and, once he was sure that they were not being observed, entered the code.

He opened the door and Isabella looked inside. They had been well provisioned. Apart from an envelope that contained two new and very authentic-looking fake Australian passports, the locker was stuffed with additional items. There were hats and gloves and thick coats in anticipation of their drive through Tibet. Inside a leather satchel were guidebooks to Tibet and China, a cell phone with a collection of SIMs and a USB cable that had been wrapped around it, wads of banknotes, a credit card, visas and train tickets, and, finally, a slip of paper with a telephone number and instructions to call it when they arrived at their destination. There were also two tickets for the flight from Kathmandu to Lhasa, necessary since there were no open border crossings between China and India.

Finally, there was a key with a Land Rover fob and directions to a Discovery that had been left in the short-term parking for them. The rugged four-by-four was perfect for the day's drive that was necessary to carve a route through the high country to Kathmandu. They set off, the temperature dropping the higher they climbed.

The clouds delivered on that promise as they arrived in Bhaktapur, dumping a foot of powder on to them as they negotiated the busy roads to Kathmandu. They deposited the Discovery in the long-term parking lot and fought their way through the snow and the crowds of passengers, taxi touts and panhandlers until they were inside the terminal building.

They took the daily Air China one-hour hop to Lhasa and then, after dealing with the formalities of crossing the border, they took a taxi to the railway station. The driver was a gruff Chinese man who looked at them with a disapproving eye before chain-smoking his way through half a packet of Double Happiness Reds and switching on the radio, nationalistic Chinese music playing loudly. Isabella gazed out through the windows of the smoke-filled taxi. Lhasa felt antediluvian when set against the brash commercialism and teeming cities of India.

Heavy snow had blocked the roads and they had to run to make their connection for the 11 a.m. train; the air was thin, and Isabella was surprised at how out of breath she was when they finally clambered aboard. An official arrived to exchange their tickets for plastic key cards, explaining that the tickets would be returned when they arrived in Xuzhou East. He had them each fill out a form that confirmed that there was no reason why they should not travel at high altitude and then, with a terse suggestion that they would enjoy the trip, he left them and made his way to the adjoining cabin.

'Get some sleep,' Pope said. 'We've got a long trip ahead.'

'You, too,' she suggested. 'You look done in.'

Isabella lay on her stomach so that she could look out of the window. She watched the Tibetan yaks on the slopes of the mountains as the forty-hour journey began.

Isabella found herself alternating between wakefulness and sleep. Whenever she awoke, she would look out of the window and inevitably witness another startling change in the scenery as the train rumbled through the Chinese countryside. The first hour of the journey had seen peasants returning to their homes with shovels and hoes over their shoulders and shaggy-haired yaks staring insolently at the train as it cut through their fields. They had passed through a passage that was breathlessly described in the guidebook as the world's longest permafrost tunnel. She woke into stunned silence at the sight of the monumental beauty of the Tibetan plateau. She stared out at the mirror-smooth surface of Cuona Lake as it reflected the trees and mountains so perfectly that it was sometimes difficult to be sure which was up and which was down. They raced through the Qiangtang grasslands, the yellow plains changing to dark ochres, and then climbed up and raced down the Tanggula Mountains, making their way to Xining and the vast scrubby plains of Shaanxi province.

The train was utilitarian in comparison to the landscape through which it hurried. It was clean and decorated in neutral colours. There was nothing glamorous about the accommodation. They had two bunks in their cabin, and each was equipped with a small LCD screen of the same dimensions as might be found on an aircraft seat back, although only state TV programmes were shown. There was a single electricity point and, with a nod to the altitude, oxygen ports that accommodated small capillary hoses that could be run beneath the nose as with patients in hospital. There was storage room under the bed, as well as a compartment near the upper bunk that essentially made use of the space above where the outside corridor was.

She looked out as they passed a row of tents that accommodated the workers who maintained the line. She closed the curtains and lay back on her bunk. Pope was asleep on the bunk beneath her, occasionally snoring until he turned over and breathed more easily again. They had spoken about the conversation that he had had in the telephone box outside Nandagon Peth, and he had given her the faxed photograph that he had been sent at the gas station near Mojhri. Her childhood had instilled in her a natural wariness and her mother had reinforced this during the year that they had spent together, yet she was prepared to go with Pope if he felt it was the right thing to do. He had put his life at great risk to recover her from Syria, and that had bought him her trust. She wouldn't follow him blindly, but, as he said, there was no reason for contact to have been made if there wasn't more to be learned, at least.

Isabella had considered this as they had continued the long drive through Nepal, and she thought about it again now.

It would have been a simple enough thing for the person who had found them to have turned over their location to the people who were searching for them. And that hadn't happened. That meant something.

They clearly had information about Pope's family. The photograph was the best lead that Pope had received since they had been taken from him.

The best lead? She corrected herself. More than that. It was their *only* lead.

They had nothing else to go on. Pope had struck out with his efforts in Mumbai. They needed to be doing something, to be moving in a direction that might bring progress.

The conversation and the photograph were not much, but they were more than they'd had before.

The leather satchel that they had taken from the locker at New Jalpaiguri was at the foot of her bed. She opened it and looked inside. It contained everything that they would need to complete the journey to Shanghai. The fake Australian passports, describing them as Mr Harry Boon and his daughter, Miss Juliet Boon, had been accepted without issue at the immigration kiosk. The same was true for the two visas for onward travel into China and the tickets for this train journey.

Whoever their benefactors were, they were efficient and professional.

The cabin was cold, so she pulled the blanket up to her chin and closed her eyes.

⌣

She awoke from another two-hour doze and found that they were in a station. A sign indicated that they were at Xi'an. She slid her legs over the edge of the bed and dropped down to the floor of the compartment.

Pope was still asleep.

She opened the door and went to the vestibule at the end of the carriage. The door to the platform was open, and she stepped down. It was cold, her breath steaming before her face. It was one in the morning, but the platform thronged with passengers, rough-faced Tibetans getting off and Chinese people getting on. The broad concrete platforms were well stocked with newspaper kiosks and mobile trolleys whose owners proffered fried chicken. One of them saw her staring out at him and, hawking up a ball of phlegm, spat it in her direction.

The train staff were going about their business, refuelling the engine and fitting hoses to the carriages so that the latrines could be emptied.

A whistle sounded and the passengers stretching their legs on the platform started to embark once again.

She went back to their cabin.

Pope was awake. He was sitting on the edge of the bed. He had taken off his shirt and Isabella could see the firm lines of the muscles in his chest and the bulge of his arms.

She pointed at his arm. 'Can I take a look?'

He nodded and slid around so that she could address the wound more easily. She removed the dressing. His triceps was healing. The doctor at the hospital in Kankavli had told her what to look for: redness or swelling around the wound; a fever; drainage that did not stop with direct pressure; wound tissue that appeared yellow, white or black in colour. There was none of that. The new flesh looked healthy and the contusion was fading, the bruise passing from purple to yellow and then disappearing completely.

'It looks better,' she said.

She dropped the dirty pad into the compartment's waste bin and fixed on a fresh one.

He stood and flexed his arm. 'You get some sleep?'

'Yes,' she said.

He looked much better. She was pleased. Pope had looked frayed by the time that they had finally made it on to the train, but, with the benefit of a few hours' sleep, he looked more rested than he had for days.

'Do you know where we are?' he asked.

'Xi'an.'

He turned to the timetable at the back of the brochure that they had been given. 'Ten hours to Shanghai,' he said. 'You want something to eat?'

'Yes,' she said.

The dining car was next to their carriage and it was open despite the early hour. The menu was limited to bottled water, soda, beer, snacks, beef jerky and sweets. But Isabella saw an attendant bringing out a plate of pan-fried pork and, when the waiter attended to them, she ordered one for herself. Pope ordered noodles that came in cardboard containers that were the size of large salad bowls. The waiter scribbled down their order and disappeared.

The train pulled out of the station and picked up speed, passing through the darkened city.

'The man you spoke to,' Isabella said. 'You trust him?'

'No,' he said. 'I don't trust anyone. Not after what happened in Syria.'

'But?'

'But we don't have any other options open to us. And he's been true to his word so far.'

'So we're meeting someone to make an exchange?'

'That's what he said.'

'But we don't know anything else. Who is it we're meeting?'

'A man and a woman.'

'But who?'

'No, we don't know that.'

'And where do we meet?'

'We don't know that either. Shall we find out?'

Pope reached into his pocket and took out the cell phone that had been left for them in the locker at Lhasa station. He detached the cover so that he could insert the battery. He closed the case, switched on the phone and waited for it to find a signal. He unfolded the piece of paper that had accompanied the phone and dialled the number.

Isabella watched curiously as he held it to his ear. He waited for a moment and then started to scribble notes on the paper. He ended the call, opened the case, pulled out the battery and put the pieces into his pocket.

'Well?' she asked him.

'It was a recorded message.'

'And?'

'We need to pick up a bag of equipment at the station in Shanghai. And then we're meeting a man. His name is William Wheaton. He's going to be at Chen Yi Square tomorrow.'

'Do you know it?'

'No. But they said it's on the river. Very public. Lots of witnesses. That means Wheaton must be frightened.'

'And what are we getting from him?'

'A memory stick. Once we get it, we call the number they just gave me and they'll transfer the money he wants into his account. And then we get out of China.'

'When?'

'Tomorrow,' Pope said.

PART SIX:
Shanghai

Chapter Twenty-Three

Their train pulled into its platform at Shanghai station at ten minutes to midday on the sixth day since they had fled Mumbai. It groaned up to the buffers just as a bullet train slithered away in the opposite direction from the adjacent platform. The passengers started to disembark. Pope and Isabella took their places in the queue and waited for the carriage to empty out. There had been instructions in the bag that they had collected in Jalpaiguri that they should reprovision themselves in Shanghai. They followed the crowd into the station's main building, a vast hall with a clear ceiling and shops along both sides. Pope led the way through the crowded atrium to the luggage office on the first floor, near to the south entrance. Pope said that he had a bag in one of the lockers, and the dour woman behind the desk wrinkled her nose and gestured that they could go through.

They found the locker and Pope entered the code. The display reported how long the locker had been used for and demanded twenty yuan before it could be opened.

'Ten hours,' Pope said, pointing to the display. 'Whoever we're working for, they've got someone else in the city.'

Pope fed in a twenty-yuan note, the door opened and he took out the backpack that had been stored inside.

There was no one else in the room, so he put the pack on the floor and unzipped it. There was a new Bluboo Xtouch cell phone, with a SIM card attached to the box by a piece of tape. The boxed phone was sitting atop a stack of banknotes. He took one of the bundles out. The notes were fifty-yuan bills, and there must have been a hundred notes. Five thousand yuan. There were eight bundles comprising the stack.

'Forty thousand yuan,' Pope said. 'Four and a half grand. Very considerate.'

There was a zipped pouch at the front of the backpack. Pope opened it and reached inside. His fingers brushed up against something coldly metallic.

'What is it?' Isabella asked.

Pope opened the pouch all the way to reveal the pistol inside.

'Glock?' she said.

Pope nodded. 'G43.'

Isabella recognised the single-stack nine-millimetre with the stippled beaver-tail grip. It was highly concealable, very accurate and it suited most hand sizes. That was the upside. The downside was that the magazine held just six rounds with another in the chamber; seven shots wouldn't last long in a running gunfight.

'Ammunition?'

Pope took out a box of nine-millimetre rounds and spare magazines. 'They really do think of everything.'

The final thing inside the main compartment was a sealed envelope. He slid his finger inside and tore it open. There was a printed reservation for two rooms in the Shanghai Hilton.

Pope zipped the backpack up again and carried it down to the subway that was beneath the station. They took line one towards Xinzhuang and got off at Changshu Road. They walked north along Huating Road and then Changshu Road and finally, after a few more minutes, arrived at the hotel. It was a forty-three-floor behemoth that overlooked the Yan'an Elevated Road. Pope checked them in, dispensed with the offer of help from the bellboy and led the way to the elevator. Their rooms were on the thirty-fifth floor.

Pope unlocked the first room and opened the door.

'You going to be all right here?'

Isabella looked around. The room was expensively furnished, but in a bland style that could have been found in any high-end hotel anywhere in the world.

'This is fine,' she said.

Pope left the key card on the bureau.

'Get some sleep,' he said. 'It's going to be a long day tomorrow.'

She followed him to the door and closed it behind him.

She went back to the window and looked out into the gloomy afternoon. Shanghai was gloriously futuristic, very different to the rest of the country as seen from the window of their train.

Isabella undressed, stood under the shower for ten minutes and then fell back on the bed. She was tired and Pope was right. There was no way of knowing what the following day would bring. They knew very little about the man whom they had been sent to meet, and they only had a little time to scout the meeting place and consider a plan.

That would all come tomorrow. For now, though, she closed her eyes and waited for her questing mind to calm.

She was asleep within five minutes.

Chapter Twenty-Four

I sabella woke at four in the morning.

She passed across the room to the window and watched the lights of a jet as it flew overhead, then looked out at the Oriental Pearl Tower dominating the skyline to the east, the distinctive spheres, each bisected by red bands, representing pearls falling on to a jade plate. The two largest spheres, positioned along the length of the tower, were illuminated and shone brightly over the cityscape. She saw the wide dark curve of the Huangpu River and the space-age night scene in Pudong.

The hotel was equipped with a large sports complex, and she decided to go down to it and take the opportunity to wake up properly with a little exercise. She charged a new swimsuit to the room account, changed into it and went through into the luxurious pool. It was large, twenty-five metres long and wide enough for six lanes. She was the only person down here. She climbed down the steps, the cold water gradually enveloping her, and then pushed away from the wall and dived down to the bottom. She surfaced and started out, moving through the water with powerful, crisp strokes. She reached the far end, performed a smooth tumble turn and kicked out again. She had not been able to exercise ever since they had left Mumbai, and she had missed the familiar endorphin buzz.

She settled into a steady rhythm, losing herself as she powered up and down her lane. She had always been a strong swimmer, but just lately her endurance had seemed to increase. She had first noticed it during her swims in the sea off the coast of Palolem. She seemed to have more energy than she remembered. She had always trained hard, and now she was seeing the benefits.

She started to daydream, and as was so often the case, she found herself thinking about her mother. She increased the frequency of her strokes and eventually even those thoughts faded away as she powered through the water, hypnotised by the metronomic rhythm, the breath on every third and the rush of the chemicals that flooded her brain.

Isabella knocked on Pope's door when she returned to her room. There was no answer. She unlocked her own door and saw two slips of paper with his handwriting on it. The first said that he was going out and would be back at seven. The second, evidently slipped beneath the door later than the first, said that he was in the Lobby Pavilion for breakfast and would wait for her there.

She dried her hair and took the elevator down to the ground floor. The restaurant was the hotel's most informal, with comfortable chairs arranged around four-person tables. Pope was sitting alone at a table at the back, his seat pointing into the room. He saw Isabella and raised his hand in greeting.

She crossed the room and took one of the empty seats next to him. There was a plate on the table that bore the remnants of a continental breakfast, together with a cafetière and a glass of half-finished orange juice.

'Did you sleep well?' he asked.

'Yes,' she said. 'You?'

'Not really. Couldn't stop thinking about today, so I just got up in the end. Didn't want to wake you.'

'I've been up since four.'

'Doing what?'

'Exercising. Where did you go?'

'I made some preparations,' Pope said. He looked over at the buffet. 'You want to get something to eat?'

'I'd rather get on with this,' she said.

'Go and get a muffin or something,' he said. 'You need to eat.'

He was right. She was hungry, so she did as she was told. The buffet was generous, and she collected two croissants, a banana and a glass of pineapple juice. She brought them back to the table as Pope was unfolding a map. She shuffled her chair around as Pope spread it out on the table. It was designed for tourists, with all the key points of interest denoted by out-sized icons. The legend at the top of the page read 'Shanghai City Centre', with a box to the right of the page locating all of the main hotels, including their own. She saw how the city was split by the broad blue stripe of the Huangpu River, ranging nearly half a mile between the east and west banks.

Pope laid his finger on the map. 'We're meeting Wheaton here,' he said.

Most of the land was coloured yellow, bisected by a grid of white streets, except for a shoulder of green on the western bank of the river. It was labelled 'Huángpu Park' in the north and, below that, 'The Bund'. That was where Pope was indicating.

'It's a promenade,' he explained. 'Runs north to south with the river on the right and the East-1 Zhongshan Road on the left. The precise spot is here, Chen Yi Square, next to the Bank of China.'

He moved his finger, landing it on an area adjacent to the Bund Sightseeing Tunnel and around five hundred feet north of the Yan'an Road Tunnel.

'I've been there this morning. It's just a square, looks like it'll be busy with tourists when we meet. Lots of people, lots of witnesses to make sure Wheaton's safe when he makes the exchange. There's a coffee stall there, too. I'm guessing that's where he'll want to do it.'

Isabella munched on the croissant. 'What's our plan?'

Pope looked down at the map. 'He could come in from any number of ways. He could use the Bund from the north or the south or he could come in from any of these roads that feed into Zhongshan. There's no way of knowing.'

'And we don't know what he looks like,' she added.

'Correct.'

'So what do you want me to do?'

Pope reached down to the bag by his feet. Isabella saw that it was marked with Mandarin script and, below that, an English translation: 'New World Department Store'. He picked up the bag and gave it to Isabella. She rummaged inside it and found a new set of clothes, a boxed Xiaomi cell phone and a pair of in-ear headphones.

'I went shopping. They open early. I think the clothes will fit,' he said, a little unsure. 'They'll help you blend in. I want you to watch from the northeast corner of the square, on the Bund. It's elevated – you'll have a good view from there. If you see anything that bothers you, you tell me. We'll keep a line open on the phones: this one for you, and the one we were given for me. I'll loop our friend into the call. It'll save time if he can hear the conversation I have with Wheaton.'

'Fine.'

'And I'm going to give you the Glock. I'm not sure how careful Wheaton is going to be, but I don't want to scare him off. And I know I can trust you with it. If there's any trouble . . .' He left that hanging. 'Well, you know what to do.'

Isabella was satisfied with the plan. There was little more that they could do to prepare themselves when they knew so little of what the exchange might entail.

Pope finished his coffee and checked his watch. 'It's eight,' he said, pushing the chair away and getting to his feet. 'We should think about getting over there.'

'When do we meet?'

'Midday. Four hours.'

Chapter Twenty-Five

The Bund. It was also known as Waitan and was the waterfront area that centred around the East-1 Zhongshan Road within the city's old International Settlement. Isabella had the map, and she looked down at it as she followed the western bank of the wide Huangpu River. Both sides of the water were faced with the high, glossily modern skyscrapers that had been developed over the course of the last few decades. There was a lot of traffic on both Zhongshan and, on the eastern bank, Binjiang Avenue. Just as Pope had predicted, the promenade was busy with sightseers and locals enjoying the warm midday sun.

Isabella walked south, up against the barrier that guarded against the drop into the sluggish waters of the river. She was wearing the bland and featureless clothes that Pope had purchased in the mall: jeans, a zip-up top and a cap that she wore forward to cover as much of her face as possible. She also had the backpack that had been left for them at the station. It looked like the kind of thing that a young tourist might wear. She had the Glock inside the pack. She concentrated on maintaining her anonymity, idling along behind a group of young tourists who were following a guide, the woman's flag bobbing up and down fifteen feet away from her. She hoped that anyone observing might think that she was part of that group.

Isabella glanced ahead. Pope was a hundred feet away, just entering the square. The wide space was dominated by the skyscraper that accommodated the Bank of China to the west and by a bronze sculpture of Chen Yi, the community mayor who had been the first man elected to the post in 1949. He stood atop a marble dais, his left hand in his pocket and his right arm by his side. Pope paused in front of the statue. He bent down to fiddle with the laces of his shoe.

Isabella drifted back towards the rail, slowing her pace. She could see Pope and the stretches of the wide boulevard to the north and south. She watched the men, women and children as they walked by. There were hundreds of people here. Thousands, probably. It was a little before midday. A busy part of the day. It was easy enough to gain anonymity by staying within the crowd, yet, on the other hand, should anything be amiss, it was very public; the opportunities for anyone to do harm would be minimised by the sheer number of witnesses. That was of benefit to them and to the man whom they had come to meet. It was an excellent place to plan a rendezvous. Wheaton was careful. That was good.

Pope had said that there was an outdoor cafe in the square and she looked down on it: a collection of chairs and tables set out around an Airstream trailer made out of gleaming aluminium. Customers made their way to the tables, where they were served by white-shirted waiting staff.

Pope went to a spare table and sat down.

His voice buzzed in the earbuds that she had pushed into her ears. *'I'm here.'*

'I can see you.'

'Anything?'

She glanced around again. 'Nothing's standing out.'

'Stay back. If you see anything that makes you worry, let me know.'

131

'I know,' she said. 'I know what I'm doing.'

'*I know you do. I'm going to loop our friend into the call now.*'

'Understood.'

Isabella was alert, scanning the faces of the Western men who passed her by. No one stood out. Perhaps Wheaton would approach from the south.

A ferry chugged across the water, distracting her for a moment as it sounded its mournful horn.

⌣

The asset's given name was Eric Curry. His codename within the programme was Moros, but the Curry persona had become a good fit; the quirks and habits of his alter ego came naturally, worn as easily as a comfortable jacket. Curry worked for a software company as a travelling sales rep. He was always on the road, visiting prospective customers all around the world. He had arrived in Shanghai four days ago for a series of meetings. They were all legitimate. He would meet a potential new client this afternoon to discuss a licence agreement that would, if agreed upon, cement his position as the company's third most productive salesman.

It was the final meeting of the trip, but it would come later. The real purpose of his visit needed to be attended to now.

They had received intelligence that the exchange was due to take place in the square below.

Five minutes.

Curry went to the room's window. There were two panes of glass, one above the other. He spread duct tape over the lower pane, and, using the rubberised butt of a small hammer, he tapped on the glass to shatter it. The tape held the pieces in place. He put on a pair of gloves and picked out the broken glass, starting with the larger fragments and then working his way around the frame until it was all gone. He lay down flat on his belly and slithered forward. The office had been carefully scouted and provided an excellent vantage. He could see down into the square, with the bronze statue of the Communist Party functionary and the locals and tourists who passed along the wide promenade.

He rolled on to his side so that he could get at the bag that he had brought with him. He unzipped it, reached inside and withdrew the component parts of the sniper rifle that had been delivered to him. It was a QBU-88, the designated marksman rifle deployed by the Chinese People's Liberation Army. The rifle, also known as the Type-88, was a gas-operated, semi-automatic weapon. It wasn't optimal, by any means. It filled the niche between the infantry rifle and the sniper rifle, being intended for aimed semi-automatic fire at a range of between three hundred and eight hundred yards. But he had fired rounds from dozens of different rifles during his training, and he was confident that he could make this shot.

The weapon was equipped with a Chinese military rail on the receiver; he took a 3-9x40 standard day optic and mounted it. He attached the quick-release bipod and, as happy with his setup as he could be, rolled back on to his stomach with the weapon arranged in front of him. He took out his binoculars.

Aleksandra had wanted to go with her husband, but he had said no. She told him that she didn't trust his connection. She said that they didn't know anything about the courier who was being sent to make the exchange. Will tried to soothe her, reminding her that the exchange was being made in a public place and that it would be safe, but Aleksandra had seen how anxious he was, and that made her anxious, too. But she had agreed to his plan: she would meet him at the railway station an hour after the exchange had been made.

She packed their case, checked out of the hotel and took a taxi to the station. They were going to Beijing, at least to begin with. They had chosen China because they wanted the reassurance that they would not be extradited back to the United States should they be discovered. The counter to that reassurance was the concern that, should their presence be revealed, the Chinese government would not let them leave, either; the Chinese had a booming biogenetics programme of their own, and the information that they had stolen made them very valuable indeed.

They had decided that they would take a flight from Beijing to Johannesburg. Extradition would be possible from South Africa, but, insulated by the money that they would shortly receive, it would be possible to buy a place and live off-grid. They would be able to disappear. There would be security, and happiness, in anonymity.

Aleksandra looked around. The station was busy around her. She waited in line for the ticket desk. There were several tellers serving the waiting passengers, but it took twenty minutes to make her way to the front.

She looked at her watch.

Just before midday.

That was the time that had been set for the rendezvous.

The location of the appointment wasn't far from the station. Aleksandra tried to picture it, what might be happening, what Will would be saying to the man who had come to collect the data in exchange for the money that they had negotiated. Their failsafe had not been agreed in advance with the buyer. They knew that might cause problems, but they wanted the additional peace of mind and they were prepared to gamble for it.

They were not interested in welching on the deal. They didn't need another set of enemies. Instead, they would find an Internet cafe when they got off the train in Beijing and Will would upload the key so that the buyer could access the information.

Aleksandra felt a tap on her shoulder, turned and saw that the woman behind her was glaring and gesturing towards the now vacant window ahead. She smiled sheepishly and stepped up. She didn't speak Mandarin and the surly teller made no effort to speak English, and it took careful negotiation before she was able to buy the two one-way tickets to the capital.

The woman whom she had inconvenienced shook her head derisively as Aleksandra wheeled the suitcase away. There was a cafe in the concourse and she bought a cup of coffee and took it to one of the outside tables. She sat down and checked her watch again.

Twelve.

The meeting should be taking place now.

It would take fifty minutes for Will to get across town on the subway.

The train was at one fifteen.

Plenty of time.

Chapter Twenty-Six

Pope faced the water so that he could see to the left and the right. The square was busy with locals going about their business and tourists enjoying the morning. He looked up and saw a bulky CCTV camera on a pole on the other side of the square. It was a dome camera, and as he watched, it rotated through 360 degrees.

He noticed Isabella keeping her distance just like he had told her to do. He had wrestled with the good sense of bringing her with him, but he had quickly realised that trying to have her stay behind was going to be impossible. She was determined to be involved and, save locking her in a room somewhere, he knew there was little that he could do to persuade her to wait. And, he conceded, it was useful to have a second pair of eyes. She was young, but she had been given excellent training and had more experience than plenty of intelligence agents he had worked with. She had demonstrated all of that in Syria. It was not lost on him that she had saved his life when they had been compromised in the desert just before they crossed over the border to Turkey. And she had intervened just as he was getting his arse handed to him by the woman who had jumped him in Montepulciano. It was pointless to pretend otherwise: she had already more than proven her worth.

He took out the cell phone that had been left for them at the Shanghai train station. The line was open with Isabella on the other end; he conferenced in the number that had been left for him.

'*Mr Pope.*' The voice was distorted as before.

'I'm here.'

'*What do you have for me?*'

'Not much. No sign of Wheaton.'

'*He's in Shanghai. We've confirmed it.*'

'But not here.'

'*Let's give him a little time, shall we? He's a nervous man.*'

'Assuming he shows up, how do you want me to play it? What if he has what you want?'

'*Do you have the cable that was with the phone?*'

'Yes.'

'*Look at the phone.*'

Pope did as he was told.

'*You see the micro-USB port on the top of the phone?*'

'Yes.'

'*Plug the cable into the port.*'

Pope took the cable from his pocket and pushed it home. 'Done.'

'*The phone has been rooted. That just means we've played with the code a little. Wheaton will have a USB drive. You attach the drive to the other end of the cable and that's that.*'

'What happens then? You upload the data?'

'*Correct.*'

'No,' Pope said. 'Are you joking?'

'*What do you mean?*'

'I mean I don't think so. If you have the data, you've got what you need. There's no reason for you to help me after that.'

'*You have to trust us, Mr Pope.*'

'With respect, I don't even know your name. And I'm old enough to know that you don't trust anyone, not in this game.'

Isabella's voice interrupted the call. '*Someone is coming your way.*'

'Where?'

'*From your six.*'

Pope turned around and saw the man. He had approached from the south, pausing on the promenade before angling to his left and taking a diagonal that brought him right up to the tables. He stopped there, nervously massaging an ear lobe, and then he noticed Pope looking at him. He took a half step towards him, paused again, looked behind him and then continued.

'He's coming,' Pope said into the phone. 'You'll get the data when I deliver it to you in person and not before. If that's a problem, say so now and I'll walk away.'

The man walked across the square towards Pope's table.

Pope stared up into the CCTV camera. 'You're watching, aren't you?'

There was no answer.

'I know you are. So you'll see this.'

He got up from the table.

'I'm about to go,' he said into the phone.

'*No,*' the voice retorted, the anger and frustration evident even through the electronic distortion. '*Fine. We'll do it your way. Leave the call open. I want to hear what he has to say.*'

Pope put the phone down, sat back in his chair and turned all the way around.

The man was a few feet away. He stopped when he reached the table. 'Is this free?'

'Help yourself,' Pope said.

The man stood where he was.

Pope looked up at him. 'Mr Wheaton?'

The man swallowed, his larynx bobbing up and down. 'Yes. And you?'

'My name is Michael. Why don't you sit?'

'I have to be careful. I'm sure you understand why.'

Pope watched the man as he spoke. He was slender, with neatly cut hair and eyebrows that looked like they had been trimmed. His fingers were long and thin, the nails chewed down to the quicks.

'I understand. And the sooner we do this, the sooner you can leave. Sit down. You're standing out.'

Wheaton pulled the chair out and sat. He clasped his hands together and kneaded them nervously. 'Are you ready to make the transfer?'

'I just need to speak to your buyer and the money will be transferred. How about you?'

Wheaton reached into the inside pocket of his jacket and took out a USB drive. He reached across and dropped it on the table next to Pope's hand.

'That's half of what you need,' Wheaton said.

'Half?'

'That's the data. But it's encrypted. It stays that way until I leave the country. When that happens, and I'm sure I'm safe, then I'll give you the key to unencrypt it.'

Pope had no idea whether that was acceptable.

'I'm not negotiating,' Wheaton said as Pope paused. 'Take it or leave it.'

'One minute,' he said. He turned his head a little and spoke into the microphone. 'Did you hear that?'

Wheaton started to protest – 'They were listening?' – but Pope hushed him with a raised hand.

'*Was that a stick he gave you?*'

'Yes,' Pope said.

'*Let me think about it. Don't let him leave.*'

Isabella drifted along the promenade, maintaining distance between herself and the square. She could see Pope and the man at the table and, thanks to the open connection, she could hear the conversation that he was having.

She watched them carefully. Pope was bigger, taller and broader across the shoulders. Wheaton was slender, almost effeminate. His nervousness came through in his voice. Pope had taken the seat at the table with his back to the cafe, granting himself a clear view into the square. That was not coincidental; Isabella's mother had taught her to do the same thing, how important it was to choose the seat with its back to the wall so that you could see who else was interested in your conversations. Wheaton was discomforted by the fact that he couldn't see behind him and frequently turned his head to look out into the square.

She listened to their conversation.

'*That's half of what you need.*'

'*Half?*'

'*That's the data. But it's encrypted.*'

Isabella's attention was distracted from the conversation. She had been looking west, into the square, and something had caught her attention. She stopped walking and looked more carefully. What was it? She glanced up at the tall buildings on the other side of the busy road.

She thought she saw something.

And then she saw it again, clearly this time.

A glint.

A starburst as the noon sun bounced against something reflective.

Curry arranged himself so that he could hold the rifle comfortably: his left hand was forward, cradling the fore-stock; his right arm reached around so that he could slide his index finger inside the trigger guard; his shoulder was pushed up against the stock; he put his eye to the sight.

He scanned the square and the promenade. He nudged the rifle right to left, allowing the cross-hairs to settle on the heads of the men and women below before nudging it away again. He drew the range back, locating the table where the two men sat facing each other. He recognised Michael Pope and laid the cross-hairs over his face and watched as he spoke, gesturing as he did so. The second man had his back to him, but he had watched him make his way across the square.

He spoke into his lapel mic. 'Angler is here.'

'*And Parasol?*'

'No. Just him. I have the shot. Am I clear?'

'*Weapons free. Repeat: weapons free.*'

Curry had orders to take both Wheaton and Pope out. Wheaton was the primary target. Curry adjusted his aim accordingly. The safety switch was on the bottom of the receiver, just behind the magazine opening, and Curry clicked it into firing mode.

Pope waited until he heard the voice in his ear again.

'*Tell him we'll pay half now, half when the data is unlocked.*'

Pope relayed the message. Wheaton nodded; he must have been expecting the counter.

'*Do you have the stick?*' the voice asked in Pope's ear.

Pope reached across for it. 'I have it.'

'*We're sending the money now. Tell him to check.*'

Pope turned to Wheaton. 'They're paying you. Check your account.'

Wheaton took out his own phone and busied himself making a series of taps on the screen, navigating through his banking app.

Pope glanced up at the Bund. Isabella was still there, standing against the wall. She wasn't looking at him, though. Her attention was beyond the square, focused on something on the other side of the road.

Pope turned in the same direction, but couldn't see anything out of the ordinary.

Pope spoke quietly into the microphone. 'Isabella?'

Wheaton put his phone away. 'The money's there,' he said, buttoning up his jacket and standing. 'Thank you.'

Isabella screamed into his ear: '*Sniper!*'

Chapter Twenty-Seven

Pope swung around to look into the square, instinctively searching for a threat, anything that might explain the message.

A flash in his peripheral vision.

The quickest flash of light from a window of one of the buildings.

And then he felt a sudden damp warmness on his face.

The boom of the rifle came another fraction of a second later.

He turned back. Wheaton's lifeless body lolled forward against the edge of the table. A bullet had entered his skull at the back of his head and had blown it apart as if it were an overripe melon.

The gunshot had brought a moment of shocked silence, but now there were screams.

Pope pushed away from his chair and rolled aside a fraction of a moment before the second bullet hit. It sliced through the metal slats of the chair, mangling them, and thudded into the ground beneath it.

The crack of the shot followed.

He heard Isabella's voice in his ear again. '*Pope!*'

He was out in the open and knew that he had to move. He pushed himself up on to his hands and knees and started to scramble away, his boots sliding through the sudden blood that had been spread over the ground like sticky jam. He found traction and pushed with his legs until he was upright, taking three steps and then diving into the inviting cover offered by the corner of the Airstream.

It might not be enough. The walls of the trailer would be thin, and the calibre of the bullets that had been fired had to be on the larger side of the spectrum. He guessed the sniper was using heavy-calibre rounds and, if that was right, they would slice through the wall of the trailer as if it were paper.

He shuffled farther into cover, trusting that the fact that the sniper wouldn't be able to sight him would be protection enough.

His earbuds had been disturbed by his lunge into cover. He pressed them back into his ears.

'Isabella,' he said into the microphone. 'Isabella – can you hear me?'

Nothing.

He heard the distorted voice instead. '*Control – report.*'

'Sniper,' Pope said. 'Wheaton is down.'

'*Do you have the drive?*'

He patted his pocket and felt the hard little ridge of the memory stick. 'Affirmative.'

'*Do you know where the sniper is firing from?*'

'One of the buildings to the west of the square. I'm in cover, but he'll have a clear shot if I move.'

'*Hold position. I can see you.*'

He looked back to the CCTV camera on the other side of the square. It had panned around so that it was pointing directly at him.

'*I'll arrange a distraction,*' the voice said.

Curry clicked his radio to transmit.

'Target is down,' he reported.

'*Extent of injuries?*'

'Angler is dead. Headshot.'

'*What about Archangel?*'

'Negative. He is in cover. I have no shot.'

'*Did he make the exchange?*'

'Affirmative.'

There was no immediate response. Curry ignored that, settling into the routine that had been drilled into him. He quickly reached forward and collected the two spent casings.

The radio crackled again. '*Are you compromised?*'

'Negative. Not as far as I can tell.'

'*Then maintain position. Blaine is inbound. Provide coverage.*'

'Affirmative.'

Isabella sprinted across the promenade.

The square was a confusion of frantic activity. The men and women who had witnessed the shooting were scattering in all directions, and there was an ugly cacophony of noise: screaming from onlookers who had seen what had happened mixed with angry car horns from the road as pedestrians spilled off the pavement in an attempt to get clear. The dead body slumped over the cafe table was like a stone dropped into the middle of a smooth pool of water; ripples were rolling out in all directions and, as those nearby realised what had happened, panic began to spread.

Isabella had looked down at Wheaton when the first shot had been fired. The bullet had come from a high angle, entering the top of his skull and exiting through his cheek before it crashed into the table and split it down the middle. The shot had been fired from the building, high up, from where she had seen the glint of light. The tower bore the insignia of the Bank of China.

'Pope,' she said into the microphone. 'The shooter's in the Bank of China building. Two-thirds of the way up.'

What next? Would the sniper be satisfied now that his or her first target had been eliminated? Would they be making an escape, or would they be sighting for a third shot?

'Pope,' she said again.

'*I'm here. Can you see them?*'

'I saw the reflection off their sight. If they're still there, they've got you covered.'

'*Hold your position, Control,*' the distorted voice said again. '*I'll tell you when to move.*'

Isabella noticed something unusual. Most of the men and women who had been in the square were cowering in cover or running away along the Bund to the north and south. Her eye was drawn to one man in particular. Instead of running away from the scene, he was walking purposefully towards it.

She stared at him: he was wearing a business suit, the kind of attire that meant he could melt into the background in a place like this. He might have done just that, apart from his demeanour and the fact that his hand reached inside his jacket to bring out a submachine gun that he was wearing on a strap.

'Pope – there's another one.'

'*What do you mean?*'

'A second shooter.'

The man kept coming, walking briskly towards the steps that led down into the square.

'*Where?*'

'Coming from your six.'

She took the Glock from her bag. The man was fifty yards away from her, proceeding north from the other side of the square. It would be a difficult shot for her to make, but she would at least give him something to think about.

She raised her arm and fired.

The shot went high and wide.

The man dropped to a crouch and, before Isabella could fire again, he brought his own gun around and squeezed off a burst.

She dropped to the ground and rolled to the side.

The barrage passed close by overhead.

She scrambled to her hands and feet as she heard a second burst and flung herself behind an outcropping in the wall.

Her face was stung by a storm of dislodged stone chips.

'*Isabella?*'

'He's got a submachine gun,' she said.

'*Stay in cover.*'

'If he gets to the steps, he'll be able to see you.'

The distorted voice spoke. '*Hold in place, Control.*'

'*Where's your fucking distraction?*'

Isabella was secure behind the bulge in the wall. She turned and looked up over the edge towards the East-1 Zhongshan Road. It was one hundred and fifty feet from the promenade to the street. It seemed like the safest route for her to take. She would have to cross a margin of grass with topiary and neatly ordered hedges. The statue of Chen Yi would provide her with cover from the man with the submachine gun for at least some of the time it would take her to cross. She would have to trust that the sniper had left his eyrie or was concentrating on Pope.

She closed her eyes and took two deep breaths.

She opened her eyes again, put both hands on the wall and, with a push from her legs, vaulted easily over it and dropped down on to the other side.

And then she ran.

Chapter Twenty-Eight

Curry saw everything.

Jacob Blaine on the Bund, approaching from the south.

The sun sparking off the aluminium trailer behind which Archangel was still hiding.

The muzzle flash of Blaine's submachine gun as he sprayed rounds at a target on the other side of the square.

A sudden blur of motion as a figure vaulted the wall and started to run through the gardens on the north side.

He nudged the rifle around, quickly finding the figure in the scope. It was the girl. Angel. She was a target, too. She was moving west, towards him. The gardens offered minimal cover and she had one hundred and fifty feet to cross before she could reach the relative safety of the road. One hundred and fifty feet and no cover. She was moving quickly, but that wouldn't matter. Curry was an excellent shot. This wouldn't be difficult.

He tracked her, leading just a little, and wrapped his finger around the trigger.

The blare of the alarms was sudden and disorientating. It was everywhere, all at once, and then, almost immediately, the overhead sprinklers opened and sprays of water gushed down.

He looked up, straight into a torrent of water.

He looked away, wiping the water from his eyes. 'This is Curry,' he reported. 'I've been compromised.'

He didn't wait for a response. The protocol was clear and unambiguous. He disassembled the rifle and put it back into the bag he had used to bring it into the office.

'*What do you mean?*'

'The fire alarm has been tripped. The sprinklers have been activated.'

He stood, checked that he had not left anything that might incriminate himself and started back to the door.

'*Understood. Leave the area.*'

'On my way.'

He opened the door and hurried along the corridor to the emergency stairs.

Blaine's voice came over the radio. '*Both targets are running,*' he said. '*No sign of the police. Am I cleared to pursue?*'

'*You're cleared. Take them out. Both of them.*'

⁀

Jacob Blaine jogged briskly towards the square.

His codename within the programme was Morpheus. Pride was not something that mattered to him, but the efficient fulfilment of his orders was something from which he derived satisfaction.

Two targets. They had known that Archangel was most likely not alone, and now they knew for sure.

Pope *was* with the girl. She had been with him in Mumbai, too. All of the targets had been assigned codenames.

Litivenko was Parasol.

Wheaton was Angler.

Pope was Archangel.

Rose was Angel.

One down. Curry had seen to that.

Blaine would account for two more.

The girl was running, fearful of the spray from his submachine gun. Blaine had authorisation to eliminate her, too, and he would do so without compunction if the opportunity presented itself. But she was hidden beneath the line of the promenade now, and there was no more time for even the briefest of diversions. He and Curry had been given two priorities: Wheaton and Pope.

He continued along the Bund until he reached the gap in the parapet to his left that allowed access to the steps that led down to the square. Pope was sheltering behind the Airstream trailer that was employed as a cafe. The tables set out around the trailer had been abandoned, many of the chairs overturned in the panicked rush as people fled the area. Wheaton's body was still at the same table, slumped down and with his arms hanging limply to either side. Curry's round had made a terrible mess: blood had been splattered across the surface of the table, with one long gout splashed out across the ground for several yards.

Blaine started down the steps. Pope was penned in. He dared not step out of cover for fear of another shot from Curry's rifle. But his position did not offer him refuge from Blaine. He could see him crouched down with his back pressed to the side of the Airstream. Blaine was able to shelter behind the stone baluster as he descended the steps to the square. He pressed himself up against the baluster and looked over the top.

He let the submachine gun rest on its strap, reached into his pocket and took out an M67 frag grenade. He checked back up the steps to the Bund and, satisfied, gripped the pull ring with the fingers of his left hand while maintaining a firm hold on the body of the grenade and the safety lever with his right.

He started to pull the safety ring away from the grenade, but, before he could do it, he heard the sound of alarms from the other side of

Zhongshan Road. More than one alarm; it sounded as if the alarms of every building west of him had started to blare all at once.

Pope slid out from behind the trailer and ran.

Blaine put the grenade away and reached for the MP5.

He took the steps two at a time and sprinted in pursuit.

Chapter Twenty-Nine

Isabella reached the road before Pope. It was busy with traffic and, in the near distance, she could hear the sound of sirens. Both lanes were crawling, the drivers slowing so that they could look at what was happening in the square.

She took cover behind a bus shelter. The alarms were deafening. It seemed as though the alarm of every single building for fifty metres in each direction had been triggered. Workers from the buildings were beginning to emerge on to the street, quickly creating a melee of confusion and noise. Many of them were wet through. If this was the diversion that had been mentioned, it was a good one.

Isabella looked back. Pope was running hard, about to reach the steps that would bring him up to her level.

The man with the submachine gun was behind him and closing fast.

Isabella stepped out from behind the shelter, aimed the Glock and fired.

The shots bit into the ground near the shooter, forcing him to take cover behind the trailer that had recently sheltered Pope.

Pope reached the road. There was a motorcycle courier nearby. He veered towards him and, without ceremony, clotheslined the man off his vehicle.

Isabella recognised the bike; it was a Kawasaki KLR650. It was perfect for a courier: cheap, nimble and reliable. Pope leaned down and heaved it upright, then slid on to it. He gunned the engine and the bike skidded around and then jerked towards Isabella.

There was a rattle of gunfire from behind them and then the crashing of glass as two of the big plate windows on the far side of the street were struck, the panes falling in fragments to smash on the path. The detonation of the glass drew loud screams from the workers standing nearby.

Isabella risked a glance back into the square and saw the shooter again.

He had come out of cover and now he was aiming another volley at them.

Isabella heard a new noise – police sirens – and saw flashing blue to the north, the lights pulsing against the sides of the office blocks. Two police motorcycles sped along the pavement towards them.

Pope stomped on the brake and slid the rear end around again so that Isabella could get on. She jumped on the back and wrapped her arms around his torso.

She looked back to the square. The man with the submachine gun had ascended the stairs to the road. He was on their level now. Their eyes locked across the queue of traffic for a long moment before he aimed once more.

'Go!' she yelled.

Pope cranked the throttle around. The engine burbled, the rubber bit and they leapt ahead. He turned the handlebars and yanked back. Their weight was over the back of the bike and it was easy to lift the front wheel; they lurched forward, bounced up on to the back of an empty car transporter and from there they hopped the concrete divider that separated the southbound and northbound lanes and crashed back down on to the asphalt on the other side.

Pope turned south and gunned the engine, racing against the flow of the slow-moving traffic.

The shooter fired another burst. There was too much in between him and them, and the volley blew out the windows of a parked bus just as they accelerated past it.

Pope picked a path between the cars, their passage heralded by a tumult of outraged horns.

Isabella saw a flash of motion in the left-hand mirror.

She turned her head to look back.

She saw two things that concerned her.

The first was the two police motorcycles that were now closing on them quickly. They were being ridden along the pavement, the few pedestrians who had not yet fled the scene flinging themselves out of the way as they went by.

The second was the shooter. He was running hard, at a flat-out sprint. He kept coming, on and on and on, his legs beating a metronomic pace and seemingly without the need to stop and recover.

Fifty feet.

A hundred.

Two hundred.

He was uncannily fast, but they were faster and they were pulling away.

He could see that, too, so he changed tactics.

The first police motorcycle reached him. He grabbed the rider and hauled him off, letting him fall to the ground just as he vaulted on to the saddle, keeping the bike upright. He gunned the throttle and sped up, closing on Isabella and Pope and pulling away from the second police rider.

Isabella heard the distorted voice in her ear: '*Go right.*'

Pope heard it, too. He pressed down on the brake, skidding off Zhongshan and accelerating west on to Guangdong Road. The traffic was dense here, too, and he darted in and out of the spaces between the cars, trying to maintain the distance between them and their pursuers.

Blaine could only just hear the sound of his handler's voice over the throb of the motorcycle's engine.

'*Report.*'

'I'm in pursuit.'

The police bike he had taken was a Honda ST1300P. It was more powerful than the dual sport bike that Pope and the girl had taken.

They skidded around to the right, on to Guangdong.

Blaine followed.

He started to reel them in.

Pope braked again and skidded left, accelerating into the narrow passage between buildings. A flight of stairs led up to a short landing and then a dog-leg right-hander.

Pope ascended, his bike bouncing up the steps, and Blaine followed.

Chapter Thirty

A family scattered left and right, the mother muscling a stroller out of the way as the two motorcycles clambered up the steps. *'Follow the path to the right.'*

Pope did as he was told and then paused at the top of another flight of steps that led down to Sichuan Middle Road. The steps were jammed with people. There was no obvious way down.

Isabella looked back.

'He's still coming,' she said.

'Go down, Control.'

'Hold on.'

The steps had been cut into the side of a steep hill, the slope of which was fenced off to the left and right. Pope gunned the engine and sent the bike through the left-hand fence. He pressed down on the brake, locking the rear wheel, and they slithered down the grass.

The shooter followed them.

'Turn left.'

'He's catching us.'

'I'm working on that.'

Pope opened the throttle again, turning right at the Union Building. He picked up speed towards the river.

'*Head for the Waitan Tunnel.*'

The plate window of a noodle shop was blown out of its frame. Glass crashed on to the road and, a fraction of a moment later, Isabella heard the echo of gunfire as it resounded from the walls of the tall buildings around them.

She craned her neck to look back again.

The bike was closing.

'Pope—' she said.

'This is all we've got.'

Another volley of automatic gunfire shredded the car to the right of them, knocking out the rear window and punching through the roof.

'He's gaining!'

She remembered the Glock; she had it in her left hand, pressed to the side of Pope's chest. She turned so that she could aim behind them, raised the pistol and fired. The shot was unaimed, and not helped by the swerving and bouncing of the bike as it bumped up and down the kerbs, and it went high.

Isabella heard the high-pitched roar of an engine. She looked back. The motorbike had switched position, and now it was on their right, racing along the path towards them at high speed.

'Pope—'

The shooter was barrelling straight down the pavement, ignoring the pedestrians who were forced into taking frantic evasive action.

The engine picked up revs. Isabella was forced to grab Pope with both hands to avoid falling off as he swerved left and right, pressed back by the sudden burst of acceleration. The shooter was travelling more quickly than they were and he continued to close. Isabella looked back and saw that he had caught up with them; his bike was adjacent to the rear wheel when the man took one hand off the handlebars and aimed his MP5 at them. He opened fire as Pope swerved to the right; most of the bullets went just wide, but Isabella felt the thud-thud-thud as at least some of them lodged in the padded upholstery of the seat.

There was nowhere for them to go.

The shooter closed again, drawing alongside them. He raised the MP5 and . . .

Nothing happened.

He must have run dry.

He tossed the submachine gun behind him, accelerated alongside again and then swerved into them.

The motorbikes clashed and jammed together. The shooter reached across with his right hand and tried to grab the handlebars of their bike. Pope fended him off. The man tried again.

Isabella acted instinctively.

She clambered up on to the saddle, her feet pressed together, and hopped on to the back of the shooter's Honda.

Isabella still had the gun. She tried to bring it up so that she could press it against his head.

The man kicked down on the brake with his right foot. The rear tyre locked, smoke billowing out around the saddlebag and luggage rack.

Pope raced away.

The shooter caught Isabella's wrist and yanked. She dropped the Glock and tried to lock her left arm around his throat even more tightly.

The shooter pulled down on her right arm, bending her elbow over his shoulder. Bolts of pain lanced into her brain as the joints started to pop. The man pulled harder, but the effort was a distraction and he lost control of the bike.

The rear tyre slid out and the bike went down on to its side. The man released his grip on Isabella's wrist and she fell free of him and the bike, sliding along the asphalt on her backside. The man and the machine skidded ahead until their momentum was arrested by a firm bump into the side of a stalled car.

Isabella got up. She touched her hand to the back of her legs and felt the scrape of road rash. She panted for breath, assessing her surroundings. They had fallen in the middle of a busy junction. Sichuan

Middle Road ran into a crossroads with Sichuan South Road. The multiple lanes of Yan'an East Road passed on a flyover above them. The traffic on their level had stopped. A bus sealed the exit to the east and tightly packed cars blocked the way to the south and west. She could hear the sound of Pope's motorcycle, but he was hidden from view behind the bulk of the bus.

The shooter disentangled himself from the bike. The impact of the crash had buckled the front wheel. It wasn't going anywhere. The man stood, shook out his arms and rolled his neck. His pants were shredded, and the skin beneath had been rubbed red raw. The skin of his palms, too, had been abraded where he had put his hands down to try to stop the slide.

He ignored all of that and started to walk towards Isabella.

She turned to look for the Glock. She couldn't see it.

She retreated.

The parked vehicles penned her in.

The man closed in.

Chapter Thirty-One

Isabella backed away.

The man looked to be in his twenties. He was wearing a slim-fitting suit and was shaven headed. His skin was smooth and clear. It would have been difficult to describe him as attractive: he had heavy brows, his eyes were spaced a little too far apart, his nose was longer and thinner than usual and his ears stood out from the sides of his head. He was not especially tall, nor was he built any larger than average.

Isabella took it in as she maintained the distance between them, but her attention was snagged by the expression of bland normality that he wore on his face. It was as if this extraordinary scene – the murder of a man in broad daylight and then an armed pursuit through the streets of the world's largest city – was the equivalent of a lazy Sunday afternoon jaunt to the shops. He moved with a loose ease that suggested that he was completely comfortable with what he had done and what he obviously intended to do next.

Isabella bumped up against the side of the car that was blocking the way behind her. It had crossed the junction from the south and crashed into a Nissan going west. She glanced left and right. There was a gap between the two cars, littered with broken glass.

Isabella started to edge left, towards the gap between the crashed cars.

'Look around you,' she said. 'There are witnesses everywhere.'

The man didn't take his cold eyes off her. He kept coming.

They both heard the sound of the bike at the same time. The man turned just as Pope appeared around the side of the bus. Pope drove right at him, yanking the handlebars and throwing the bike into a skid. The bike went sideways and slid into the man's legs. The impact was sudden, the weight of the bike striking the back of his legs, knocking him off his feet so that he crashed down to the ground as the bike continued its slide beneath him.

Pope righted the bike and smoked the rear wheel as he turned back to the east.

'Quickly!'

The shooter had landed flat on his back, a heavy impact that seemed to have knocked the wind out of him.

Isabella sprinted across and vaulted on to the back of the bike.

The man pushed himself up on to his hands and knees.

'Go!'

Isabella held on tight as Pope lit up the wheel again. He flung them ahead, crashing over a kerb hard enough to launch the bike into the air. They thudded down again on a grassy expanse that bracketed an access road leading towards one of the tunnels that threaded beneath the river. They left the grass, the tyres squealing as they bit on to the asphalt. The tunnel had four lanes: two for eastbound traffic and two for westbound.

Pope flung the bike to the left and right, and Isabella had to hold on as he opened the throttle all the way.

'*Take the tunnel*,' said the voice in her ear. '*I'll contact you on the other side.*'

Pope crashed over the central reservation until he was in the correct lane. The traffic was busy, but Pope negotiated it aggressively, ignoring the angry horns that sounded in their wake. The wind rushed around them both, drying the moisture in Isabella's eyes and stinging her skin.

The road was clear ahead and Pope was able to accelerate. They flashed into the tunnel, the overhead lights passing above them in a series of ever-faster lines.

Isabella turned to look back.

Nothing.

'We've lost him.'

———

Blaine got up. He had managed to jump just as the bike had slid at him, and that had probably prevented one or two broken legs. But the bike had still clipped him, and it had flung him down on to the surface of the road with enough force to daze him. He could hear a buzzing in his ears as he tried to stand.

A man arrived next to him, reaching down. He said something, but Blaine didn't hear him properly. The man put both hands beneath Blaine's shoulders and helped him up. Blaine's reaction was automatic: he windmilled both arms to slap the hands away, grabbed the man by the lapels of his jacket, butted him in the face and then dropped him to the ground.

There was a scream; Blaine turned to see a woman caught between wanting to run to the fallen man and her fear of him. A wife, maybe. A girlfriend. Blaine didn't care. It didn't matter.

He started to jog, leaving the junction and going south along Sichuan South Road.

He made sure his throat mic was still attached to the collar of his shirt.

'This is Blaine.'

'*Report.*'

'I lost them.'

'*How?*'

'The girl. She is resourceful.'

There was a pause. Blaine could hear the sound of sirens behind him. He picked up the pace. He remembered a bus stop opposite the Guangming Finance Mansion. He would take a bus and get as far away from here as he could.

'*Exfiltrate, Blaine. You can't be there.*'

'Acknowledged. Blaine out.'

Chapter Thirty-Two

Pope waited until he could see daylight and then stopped the motorbike, blocking the lane. He told Isabella to get off. He walked back to the car that was trapped behind them. The driver had opened his own door and was halfway out when he saw Pope. He tried to get back inside again, but he was too slow. Pope reached down, grabbed the collar of his jacket, hauled him out and dumped him on the road.

Pope got into the front seat. Isabella hurried around to the other side. Pope put the car into drive and negotiated a path around the parked bike. They set off again, the daylight blending with the artificial light until they emerged into the early afternoon's brightness.

Pope looked ahead, but there was no sign of anything that suggested that the enemy had been able to get across the river in time to continue their pursuit.

He heard the distorted voice in his ear. '*Pope?*'

'The sniper and the man on the ground – they were the same as the woman in Italy?'

'*They are the products of the same research. Wheaton works – sorry, worked – on the programme to develop them.*'

'Did you know they were going to be there?'

'*No. We had no idea. We wouldn't have sent you if we did.*'

'So how did they know?'

'*We're looking into that.*'

Pope took the opportunity to take a deep breath. 'We need to have a conversation.'

'*We are. Right now.*'

'Not like this. Face to face. I don't like being used as an errand boy.'

'*That's not how it is. We're helping you. It's not all one-way.*'

'It's not going to be anything at all unless you can persuade me that you can be trusted. And I can't trust you like this. I need to look you in the eye.'

There was no answer.

'Last chance. You agree to meet me or we're done. I'll throw the stick in the river and find them without you.'

There was no response.

'You still there?'

'*I need the stick, Control.*'

'And I'll give it to you. But it has to be face to face.'

'*Fine. Go to Beijing. I'll meet you there.*'

'Where?'

'*The Rosewood. I'll reserve a room for you. Go there and wait. I'll be in touch.*'

⌣

It was two in the afternoon when Aleksandra finally stopped pretending and allowed the panic to wash over her.

The train to Beijing had departed forty-five minutes ago and William had not been here to take it with her.

She tried to persuade herself that there was a good reason for the delay.

Perhaps there had been extra negotiation to be done to accommodate the failsafe.

Perhaps there had been traffic between the location of the rendezvous and the station.

Perhaps the subway had been delayed . . .

Perhaps, perhaps, perhaps.

No.

Aleksandra knew that none of those reasons were true.

Something had happened.

Something bad.

They had discussed what would happen if William did not arrive for their meeting. Plan B. Aleksandra would take the train to Beijing and then transfer to Harbin. William would join her when he could.

She bought a ticket for the next train and joined the scrum of passengers shuffling through the gates and down to the platform.

The train was waiting.

She struggled through the crowd to the correct carriage and hauled her suitcase aboard. She stowed it, slumped down in the seat and stared at the men and women outside. She had been thinking about William, but now she found that she was thinking about herself, too.

If something had happened to him, then she was in danger.

She looked at the blank and apathetic faces in the crowd and thought of the millions of people that swarmed through the city outside. Twenty-four million. The most populous city in the world. The only person she knew in Shanghai was William, and now she had no idea where he was.

She felt vulnerable and alone.

PART SEVEN:
Beijing

Chapter Thirty-Three

Shanghai and Beijing were connected by the Jinghu High-Speed Railway. Pope and Isabella caught a commuter train from Yuyuan Garden station and then changed to the non-stop 15.32 from Hongqiao. They rode in second class, the carriage arranged into rows of three seats, a space for the aisle and then a further two seats. They had two seats together.

They tore through the countryside at two hundred miles an hour. They were both quiet. Pope took out the thumb drive and laid it on the fold-up table attached to the back of the seat ahead of him, flicking it with his finger so that it spun on its axis. Isabella was next to the window, and she gazed out as the landscape went by in a fluid blur. They took turns to go up to the buffet car for lunch. Isabella looked at the juice, teas, dried Chinese snacks and dried noodles, but she wasn't hungry. She bought two butter cookies and made herself eat them.

Pope was still playing with the thumb drive when she returned.

'What are we going to do?' she asked him.

'We'll meet our friend and then decide.'

'You think they're a friend?'

'They helped in the square.'

'The alarms?' she said.

He nodded.

'You think they did that?'

'They didn't go off by themselves.'

'How did they do it?'

'I don't know,' Pope admitted. 'The same way they found us. The same way they got a message to us. There's a lot about this that we don't know.'

***

The journey was 820 miles, but they completed it in two minutes shy of six hours. They cleaned themselves up in the bathroom, washing the dust and grime from their skin. Their contact had booked a room for them at the Rosewood, and a hotel driver was waiting for them after they had disembarked the train. Isabella sat quietly and looked out of the windows as they made their way across the city. The air was dense with pollution and the skyline was largely invisible. Vast skyscrapers that were the rival of anything in Manhattan were shrouded in smog, just the occasional glimpses revealed as the breeze stirred up the miasma. It was past nine, but the streets were still busy with pedestrians, the men and women anonymous behind pollution masks. Beijing seemed vast and impersonal, and Isabella felt the stirrings of disquiet. Pope was quiet in the seat beside her, similarly staring out at the streets as they passed slowly through them. She found that she was glad that he was with her.

***

The hotel was in the Chaoyang district, opposite the Chinese state broadcaster. The fifty-four-floor China Central Television Building soared into the dense clouds: two leaning towers, bent ninety degrees at the top and bottom to form a continuous tube.

The taxi turned off the main road and slowed down to advance into the tree-lined forecourt. The cars waiting at the kerb were all top of the line: Mercedes-Benzes, BMWs, Ferraris and Porsches. The driver stopped and a bellboy in a crushed velvet jacket and shiny black shoes ghosted up to them, opening the door and welcoming them to the establishment in perfect English. Guests were led into the elegant building, passing between two stone lions as their cars were driven away by similarly attired valets and their luxury luggage dispatched.

Pope checked them in at the front desk using their Australian passports and referring to their cover story as father and daughter. Their room had already been paid for. They were taken to their room by a deferential member of staff, who blushed as Pope tipped him.

Isabella looked around. Their room was decorated with Chinese objets d'art, and the floor-to-ceiling windows offered a glimpse out into the smog-filled canyons formed by the unsympathetically utilitarian office buildings of the financial district.

'Not bad,' Pope said.

Isabella sat down on the edge of the bed. 'When is he coming?'

'He didn't say. Get some sleep if you want.'

'I'll wait.'

Chapter Thirty-Four

They didn't have to wait long.

The clock showed half ten when there was a knock at the door. Pope got up off the bed, crossed the room and opened it.

Pope stepped aside. The man who came into the room was dressed shabbily, and Isabella's first thought was that he must have been homeless. He had an aged leather jacket with holes at both elbows and the stitching coming loose in the armpits and a series of patches on the lapels. He wore two scarves – a grey cable-knit and a blue windowpane – together with fingerless gloves and a pair of aviator shades with one arm secured in place with a short length of duct tape. He had a frayed corduroy cap that he wore pulled down low on his head and he had a laptop bag over his shoulder.

'Hello, Control,' he said.

He came farther into the room and turned to Isabella.

'Are you sure you want her in here?'

She stood, a denunciation ready on her lips.

'I don't have any secrets from Isabella,' Pope said before she could speak. 'She's already been through more than she should have on the basis of the lies that I've been told. She can listen to what you have to say and decide what she wants to do.'

'Fine. It makes no difference to me.'

'You got here quickly.'

The man shrugged. 'I wasn't far away.'

'Were you in Shanghai?'

'Yes.'

'Couldn't we have met there?'

'It was getting a little hot. This is better.'

'What do we call you?'

'Whatever you like.'

'No,' he said. 'We need a name.'

'Fine.' He reached up and tapped his finger to the centre of his cap. 'Call me Atari.'

The man's cap was decorated with the logo of the Japanese video game company. Isabella recognised the design: the curved prongs that joined at the top to form the outline of the letter A.

'Come on,' Pope said with irritation.

'You don't need to know my name. It's not important. *I'm* not important. I'm just the guy who talks to you.'

'On behalf of whom?'

'That doesn't matter, either. Look – there are lots of us, all around the world. I don't know who they are, they don't know who I am. It's safer that way. We share certain beliefs and opinions.'

The man took off the jacket, folded it neatly – Isabella thought that seemed pointless, given the state of it – and laid it on the bed. He was wearing a tatty fifties-style cardigan beneath it that he might have found in a thrift store. He went to the minibar, opened it and took out a bottle of water. He cranked the lid and swigged down a mouthful.

'This fucking smog,' he said, taking another drink. 'I can still taste it.' He went to the window, looked out and then, almost without thinking about it, closed the blinds.

'We're five floors up,' Pope said.

'And I don't like to take chances.' He turned back. 'Do you have the drive?'

Pope took the other two bottles of water from the fridge and gave one to Isabella. 'Yes.'

'Give it to me.'

'No. Not until you tell me why you want it.'

He sighed. 'What would you like to know?'

Pope opened his bottle. 'Let's go over what you mentioned before. Start with Wheaton. Who was he?'

'He worked for Daedalus Genetics.'

'I've never heard of them.'

'Why would you have? It's a biomedical research company. Based in Boston. Facilities all around the world.'

'And Wheaton did what? Genetics?'

'No, that's what his wife does. He was a computer scientist. He and Aleksandra are selling information that they stole from the company. That's what's on the stick.'

'What kind of information?'

'Therein lies a longer tale. Do you mind?' he said, nodding to the bed. He sat down next to Isabella; she caught a faint odour from his clothes or his body. 'Daedalus is working on a project to re-engineer war fighters. They call it "Prometheus". Very grandiose, I know. Its aim is to produce "metabolically dominant soldiers". Wheaton's wife is Aleksandra Litivenko. Russian émigré, very smart, expert in experimental molecular embryology.' He put both hands on the bed and leaned back, exhaling wearily. 'Look, a lot of what I'm going to tell you is going to sound like crazy science fiction. Daedalus, Prometheus, all that – I know it sounds nuts, but I promise you, it's not. It's all true, one hundred per cent straight up, and it's fucking scary. You just need to keep an open mind.'

'I don't have a problem with that,' Pope said. 'I had a woman half my weight throw me around in Italy. Isabella watched her jump off a third-floor balcony and walk away. Neither of those things should have

174

been possible. And then the shooter in Shanghai ran flat out after us for half a mile. That shouldn't have been possible, either. You could say that my horizons have been broadened in the last few weeks.'

'That'll all make this a little easier, then.' Atari took a moment, as if thinking where best to start. 'None of this is new,' he began. 'Science has been trying to improve the human body for a hundred years. Hitler tried. Stalin tried. The US. The Chinese, most recently. They've all tried to push the boundaries of what the human species can do. Some of those programmes have been hidden within legitimate research. Twenty years ago, gene therapy was used to cure a child with severe combined immunodeficiency; you introduce a virus to replace a faulty gene with a healthy one. Or kids who can't produce the enzymes we need to regulate the toxicity in white blood cells. You harvest stem cells from their bone marrow, add a working version of the enzyme, inject them back in. Presto: the kids are cured.'

'Why would anyone have a problem with that?' Isabella asked.

Atari looked askance at her, as if annoyed that she had the temerity to interrupt him, especially with such a foolish question. 'We don't. But that's not even the half of what's happening. It's the secret projects that concern us. The ones where the aim is "metabolic dominance".'

Chapter Thirty-Five

They heard a knock on one of the neighbouring doors and the call of 'Room service.' Atari paused, tensing, and waited until he heard the clatter of the trolley as it was pushed away again. 'Metabolic dominance?' Pope repeated.

Atari nodded. 'Stalin had a hard-on for it. Go back to the twenties. The Red Army suffered nearly two million deaths in the First World War; then they were sent to fight in the Ukraine, Kazakhstan, Finland, Latvia, Estonia, Lithuania, Georgia, on and on and on. They were on their knees. Stalin was ready for the first Five-Year Plan and he needed a new labour force to make it happen. He ordered the Soviet Academy of Science to produce a "living war machine". He had a vision of half-man, half-ape super-warriors. His orders were for, and I quote, "a new invincible human being, insensitive to pain, resistant and indifferent about the quality of food they eat".'

Atari got up, went back to the window and peered through a gap in the blinds.

'Stalin had a man called Vladimir Ivanosky. He was at the cutting edge in embryology, mostly concerned with breeding racehorses. He established the world's first centre for artificial insemination, but Stalin told him to change focus. The Russians sent Ivanosky to West Africa with $200,000 and orders to conduct experiments in impregnating chimpanzees. And when they were done with that, they built a centre in Georgia, where they tried to impregnate human volunteers with monkey sperm. It failed, of course, but they made marginal gains. And then they built on them.'

He let the slats of the blind close again and started to pace.

'There's another man: Nikita Ivanosky. Vladimir's grandson. He was born in Leningrad seventy-five years ago. His father was a functionary in the Soviet political apparatus and his mother was a scientist. Nikita was identified as a prodigy. Fast-tracked through school and university. Do you know about Biopreparat?'

Pope shook his head.

'The Soviet biological weapon project. Dozens of labs, all working on individual pathogens. Ivanosky was invited to participate. This was back in the seventies. He was initially concerned with the breeding of primates so that they had enough subjects to test their new toys on. But then he branched out. Started looking into their DNA. Tampering with it. What he did got buried within the larger project for political expediency. They gave him a laboratory in Sverdlovsk until they had an outbreak of the pulmonary anthrax they were messing with and they moved him to Vozrozhdeniya in the Aral Sea. It's an island. They use it to test bioweapons. Ivanosky started to make progress. They saw potential. They called his programme "FACTOR", showered it in roubles and gave him five hundred scientists and technicians. And then they started to make real progress: bacterial gene-tagging trials on human subjects, somatic treatments that produced permanent genetic changes, work to make the packaging vectors more efficient. Unfortunately for them, Ivanosky was having second thoughts. Not about the research, but about what he stood to gain from it. He wasn't a very good communist. He has always been a greedy man. He knows that if he pulls off what he's planning, *Homo sapiens* will have more in common with the Neanderthals than what comes next. He's building *Homo superior.* *Homo deus.* And he wants to get paid.'

'So he defected?'

'Just after the Wall came down. He told Biopreparat that the project had failed and they swept it up along with the bioweapons programmes when Gorbachev let Western inspectors in. They were all over the show back then, and no one noticed when Ivanosky reached out to the CIA, told them that he had made much more progress than he was admitting to the Russians and basically told them how much it would cost to get their hands on his brain. They got him and his family out through Albania. He's been working for the American government ever since. He's been passed around a lot. Not always treated right. The CIA put Daedalus together as a front, said it was working to improve efficiencies in gene transfer, but that was only half of what they were doing.'

Atari scrubbed his eyes and suddenly looked very tired.

'The Department of Defense poured money into the programme and Ivanosky started to make very significant gains. The difficulty was always keeping his test subjects alive. He ran cycle after cycle to try to make it stick. Each cycle was given a letter to mark it out. A dozen embryos in each cycle. Each embryo was given an internal codename. The first cycle had Atlas and Apollo. The third had Charon and Calypso. The eighth had Hades and Hera.'

Atari sat down again.

'The early ones all failed. Some died before they were born. Others were born with mutations. A few lasted a month or two before they developed cancer. The K cohort was the first that showed real promise. Kratos lived until he was four. The L cohort improved on that. The progress was fast enough now that they decided it was better to hide what they were doing. They packaged up Daedalus with a new division of Manage Risk.'

Isabella leaned forward. 'The private security contractors?'

Atari turned to her. 'You know about them?'

'Isabella's mother had dealings,' Pope explained neutrally.

The mention of that name brought back unpleasant memories. The five men and one woman who were responsible for the murder of Isabella's father and her separation from her mother had all gone on to work for Manage Risk. Isabella had shot two of their guards before she completed Beatrix's unfinished work and murdered Pope's predecessor as Control of Group Fifteen. Her first three murders. She had commemorated the last with the tattoo of the rose on her shoulder, completing the set that her mother had been unable to finish.

Atari went on. 'Manage Risk saw what Ivanosky had developed and they went all-in. They created a secure laboratory in an old agency black site in Macedonia and ran the project from there. And they did it. The M cohort has been stable.'

'What does that mean?'

'Ivanosky did what he said he would do. The technology is proven. You met one of the Ms. In Italy. The woman who took your family and tried to kill the two of you – that was Maia.'

Chapter Thirty-Six

H ow does Litivenko fit into this?' Pope asked.
'She was at Daedalus for a decade,' Atari said. 'She worked with Maia for all of that time. They started when the girl was ten and they were confident that the genetic improvements were stable. Litivenko was effectively Maia's personal physician. That means she had access to every last bit of data about her: everything from her physical limitations to the precise sequencing of her genome. That's the data. That's what we agreed to purchase. That's why it's so important. And it's all on the stick.' He took another swig from the bottle of water and then got up from the bed. 'Is there anything else you want to know?'

'Plenty,' Pope said. 'Why are you doing this?'

'Why am I involving myself?'

'What's in it for you?'

'It doesn't matter. All you need to know is that I'm on your side.'

He scoffed. 'So what are you saying? This is because of altruism?'

'No,' Atari said. 'Of course not. There are several reasons, none of which are relevant to our relationship.'

'Of course they're relevant,' Pope snapped. 'How do you expect me to trust you when I don't know your motives?'

'My goals are in opposition to the goals of our mutual antagonists. Neither of us – you and I – want them to succeed. We have that in common.'

'No. I need more than that.'

Atari sighed impatiently. 'I have ethical concerns about the work that is being done. There needs to be proper oversight for this kind of research and there isn't. There needs to be informed debate. And there's *nothing*. The consequences of allowing Daedalus to continue unchecked are potentially catastrophic. The data will catalyse the controls that need to be put in place.'

'How?'

'There is going to be a congressional hearing. Soon. We're gathering evidence for it.'

'So you work for a politician?'

He laughed. 'No. Far from it. But we have a tame senator who's been persuaded that he should share our view. He will ask the questions we want him to ask. The data is the evidence he needs to back up his allegations.'

Pope reached into his pocket. 'You're banking a lot on this,' he said, holding the stick up. 'But Wheaton said it was encrypted. If you can't get at it, how can it help you? Wheaton is dead.'

'But his wife isn't.'

'What if she can't decrypt it?'

Atari didn't pause. 'There'll be a failsafe. We just have to get it from her.'

'That might be possible if you knew where she was.'

'We do,' he said. He reached into his bag and took out a tablet. He activated it and turned it around so that Pope and Isabella could see the screen. It was a map of China. A pulsing red dot followed the unbroken line of a railway as it skirted the city of Shenyang. 'We've got a little malware on her phone. She switched it on an hour ago, probably because she wanted to see if her husband had left her a message; then she thought she'd switched it off. But she didn't. The phone's on, and it's telling us where she is.'

'Where is that?'

'The train from Beijing to Harbin. She must know her husband is dead. We don't know what they were going to do if they pulled this off, but they must have had a plan B if it went wrong and this must be it. There's no reason for her to go to Harbin. It's a hole. There's nothing there. But Harbin is a gateway for Sino–Russian trade. It's also the interchange for buses that go to Vladivostok. Litivenko is Russian. Her parents live in Ussuriysk. That's where she's going. That's her plan B. She's going to defect.' He collected his jacket and put it on. 'Come on, then. Are you coming?'

'You want us to go to Vladivostok?'

'Unless you're willing to give me the drive to see if we can unencrypt it without her?'

'I told you. Not until you give me something I can use about my family.'

'Exactly. So you need to come with me.' He paused and added, 'That reminds me.' He reached down and collected the tablet. 'Your wife and children were taken to Riga in Latvia. They were held there for three weeks. We don't know where – a safe house, no doubt. We picked them up again two weeks ago at the airport. A Gulfstream registered to a Bahamian corporation flew them to Atlanta.'

He tapped on the screen until he had the application he wanted and then handed it to Pope. The screen showed a paused video. It looked as if the footage had been filmed from a security camera beneath the canopy of a gas station. Pope could see the pumps and a single vehicle parked on the forecourt. He pressed 'Play' and the footage spooled. The vehicle was a big SUV with blacked-out windows. As he watched, the passenger-side door opened and a man in a suit stepped out. He opened the door behind him and stood aside as a woman got out. Her back was to the camera, but, even before she turned, Pope knew that it was Rachel. The man shut the door and held on to her arm as the two of them moved off, out of shot.

'Scrub through it,' Atari advised.

Pope did as he was told, dragging his finger across the time bar until his wife reappeared. The man stayed close at hand as she opened the door and stepped aside to let Clementine, Pope's daughter, get out. Rachel got into the car and the man in the suit and Clem walked out of shot.

'Where's Flora?'

'We think she's in the car. No reason to think otherwise.'

'Where was this?'

'Decatur.'

'And where are they now?'

'They were taken to a compound in the woods south of Stone Mountain. We're investigating it now. Farmhouse, outbuildings, nothing out of the ordinary, save that it's registered to a company in the British Virgin Isles. We know where they are now, Control.'

'So give me the address.'

'I can do better than that. I can take you there.'

'Just give me the address.'

'You'll need help. It's a safe house, and your family is an important asset for them. They are guarded. We think there's a team of five or six, well trained and heavily armed. You won't be able to take them out yourself.'

'I'll take my chances.'

'They'll kill you. And the fact that you are still alive is the only reason your family hasn't been shot. If they don't have to worry about you, there's no reason to keep them. I understand your impatience. I'd feel the same way. But you need to do this right.'

'And how would I do that?'

'We can fly you into the country. We can get you in without anyone noticing. We can arm you. And we can run interference to give you a better chance.'

'In return for what?'

'Come with me to meet the doctor before she can do something stupid like hand herself over to Putin.'

PART EIGHT:

Boston

Chapter Thirty-Seven

Dzhokar Khasbulatov clocked out and rode the bus out of Boston to Arlington. He took a seat at the back of the bus, fished his phone out of his pocket and plugged in his earbuds. He had downloaded the new Jay Z album that morning and he had only had the chance to listen to half of it during his lunch break. He had enjoyed what he had heard and was keen to listen to the rest.

Arlington was six miles to the northwest of Boston. He had lived here with his parents and his sister ever since they had arrived here from Kyrgyzstan twenty years ago. Dzhokar had been little more than a babe in arms when they had arrived. His parents had made a point of teaching him to respect his heritage whilst always reminding him that he was an American citizen and that he should be grateful to the country for the opportunities that it had afforded his family. He had agreed with them for almost the whole of his life. He had enjoyed his years at school and he had considered himself fortunate to find a job as a janitor at the Massachusetts Institute of Technology.

He had a little money, security and a small collection of friends. It should have been enough, but it wasn't. He had come to the conclusion that something was missing.

Dzhokar got off the bus on Massachusetts Avenue and walked the rest of the way along Court Street until he reached Khasan's house. It was a large property, clad in clapboard and with colourful panels on either side of the windows on the ground and first floors. The front door was beneath a porch; he pulled the screen door back and knocked. He waited for a minute, unable to stop himself from self-consciously checking up and down the street to see if he was being observed.

They all worried about it, the possibility that the police or the FBI might have been investigating them, even though they had been as careful as they could be to ensure that they did not leave digital footprints that might be traced back to them. They communicated via WhatsApp, relying on its end-to-end encryption to keep their messages private. Khasan had sent a message to the group yesterday evening to say that they should gather here tonight. Dzhokar had been excited and had allowed himself the hope that events were drawing on. They had been together for six months. Khasan had told them that they would have to be patient. Now, perhaps, their patience was to be rewarded.

Dzhokar heard footsteps and then saw the glow of a light through the stippled glass. The door was unlocked and opened a crack; he saw Khasan's face through the gap.

The door closed so that the security chain could be unlatched and then it was opened again.

'Hello, brother,' Khasan said.

Dzhokar stepped inside.

⌣

Dzhokar removed his shoes. There were four other pairs of shoes there already, lined up neatly inside the door. He recognised them: Khasan's white sneakers, Imad's Nikes, Hasan's leather brogues, Abdul's prissy loafers with tassels. They were all here before him. He put his shoes next to Abdul's, hung his coat on the edge of an open door and went through into the large room at the back of the house.

The others were there. Abdul and Hasan were watching TV, a rolling news channel that was still leading with the attacks on London. Imad was staring intently at his phone, probably on Twitter, just like he always was. The three of them and Khasan could trace their heritage back to the Middle East. They were all first-generation Americans, their families emigrating before they were born. Dzhokar couldn't claim the same background, and he sometimes felt as if the others made light of his Chechen blood, as if the quality of his piety was somehow different from theirs. There had been arguments before, and he knew they liked to prod and poke him for their sport. He had learned to ignore it, even to play along, but it still stung. He knew, though, that Allah would treat him the same as he treated them. His sacrifice would be every bit as good as theirs.

'Hello,' he said.

Imad didn't respond, but Abdul and Hasan turned briefly from the TV and acknowledged him. Dzhokar looked over their shoulders and saw that the news reporter was standing in a hangar where pieces of the shot-down airliner were being collected and reassembled. Abdul and Hasan turned back just as the bulletin switched to a 3D reconstruction of the missile detonating against the fuselage of the jet. They laughed as the animation showed the plane breaking into pieces and falling to the ground.

There was a camera mounted on a tripod in the middle of the room. It was aimed at the wall, where the black and white flag of ISIS had been fixed into the plasterboard with four small tacks. One of the Kalashnikovs that they had been given was standing on the floor, its muzzle pointed up to the ceiling. The windows had been covered with a thick blackout blind. The room was lit by an arc light behind the camera and a lamp on the table. There was a small pistol on the table next to the lamp.

'Are you ready, brother?' Khasan asked him.

'We're doing it tonight?'

'Yes. Have you memorised it?'

'I think so.'

'Very good. Sit in front of the camera. I just need a minute to get ready.'

Dzhokar did as he was told. He sat with his back to the wall, his legs crossed, and faced the camera. He ran through the script that Khasan had given him one more time. He had rehearsed it again and again since he had been given it, experimenting with putting emphasis on different words, closing his eyes and trying to tap into the passion that he had first found when he had listened to the imam at the mosque where he had met Khasan.

Khasan left the room. Imad looked up from his phone. 'Make it good,' he said. 'This is what you'll be remembered for.'

Khasan returned with a dun-coloured vest. It had been adapted to accommodate four large metallic tubes, two on either side of the opening at the front. The tubes were nestled in loops of fabric that had been stitched on to the vest, and each of them was connected to a battery that was slotted into a fifth loop that had been sewn to the back of the vest. Khasan carried the vest insouciantly; it might just as easily have been a bag of groceries.

He handed it to Dzhokar. 'You know what this is?'

'Of course.'

Khasan nodded and smiled.

'I thought we were using suitcases?'

'Vests *and* cases.'

Now the others paid attention. None of them had seen anything like this before. There had been YouTube videos, of course, and videos that had been posted on the Twitter accounts that the caliphate used to broadcast its message around the world, but the vests were incidental then. Fighters wore them in their martyrdom videos. They might sometimes be visible in grainy CCTV or phone footage shot just before the moment of detonation. The men knew what the vests meant, but it was still an abstract concept, difficult to consider. To have one here, to weigh it in the hand and feel how heavy it was, to touch the fingertips to the cylinders that had been filled with explosives and debris, it made it into something more realistic. Something tangible and real.

'Put it on. We want the unbelievers to believe you when they hear your words.'

The others gathered around. Dzhokar put his arms through the vest and then fastened the hooks to close it around himself.

'Fat fucker,' Imad said.

The garment was tight, but it had to be that way; they would wear lightweight jackets over the top so as to hide their purpose as they made their way to their objective.

'Comfortable?'

'It'll do.'

'Here.' Khasan took the pistol from the table and handed it to Dzhokar. 'Use this. Wave it around when you speak. It will make an impression.'

Dzhokar took the weapon. It was compact and fitted snugly into his big hand. He squeezed, feeling it pressed tight into his palm.

The others moved behind the camera. Abdul switched off the television and Imad killed his phone. Khasan busied himself with the settings, then went to the light and arranged it so that its illumination fell squarely across Dzhokar and the flag behind him.

'You ready?'

'Yes.'

Dzhokar took a breath. He found that he had started to sweat; the pistol was squirming in his grip.

Khasan pointed a finger at him and mouthed, 'Go.'

He breathed in and out and started to recite the speech.

'I have undertaken my operation because of the rewards that Allah has promised those who follow on his path and, Inshallah, become martyred in his name. I am doing this for the guarantee of paradise for myself and my family. And I am doing this to punish and to humiliate the Kuffar, to teach them a lesson that they will never forget.'

Khasan nodded his encouragement. The others watched on. They were intent. None of them were laughing now.

'We Muslim people have pride and we are brave. We are not cowards. We have looked at what you have done to us and we say that enough is enough. You have been warned many times to get out of our lands and to leave us alone, but you have persisted in trying to humiliate us, to kill us and to destroy us. Now the time has come for you to be destroyed. You have nothing now but to expect floods of martyr operations. We will destroy your capital and kill your people so that you can taste what you have made us taste for a long time.'

'What about the innocent people?' Khasan asked him from behind the camera. 'Surely just because the Kuffar kill our innocent, this does not mean that we should kill theirs?'

'We are doing this in order to gain the pleasure of our Lord. Anyone who tries to deny this, then read the Koran and you will not be able to deny this. It is the words in the Koran and the words of the messenger of Allah, prayers and peace upon him, and we will not leave this path until you leave our lands, until you feel what we are feeling. This is revenge for the actions of the United States in the Muslim lands. Their British accomplices have already been punished. Now it is your turn.'

Khasan gave a final nod, pressed a button on the side of the camera and ended the recording.

'Well done, brother.'

'Who's next?' Imad said.

'You, Dzhokar – take off the vest and give it to Imad.'

Dzhokar unfastened the hooks and handed the vest to Imad.

'Heavier than it looks,' Imad said as he slipped his arms through the openings and started to do it up.

Khasan was reviewing the footage on the camera's screen. Dzhokar went to him and watched over his shoulder. He saw himself and, for a moment, allowed himself the luxury of imagining what the people who knew him would say when they watched the message that he had just recorded, when it was playing on their TVs and on their devices.

What would they think of him? Would they be surprised?

He thought that they would.

The thought of that pleased him.

'Do we know when it will happen?' he asked Khasan.

'Soon. We must be patient. When I am told, I will tell you. But it won't be long.'

'Let's do it,' Imad said. 'Hit "Record".' He was sitting cross-legged on the floor, his feet clad in white socks that had ridden down to reveal his bony ankles. Dzhokar thought that he looked foolish.

Khasan adjusted the camera. The TV had been switched back on again, a replay of the president shaking hands with the British prime minister in the Oval Office.

'Turn that off,' Khasan said. 'Let's be professional. The quicker we all record our messages, the quicker we can go and get something to eat.'

The room fell silent. Khasan counted Imad in and, on cue, he started to speak.

PART NINE:
Skopje

Chapter Thirty-Eight

Vivian Bloom was collected from his hotel and driven through the city towards the airport. It was raining again, the dreary drizzle providing a useful summation of how he felt about the city and the backward country within which it resided. He stared out of the smeared windows at the dour rows of housing, the men and women slouching into the wind as the rain lashed them.

He sat back in the comfort of the bulletproof SUV and closed his eyes.

The jet was waiting on the taxiway. Bloom waited for the driver to open the door and then sheltered under the man's umbrella as he made his way across the asphalt to the steps. He climbed them as quickly as his legs would allow, but, without the umbrella above his head, he was sopping wet by the time he stepped over the sill and made his way into the cabin of the Airbus A319.

He glanced around the interior. The jet had been extensively remodelled for executive use. He had flown on the plane before. The front of the aircraft had been given over to two large executive suites, with offices and sleeping quarters. The rest of the plane was equipped for passengers, with several rows of seats. The seats were of the highest standard, with extensive legroom and the ability to be moved into fully flat positions.

A female member of staff saw him enter and, beaming a bright smile, came over to him.

'Mr King would like to see you,' she said. 'He's in his office.'

Bloom didn't know that Jamie King was going to be returning with him. He followed the woman along the corridor that extended along the port side of the jet, past two leather armchairs in which burly Manage Risk bodyguards were sitting, to a closed door.

She knocked on the door.

'Come!'

The woman gave Bloom a polite smile and opened the door for him.

The suite beyond was impressive. The office was on the starboard side of the jet, nearer to the front. There was an imposing desk and a conferencing breakout area with a fifty-inch television, which could be used for teleconferencing. King and Professor Ivanosky were sat around the table. The two men were locked in conversation: King was leaning forward, his elbows on the table, gesticulating with his fingers; Ivanosky was leaning away from him.

'Good evening,' Bloom said as he put his bag down next to the door.

King finished whatever it was that he was saying to Ivanosky and stood. 'Vivian,' he said. 'How you doing?'

'Glad to be getting out of here,' he said.

'I bet you are. It has its uses, though. Government doesn't ask too many questions. Pretty easy to hide a secret out here, even a great big one like ours. What did you think?'

'I think it's very impressive,' he said. He was about to add that he wasn't impressed with the quality of the security, but he held his tongue. It was apparent that King had just finished tearing a strip out of Ivanosky and he had no interest in being the next in line.

'What do you think of the jet?'

'Very plush.'

'Fifty million if you want one fresh off the line, like I did.' He laughed and clapped Bloom on the shoulder.

'I thought you were staying here.'

'Change of plan. I'm going back to Washington, too. Senator Coogan is making noises about bringing the hearing forward. We're going to deal with it before it gets any more messy.'

'And the professor?'

'I have meetings,' Ivanosky said disdainfully.

King crossed the room, lowered the blinds over the row of porthole windows and then led the way out of the office towards the back of the plane. There was a clutch of Manage Risk agents in dark suits, the men gathered together at the rear of the cabin. Apart from those men, however, the plane was empty.

King put his hand on Bloom's elbow. Bloom managed to suppress a sigh that almost escaped. He was tired, and the prospect of spending more than a few minutes in King's company was more than he could stand. But it would never do to admit that. King was a powerful man and Bloom had tethered his future and his vision of his country's future security to him and the things that they had planned together. The bonds were inextricable now.

That didn't mean that Bloom liked King. He did not. He had a low opinion of him. He knew that the forced bonhomie – the slaps on the back and the hail-fellow-well-met – was all an act. He knew that it was mutual: King had the same low opinion of him, too. Bloom had seen King raise his eyebrows when he had addressed their meetings, and British intelligence had intercepted a cell phone conversation in which King had described Bloom as old and 'as slow as molasses in January'.

Bloom didn't mind; they were fair criticisms. He *was* old, and he was deliberate when making decisions. He didn't like to make mistakes, especially not when the stakes were as high as this.

So no, Bloom didn't care about what King thought of him. That would be a personal grievance, and what they were doing was too important to be coloured by something as trivial as that. Bloom's problem was more serious. He knew that his own motives and the motives of his associates in London were pure. But that was not true for King.

Bloom was concerned about doing something to stop the world backsliding into a chaos where it could no longer fight off the advance of radical Islam.

Jamie King was concerned about Manage Risk's share price and feathering his own nest.

King directed Bloom to a seat and sat down next to him. Bloom realised that he was being evicted from the executive suite. The rule on the jet was that you could go aft from your assigned seat but you could not go forward.

'I reckon we ought to get ourselves a drink before we get into the air,' King said. 'What're you having?'

King raised his hand to attract the attention of the female member of staff. Bloom was about to decline when he noticed another passenger boarding the jet.

He swivelled in his seat. It was another woman. She went to one of the empty seats at the back of the cabin and sat down.

He stared at her.

Maia.

'What's *she* doing here?'

'Relax, partner. She's coming with us.'

'For what?'

'She's well enough to go back out into the field. And like I said: things are getting hot for us in DC. That's one of the reasons I'm going back. We've got someone in Coogan's office. He's gonna try to jump us with a surprise. We can't find out what it is, and I don't much like being surprised. So Maia is going to make sure that doesn't happen. Look at her: she's young and pretty. Coogan's a womaniser. Maia's particularly well qualified for what we have in mind.'

Not for the first time, Bloom felt as if he were being dragged deeper and deeper into the rabbit hole. He reminded himself of the greater good.

'I will have that drink,' he said.

'Good man.' King stood and beckoned the attendant to come over. 'I'm going to grab a couple of hours' sleep,' he said, nodding to indicate the suite at the front of the jet. 'You want to get some, too. You look tired. Have a word with Becky. She'll make up your bed for you. I'll see you when we land.'

Bloom watched King make his way down the aisle to the door. The attendant arrived at his seat and asked what he would like. He asked her to bring him a gin. He folded down his tray table so she could deposit it there.

Maia was on the other side of the cabin, and the angle of his seat meant that he was able to stare at her. She didn't seem to notice. She had a tablet laid out on the table in front of her, the glow of the screen washing her sternly attractive face in its artificial whiteness. She was concentrating on whatever it was she was looking at, her brow furrowed as her finger swiped up and down across the screen.

Prometheus was just one of the tools that they had at their disposal. It was subservient to the grander plan, but, at the same time, Bloom wondered if it wasn't just as significant. He caught himself considering the ethics of what the men and women who worked for Daedalus were doing. The woman sitting across the aisle from him was the expression of hundreds of thousands of hours of research and billions of dollars of expense. What was she? She was different from him, even if the changes were small. And genetic manipulation of the germ line was fundamental. It was heritable and permanent and had the capacity to change what it meant to be human.

He was pondering that question when Maia stopped what she was doing and stared at him. He couldn't hold her gaze and was grateful for the delivery of his drink. He took a sip and, when he risked another glance back at her over the rim of the glass, she was looking down at the tablet again.

The engines rumbled as the jet rolled towards the runway. Bloom turned back and concentrated on the ice cubes slowly turning in his gin.

He felt the need for a second drink.

PART TEN:
Vladivostok

Chapter Thirty-Nine

The 0600 Aeroflot flight from Beijing to Vladivostok was scheduled to take two and a half hours. They had three seats next to each other: Isabella was next to the window, Pope was next to her and Atari was next to the aisle.

She pushed up the blind and looked out. The interactive map said that they were at thirty thousand feet and flying over Shenyang. The solid bank of cloud below them covered the city like a shroud. There were occasional breaks that allowed her to glimpse the lattices of roads and railway lines, the never-ending construction that meant that the towns and cities bloated and spread year on year.

The railway line that linked Harbin to Beijing was also below them, and Litivenko would have travelled this way not so long before. The doctor would have diverted to the north before transferring to the bus that would then take at least another thirty hours to reach the Russian port. They would be there at least half a day in advance of her.

Isabella glanced around the cabin. The flight was empty.

Pope turned to Atari. 'Can I ask you a question?'

The man was reading a copy of the *Chicago Tribune* that he had found before they boarded. The front page was full of the news of British and American naval assets moving into the Eastern Mediterranean. 'Sure.'

'How does this have anything to do with me?'

Both men spoke quietly, but Isabella could hear them.

Atari folded the newspaper and stuffed it into the seat back ahead of him. 'There is a conspiracy. You've seen it. You've been involved in it – both of you. What you did in Syria has put you up against them. You made powerful enemies. You know too much already. If they can't get your silence by murdering you, they'll threaten your family to get it instead. There's more at stake than you know. The men and women responsible for what's happening will prosper from the world slipping into another grand war. Arms manufacturers will make billions from selling their weapons systems. Intelligence organisations get their budgets increased. Biogeneticists like Daedalus will see the ethical climate shift so they can deploy their new assets. It's in all of their interests that the situation in the Middle East is allowed to deteriorate. Men like you are pawns in the game.'

'The attacks in London?'

'You don't need to ask that, Pope. You know what happened. They were false-flag attacks. They located a front man who would have credibility within the jihadist community. They picked a preacher and said he was radicalising local boys. The front man located and indoctrinated vulnerable local boys into attacking Westminster. Martyrdom doesn't leave loose ends. The participants wouldn't be around to answer questions. You helped there, too. You killed several. One of them lost his nerve, so they killed him and tossed his body in the Thames.'

'The shoot-down?'

'The same. If I had to guess, I'd say they smuggled a Russian launcher into the country and used it to bring down the jet.'

It was a wild, unlikely story, but Isabella believed it. She had seen too much to think otherwise.

Atari was on a roll now. 'You've both been involved all the way through. You helped them to establish their story. You delivered the preacher for rendition by the CIA. He's been taken to an agency black site in Moldova. He'll confess in due course and then they'll arrange for him to be executed. Another loose end snipped. Then you established the money trail for them, another line of evidence that the media could follow back to the Islamists.'

'Salim al-Khawari,' Pope said.

Isabella thought about the man's son, Khalil, and what Pope had persuaded her to do in Switzerland.

'That's right,' Atari said. 'I'm curious. What did they tell you to do?'

'Isabella broke into his computers. They said he was funding the operations. They wanted evidence.'

'Not true, I'm afraid.'

'They told us Isabella was planting a data tap. Something that would enable them to hack him.'

'We don't think it was about extracting information. Quite the opposite. Most likely, it was a Trojan horse. It uploaded all the fake evidence they needed to prove that Salim financed the operations. All the proof they needed to link him back to ISIS. But he was just the fall guy. His error was to make a few ill-advised friendships with some unreliable Saudi sheiks fifteen years ago. He was the stooge. And you two set him up.'

'If that's right, why did the CIA raid his compound?'

'Because you were successful. They knew the evidence was in place. My guess? They wanted to take al-Khawari there and then. And that was the moment they would have dispensed with you and her, too. What happened to the rest of your team?'

'They were killed. We were ambushed outside Geneva.'

Isabella thought of Snow and Kelleher. Pope had told her what had happened.

'You know who killed them?'

'Daedalus?'

He shrugged. 'I don't know, but I think it's very likely.'

'Can you prove any of it?'

'Of course not. But we know it's happening. There are rumours online already, conspiracy sites and the like, but it's all speculation. There's no evidence. No smoking guns. Wheaton and Litivenko have given us a way in through Daedalus. Fucking that up for them will be a start. We'll work backwards from there. Unravel it bit by bit. It all leads back to the same place.'

'I could go to MI6.'

Isabella watched as Atari aimed a withering glance at Pope. 'You'd be dead before the day was out. Both of you.'

Isabella and Pope had already worked out at least some of the broader strokes of the plot that they had unwillingly assisted, but Atari's dispassionate explanation filled in the spaces between the lines. She could see it all now. Salim al-Khawari had been cast as the fall guy. He had been compromised and had fled into Syria with Isabella as his hostage. Bloom had sent Pope to kill him. Bloom had helped Pope get across the border and then assisted him in penetrating deep into the caliphate, but as soon as Salim was located and Pope went against his orders and decided to bring him out alive rather than kill him, that help had been withdrawn. Instead, Bloom had sent a helicopter loaded with agents to kill them.

'The man I took my orders from – do you know him?'

'Vivian Bloom? Of course. He's responsible for darkening the mood in your country.' Atari nodded down to the folded-up newspaper and the picture of British ships steaming across the ocean. 'Preparing the English for war. He's doing an excellent job.'

'And he knows where my family is?'

Atari shrugged. 'I doubt it. Why would he need to know that?'

Isabella felt Pope stiffen. Atari looked at him disapprovingly. 'Are you an idiot? You can't afford to go after him. He's too important to them. He's very carefully guarded. You wouldn't be able to reach him before they found you. And locating you and the girl is of fundamental importance to them now. All of the other pawns – the boys they sent, the front man, al-Khawari, his family – they've all been swept off the board. It's just you now. You could make a lot of trouble for them.'

'Don't worry, we will.'

'And we will help you do that, but we need to be strategic. We look at Daedalus. We look at Prometheus. Then we look at what their assets have been doing. Westminster. The plane. The whole conspiracy. We're going to build a case against them that they will not be able to answer. But we need you to help me do that, Control.'

'Why me?'

'Because you're perfect. You have the training. I don't. Look at me. I'm a keyboard warrior. I don't know how to do what you do, and we don't have anyone else to send. And, not to be too crude about it, but you're motivated. You couldn't be *more* motivated.'

Isabella felt Pope stiffen again. His temper was rising. 'Do you know where they are?'

'No.'

Pope stared at him, hard. 'If you're holding out on me,' he said, his voice a tight hiss, 'if my girls have to spend just one extra minute away from me, you're a dead man. Are we clear?'

'We are clear, Control. You don't need to threaten me.'

Pope heard the jangle of the drinks trolley in the aisle behind them.

'I mean it,' Pope said. 'We're not friends. I'm not doing this to help you. The only reason we're talking now is because I want them back. If you play me, I'll kill you.'

The steward pulled the trolley alongside their row. He looked past Pope and Atari to Isabella. 'Can I get you a drink, young lady?'

'Orange juice,' she said.

⌣

Atari appeared to have an unending supply of fake documents. He provided two new passports for Pope and Isabella. They were father and daughter once again, but this time their family name was Jones and their cover story was that they were going to ride the Trans-Siberian Express after the conclusion of business in the Chinese capital. Isabella had seen Atari's own passport as he handed them theirs; the cover was deep blue and marked 'Canada' above a royal coat of arms.

Atari disembarked first. He was waiting for them at the air gate and fell into step beside Pope as he and Isabella started up the slope to the terminal building.

'We need to split up,' Pope said.

'I agree. You're booked at the Hyatt.'

'You?'

'The Westin.'

'When do you want to meet?'

'Her bus gets in tomorrow morning at one. Before then.'

'The bus station at midnight?'

'Fine. It's Chkalova. I'll see you there.'

Pope put his hand on Isabella's shoulder and allowed Atari a minute to put a little separation between him and them.

They set off, following behind him.

'Cover story?' Pope asked her as they walked side by side.

'You're my father.'

'And?'

'We're here for the Trans-Siberian Express.'

'Your mother?'

'Dead. Cancer. That's why we're here. I always wanted to come. This is to help me get over it.'

'All right.'

'You don't have to worry,' she said. 'I've been lying my whole life. This isn't anything new.'

'I'm not worried, Isabella.'

They made their way through the airport, walking along utilitarian concrete passageways that were badly lit and cold. Rain lashed down outside, smearing the glass of the wide observation windows that looked out on to the apron and the runway beyond. Russia looked cold and uninviting.

They were able to walk straight up to the immigration booth. Atari was standing at the booth next to them. He was agitated.

'What do you mean?' Isabella heard him saying to the guard.

She glanced across.

'Do you speak English? I don't understand.'

There was a firm rapping on the window in front of them. 'Papers,' the guard said.

'Sorry.' Pope took the fake passports and slid them through the slot at the bottom of the kiosk window.

Isabella watched as two armed police officers stepped between the kiosks and approached Atari. The first guard reached for his wrist and grasped it; Atari shook it off.

'Look at me, please.'

The guards double-teamed Atari, pressing him up against the window and forcing his arms behind his back.

'Sir. Look at me – *now.*'

Isabella squeezed his hand and Pope turned back to the window.

'Sorry. Million miles away.'

The guard examined their passports, thumbing through to the pages with their photographs. He looked up at them and then back down at the photographs.

'What is your business in Vladivostok?' the guard asked him.

'We're here for the Trans-Siberian.'

'Very popular with tourists,' he said with a sneer that made it clear that he did not approve. 'Where are you staying tonight?'

'The Hyatt.'

'If I call them, they will have a reservation?'

'I certainly hope so.'

He nodded. 'Want me to stamp the passports?'

'Yes, please.'

The man brought down his stamp, marking both passports, and then handed the documents back. He gave a brusque nod and then beckoned the couple waiting behind them to come forward.

Pope and Isabella paused as one of the guards took a pair of cuffs and secured Atari's wrists. The man was forced up against the booth, his head pressed against the glass, but he was facing in their direction and they shared a look for a moment before he was dragged away and marched towards a door with a smoked-glass window and a sign that read 'Immigration' beneath the Cyrillic notice.

'What is the matter with you?' the guard said to them angrily. '*Go.*'

They started off. Pope held on to Isabella's hand as they passed through the narrow channel and into the baggage reclaim hall beyond.

'What happened?' Isabella asked him in a quiet voice.

'I don't know,' he admitted.

Isabella could speculate. Perhaps Atari had been in Russia before and had caused trouble. Perhaps his own papers were not as good as the ones that he had given to them. She could guess, but it didn't matter. The man would either be at the bus station tomorrow morning or he would not. Pope and Isabella would be there. They would meet Litivenko on their own if they had to.

Chapter Forty

Isabella followed Pope to the baggage area.

Their carry-on luggage was screened first. Isabella waited and observed as Pope went through. The women operating the scanners were dressed in tight miniskirts with black lace tights. It seemed inappropriate, but as she looked beyond them to where other female staff were wandering the terminal building, she saw that it was the uniform. Pope put the suitcase on the belt and passed through the X-ray arch. The woman who beckoned him to move forward pulled down on the hem of her skirt so as to maintain her modesty. The carry-on passed through the X-ray machine. Isabella was beckoned through the arch; it beeped. The woman who was struggling with her skirt stepped up and indicated that Isabella should raise her arms. She did as she was told and the woman quickly and expertly frisked her. She ran her hands along her arms, down the sides of her torso and then down both legs.

When she was done, she sent Isabella back through the arch and, as she passed back through again, it bleeped for a second time. The woman pointed to a place beneath her throat; Isabella understood and took out the necklace with the locket that Pope had given her. It had belonged to her mother. He had retrieved it from the Americans after Beatrix had blown herself up. The woman took the locket between her thumb and forefinger and opened it. There was a picture of Isabella as a much younger child inside. The woman looked at it for a moment and said something in Russian. Isabella didn't understand what it was, and as she shrugged her incomprehension, the woman shook her head, fastened the locket again and then stepped aside.

Tourists would not have arrived without luggage, so they had bought suitcases and suitable clothes in Beijing. They had removed the labels and crumpled the clothes a little, keen to ensure that it wasn't obvious that everything was brand new. They had travelled light up until that point, but Pope had explained that it was likely that their luggage would be checked by the secret police. It would look suspicious if the father and daughter who were here to enjoy a trip on the Trans-Siberian arrived with nothing.

The cases took fifteen minutes to emerge on to the carousel, and as Pope transferred them to the trolley, Isabella noticed that the cellophane sheeting that they had been wrapped in had been removed. Pope gave her a thin smile to acknowledge that he had noticed it, too.

The arrivals hall was cold and empty. Pope stopped at a concession and bought them two large bottles of water. He stopped at an exchange desk and converted some of their dollars into roubles. He led Isabella between the barriers that held back the few waiting onlookers: family members there to greet loved ones, taxi drivers holding up boards with the names of their prospective passengers.

'We need to stay alert while we're here,' he said to her. 'The secret police are everywhere and they follow tourists. There's no need for us to worry about them as long as we stick to our story.'

She said that she understood and, satisfied, he led the way outside.

They bought tickets for the Aeroexpress. The airport was in Artyom, twenty-five miles north of the city. A ticket on the train cost two hundred roubles for the fifty-minute transfer. Isabella looked out of the cracked and dirty window at the city beyond. It was grey, with lines of brutal Soviet housing blocks squeezed into the spaces between brand new condominiums and older mansions.

They disembarked the train and took a cab to the hotel. The traffic was heavy, and the drivers were aggressive; their driver, a grizzled Russian who had not uttered a word to them save a grunt of acknowledgement when Pope asked for the Hyatt, cursed and fulminated as he was forced to brake to avoid a bus that cut across their lane. Isabella saw a statue of Lenin pointing east towards the United States. They crested a hill with a view of the city. The Golden Horn spread out on either side, the arms of its twin peninsula reaching for distant Russsky Island. The dock accommodated a whole line of Russian cruisers that had been tied up along a long series of jetties. One of the warships was equipped with four rocket launchers on each side, and the missiles must have been enormous if the size of the silos was a reliable judge.

The driver pulled up outside the hotel and took the two suitcases out of the trunk. Pope thanked him, paying him and adding a tip. Isabella noted the colour of the bill and saw that the tip was generous but not *too* generous. Neither too small nor too large, the kind of amount that would be gratefully received without sticking in the mind for excessive parsimoniousness or extravagance. Her mother had taught her the importance of that. You didn't want to be memorable. That could be dangerous in a place like this.

———⌣———

The Hyatt was an ugly building close to the Golden Horn Bridge.

Atari had booked two adjacent rooms. Isabella's was old and tired. The refrigerator was ancient, chugging away noisily with a pool of moisture gathering on the floor around its base. The room was small, with not much space on either side of the bed, and the paint was peeling away on one of the walls, patches of damp revealed beneath it. There was no air conditioning, and everything was unpleasantly stuffy. Isabella went over to the window and opened it, allowing a waft of damp air to seep inside. The view outside was obscured by the decorative curlicue of a wrought-iron figure, but, looking down, Isabella could see men and women going about their business, restaurants and shops, and, higher up, boxy air-conditioning units fixed to the walls and satellite dishes attached to the roofs.

She turned. The bellhop was waiting at the door.

Pope appeared behind him. 'Thank you,' he said.

The man waited.

Pope took a note from his wallet and gave it to him.

The man grunted and left.

Pope came inside and shut the door behind him.

'Pleasant rooms,' he said, making no effort to mask the irony.

She sat on the edge of the bed, picked up the remote, clicked on the television and channel-hopped to a news channel. The midday bulletin was just beginning. The anchor was discussing reports that the British government was sending five Royal Navy warships and two thousand personnel to the Eastern Mediterranean. HMS *Ocean*, one of the Navy's amphibious assault ships, was being sent to join the nuclear-powered Trident submarine that was also said to be in the region. The anchor said that heightened activity was also being reported at the Royal Air Force base at Akrotiri in Cyprus. There were reports that Special Forces were already active within Syria.

'What will happen now?' Isabella asked.

'Too much momentum for it to stop now,' Pope said. 'You don't move assets like that into theatre if you don't intend to use them.'

'There'll be another war?'

'It's inevitable.'

Pope turned away from the screen, opened the doors to the balcony and stepped outside. It had stopped raining now, but it was cold and damp, with a low bank of heavy grey cloud slowly rolling over the ugly buildings. Pope had purchased a packet of local Java cigarettes from the hotel bar and he tore off the cellophane wrapper, took one out and lit it.

Isabella came outside with him. 'I didn't think you smoked.'

'I don't.' He took the cigarette from his lips, held it up so that he could look at it and then flicked it over the balcony. 'You're right. Stupid habit.'

'Just breathing the air here will damage your lungs,' she said, turning to rest her elbows on the metal balustrade.

'I need to go out,' he said. 'We need a car. I saw a Hertz down the street.'

'What do we do tonight?'

'Get there at midnight. Atari is there or he isn't.'

'If he isn't?'

'We do it ourselves. We meet her off the bus.'

'And?'

'Try to persuade her that she can trust us.'

'And if she doesn't?'

'I haven't given that much thought yet. I will.'

Chapter Forty-One

Pope hired a Hyundai Solaris. He collected it from the hotel's underground parking lot and picked Isabella up from the front of the building. It was eleven at night and the weather was a continuation of the damp cold that had greeted them as they had arrived in the city earlier that day.

Isabella had slept reasonably well through the afternoon. It didn't appear as if Pope had been so fortunate. She had seen his silhouette on the adjacent balcony as she went to get some fresh air. He had his phone pressed to his ear; she guessed that he was trying – and failing – to get in touch with Atari. He drove in silence, staring at the empty road ahead. He was anxious. Isabella left him to his thoughts.

They arrived at the bus station at 11.50. It was on the south side of the city, directly opposite the grand railway station. The parking lot was almost empty, and Pope slotted the car into a space that offered them a view of the terminal building and the bays where the buses disembarked their passengers.

They sat in the car, staring ahead through the rain-slicked wind-shield. The odd car or delivery lorry swished over the wet asphalt, the single light that lit the waiting room reflecting off the surface. There was a car in the taxi rank, smoke drifting out of the half-opened window as the driver exhaled.

She couldn't see Atari.

Isabella broke the silence. 'Did you speak to him?'

'I couldn't get through.'

'So how are we going to do this?'

'Let's see if he's here. If he isn't—'

He stopped. Another car drew into the rank behind the taxi. It was a Mercedes-Benz Geländewagen, a luxury four-wheel-drive SUV with blacked-out windows that obscured the cabin.

'That's not good,' Pope said.

'Why?'

'The FSB drive G-wagens.'

'Who?'

'The Federal'naya Sluzhba Bezopasnosti Rossiyskoy Federatsii. Putin's secret service. They used to be the KGB.'

'Are you sure?'

'I hope I'm wrong. But it doesn't feel good. They might have come to pick her up.'

They waited for an hour. The blacked-out Mercedes-Benz stayed where it was, and no other vehicles arrived.

Atari was not going to join them.

Isabella was staring out of the window into the dark night when she heard it: the rumble of an engine and then the wheezing of brakes. She swung around, craning her neck to get a better look at the incoming vehicle. It drew into the first bay, the one nearest to the terminal, and she was able to see the electronic display on the flank. There were words in Mandarin, Russian and English.

HARBIN – VLADIVOSTOK

'It's ten minutes early,' Pope said.

'Do you remember what she looks like?'

Atari had shown them a series of selfies that must have been uploaded from Litivenko's phone.

'I remember,' Pope said.

Isabella looked across to the G-Class. The passenger-side door had opened a crack, a sliver of light leaking out from the inside.

She turned back to the bus. They had both studied the photographs of Litivenko that Atari had provided them, and now they peered through the rain and the gloom as a handful of men and women clambered down the steps to the ground. Pope was leaning forward in his seat, squinting hard, but it was Isabella who saw her first.

'There,' she said.

She came down the steps last of all, gingerly negotiating the gap to the ground. She was wearing a plain beige jacket and blue jeans and she had a beanie hat pulled way down so that it rode just above her brows. Isabella could see the blonde hair that spilled out of the back of the beanie.

Litivenko went to the side of the bus and waited as the driver dragged suitcases from the luggage compartment. She took a small case and wheeled it to the taxi rank. The cab that had been waiting had been taken by one of the other passengers. The others had dispersed, some waiting for connecting buses and others setting off on foot.

Litivenko checked her watch, glanced at the display that showed the times of the departing buses and started to walk to the empty waiting room.

'Here we go,' Pope said.

The doors of the G-Class opened and the driver and passenger stepped out. They were wearing padded jackets, jeans and heavy boots. They moved quickly and with purpose, crossing the pavement and intercepting Litivenko as she came alongside their car. One of the men spoke to her, gesturing to the Mercedes-Benz. She shook her head and tried to step around him, but he caught her arm and dragged her to the side. She let go of the suitcase and started to hit him with her free hand. The second man joined in, taking her other arm and forcing it behind her back. They cuffed her and hauled her to the back of the car. The passenger opened the door and shoved her into the back, sliding in with her. The driver collected the suitcase and put it into the back of the car. He slid inside the car and pulled away from the station. The Mercedes-Benz tossed spray on to the pavement as it accelerated away.

Pope reached forward and started the engine.

Chapter Forty-Two

The Mercedes-Benz headed north along Aleutskaya. The road was quiet, with just a handful of other vehicles heading north and south. Isabella looked out at the shops and businesses on either side of them and then a narrow slice of park to the left. The G-Class was fifty metres up the road; Pope was allowing them plenty of space to reduce the chance that they might be made.

'Where will they take her?'

'They'll have a headquarters in the city somewhere,' he said.

'Do you know where that is?'

'I have no idea.'

'So?'

Pope didn't answer. Instead, he reached across to the central console and zoomed out the satnav's map so that he could see more of the city.

He looked forward.

They were approaching a junction: Aleutskaya continued to the north, with Fontannaya leading off it from east to west. A set of overhead traffic lights controlled the traffic. They were suspended over the road on cables, and they were showing red. The Geländewagen's tail lights flicked red as the driver touched the brakes. The car rolled to a stop beneath the lights.

'Is your belt on?' Pope said.

'Yes.'

'I'm going to rear-end them. Not too hard, but the airbags might deploy. I'm going to play dead. Ask them to help me. Tell them your father's had a heart attack. Get them to come over here.'

The lights changed to green and the Geländewagen started to pull away, but the Russians were moving slowly compared to their Hyundai. Isabella braced herself, holding her breath as they drove into the back of the bigger car. They were travelling at thirty miles an hour, and the bump, when it came, was surprisingly heavy. There was the crunch and tear of metal and the shattering of glass, all a fraction of a second before the sudden exhalation of gases as the airbags deployed. Isabella jerked forward, her face and chest absorbed into the pliant cushion before she was jerked back into her seat again.

She stayed there for a moment, feeling the bite of the seat belt against her clavicle. The cabin was filled with motes of cornstarch and talcum powder, the tiny particles that lubricated the bag.

'You okay?' Pope said.

She glanced across at him. His own airbag was deflating, but he had arranged himself so that he was slumped over to the side, held in his seat by the belt.

'Fine,' she said.

She unlatched the glove compartment and quickly looked inside. There was a can of Blue Star de-icer. She collected it, took off the top and then pushed it into her sleeve so that it was against the inside of her wrist.

'Be careful,' Pope said.

She gathered her breath, unclipped the belt and opened the door.

The Geländewagen had been moved forward by the bump, over the stop line and halfway into the junction. The rear fender had crumpled and the nearside brake lights were out, but save that, it didn't look as if it had been badly damaged. Their Hyundai was in worse shape. The fender was hanging from one fixing, the hood was crumpled like an unmade bed and steam was jetting from the punctured radiator.

The driver's door opened and one of the two men she had seen at the bus station stepped out. He swung around, saw her and fired out a stream of Russian invective.

Isabella staggered forward, feigning weakness. She braced herself against the side of the car.

The man approached. He spat out more Russian.

'My father,' she said in English. 'Please – he needs help.'

The man spat out another guttural sentence that ended with a stab of the finger towards the back of the G-Class.

'I'm sorry,' she said. 'I don't speak Russian. My father. He needs a doctor.' She turned her head and looked up at him, mixing what she hoped might pass for shock and panic. 'Ambulance?'

The man cursed, turned to the car and called out. The rear door opened and the second man emerged. The two Russians shared a quick conversation, punctuated by angry gesticulations in Isabella's direction and at the mangled car. They both came closer.

The passenger went all the way back and looked into the car. Pope stayed where he was, his arms loose by his sides and his head resting against the dashboard.

The driver approached her. 'You are English?'

'Yes,' she said. 'My father – please, can you help him? I think he had a heart attack.' She emphasised the point by tapping her right hand against her chest.

The driver called out in Russian, perhaps relaying the information.

She heard the sound of Pope's door as the passenger opened it.

The driver drew nearer to her. He put his hand on her shoulder.

Isabella heard a grunt of protest from behind her and the sound of a landed punch. She saw alarm in the driver's face. She shook her arm, letting the can slide down into her palm. She aimed and pressed down on the nozzle. The man was close and the spray hit him in the face, the glycol and methanol blasting him in the eyes and nose and mouth. He exclaimed and stepped back, his hands instinctively going to his face. Isabella followed him, crouching down and sweeping his legs. He hit the road hard, the back of his head cracking against the edge of the kerb.

Isabella turned. Pope was out of the car, wrestling with the man who had come to check on him. The Russian was bigger than Pope and, as she watched, he fixed Pope in a front headlock and started to drive his knees into Pope's gut.

Isabella dropped down to her knees and opened the driver's jacket. He was wearing a shoulder rig with an MP-443 Grach in the holster. Isabella had fired the sidearm before; it was an ugly weapon that fired a 9×19mm cartridge. She took it out, got to her feet and aimed.

'Hey,' she called out.

The man still had Pope in the headlock.

'Hey!'

He glanced over at her, saw the gun and ignored it. He raised his right knee again, the impact landing deep in Pope's gut and lifting him off his feet.

Isabella aimed low and fired. The nine-millimetre round cracked into the asphalt a foot from the Russian's feet.

That got his attention.

He released the headlock and raised his hands to his head.

Pope straightened up, wheezing and coughing from the battering that he had taken. He put both hands on the Russian's shoulders, grabbing handfuls of his jacket and then butted him in the face. The man went down, landing on his backside. Pope took a step towards him and then drove the point of his knee into the side of his head. The Russian toppled on to his side and lay still.

Pope frisked him quickly, collecting a second Grach and a bunch of keys. Then he hobbled slowly to the G-Class.

'You okay?'

'Been better,' he groaned. 'Get in the back.'

The rear door was open. Isabella shoved the MP-443 into the waist-band of her jeans and slid inside.

Litivenko was on the other side of the cabin. Her hands were cuffed behind her back. She had turned to face Isabella so that she could try to reach the door handle. Isabella wasn't sure what she was hoping to achieve; even if she had opened the door, she was still shackled. How was she proposing to get away?

'It's okay,' Isabella said.

The woman gaped at her uncomprehendingly.

Pope got into the driver's seat and slammed the door. He started the engine and pulled away, turning left on to Fontannaya.

'Dr Litivenko?' he said.

'Who are you?'

'We're on your side,' he said.

'Let me out.'

'I will. But I'm going to get you away from here first.'

Chapter Forty-Three

Pope drove them north, out of Vladivostok.

'Who are you?' Litivenko asked again.

'My name is Michael Pope.'

'And her?'

'I'm Isabella Rose,' Isabella said.

'We're on your side,' Pope added.

'Where are you taking me?'

'Away from what just happened. Those men weren't friends, were they?'

'Secret police,' she said.

'Did they say anything?'

'They wanted to talk to me.'

'We saw what happened. You don't want to go with them?'

'Not if I can help it.'

'I didn't think so.'

'What do you want? Are you with the company?'

'With Daedalus?' Pope said. 'No.'

'So what do you want?'

'Let's get out of the city,' Pope said. 'We'll find somewhere safe to stop and I'll get those cuffs off. Then we can talk.'

———— ⌣ ————

It was two in the morning and traffic was light.

That was in their favour. Pope drove carefully, following the sat-nav to the three-mile bridge that crossed the Amursky gulf between Vladivostok and the De Vries Peninsula. The darkness of the bay filled the spaces in both directions as they headed out to the centre of the span. Pope had not discussed what they would do in the event that they were able to reach Litivenko, and Isabella didn't want to spoil the silence now to ask. She could guess, though: there were several ways that they could have left Vladivostok, but none of them – not the airport, or the ferry terminal – would have been safe. Their attack on the FSB agents would have been relayed to headquarters now, and it was reasonable to assume that their first actions would have been to lock down those facilities. This bridge would be checked, too, but Pope was evidently gambling that they would be across it before they could react.

They rejoined the A-370 on the other side of the water without incident, and Isabella allowed herself to relax. Pope followed the road north for five miles until they reached the town of Shmidtovka. The lights of the settlement were revealed as they crested a hill: it was mod-est in size, with chimney smoke drifting up through the sodium glow. Isabella wondered if he would stop here, but he carried on, continuing on the A-370.

'Where are we going?' Litivenko asked him.

'Korsakov.'

'No,' she said. 'Take me to Ussuriysk.'

'Why there?'

'It's where I was going. My parents live there.'

'It's not safe.'

'What do you mean?'

'You think the FSB doesn't know that? That's the first place they'll look for you. It might be under surveillance already.'

'It must be nice to know so much, Mr Pope.'

'We go around Ussuriysk on the way to the coast. I'll stop the car when we get nearer to it. If you want to leave, you can. I wouldn't recommend it, but I'm not going to hold you against your will.'

Pope reached into his pocket and took out the bunch of keys that he had confiscated from the Russian agent. He reached back and handed them to Isabella and she thumbed through them until she found a small key with a single hooked tooth. Isabella indicated that Litivenko should turn around. The doctor had been restrained with rigid solid bar cuffs. Isabella tried the key in the first lock; it slid in and, when she turned it, the cuff sprang open. She opened the second cuff.

'Thank you,' Litivenko said to her as she rubbed her wrists.

'Better?'

'Yes.'

'You can tell me to stop whenever you like. I'll stop now if you like.'

'How long to Ussuriysk?'

'An hour,' Pope said. 'What do you want to do?'

'I'll think about it. You can start by telling me who you are and why you're here.'

'We have some things in common, Doctor,' Pope said, staring into the darkness ahead of the car. 'You and your husband did a deal to sell data. We're here on behalf of the people you were dealing with. I don't know how to describe them. We met a man who worked for them.'

'Scruffy?'

'Very.'

'I never met him,' she said. 'But my husband said he looked like he slept in a dumpster.'

'That's not unfair.'

'How did you find me?'

'He's good at finding people. He's taken control of your phone. We've been following you since Beijing.'

Litivenko didn't reply for a moment. Isabella looked across at her and saw that she was gritting her teeth. 'And, what, you work for him?' she said eventually.

'I wouldn't say that.'

'What would you say?'

'That it's not a relationship I'd choose to have. He's helping us with something in return for us helping him.'

She paused again. 'How long have you been working for him?'

'A week.'

'Were you in Shanghai?'

'Yes.'

'When it happened . . .' The words trailed off.

'Yes,' Pope said. 'There was a sniper. They shot your husband. It was right in front of me . . . He didn't suffer. He wouldn't have felt a thing. I doubt he even knew what happened.'

They drove on in silence for another five minutes. Isabella glanced over at Litivenko and, even in the gloom of the cabin, she could see that the doctor was crying quietly. Pope said nothing, concentrating on the road ahead. They passed signs for Alekseevka and Razdolnoye.

Litivenko reached up and dabbed her eyes with a tissue, composing herself again.

'You said they're helping you. Helping you to do what?'

'My family has been taken from me. Abducted. It's very likely that they were taken by the people who killed your husband. Our mutual friend is offering to help me find them. I'd rather have nothing to do with him, but I don't have anything else to go on.'

They passed a road sign. Ussuriysk was two miles away.

'We're nearly there,' Pope said. 'You have two choices. Work with us or hand yourself over to the Russians.'

'Or leave and go somewhere else. Somewhere no one will be able to find me.'

'With respect, Doctor, I don't think you're very good at this. Either the Russians will find you or the bad guys will. You won't be able to leave the country.'

'So you're saying I have to trust you? I can't do that, Mr Pope. My husband's dead because we trusted you before.'

'You weren't dealing with me then.'

'So you say.'

'Fine. I'll take you to the police station and you can hand yourself in. The secret police will get there soon enough.'

'You keep saying how bad that would be for me. Maybe you're wrong. Maybe that's the best option. At least they'll keep me safe.'

'In a gulag.'

'No, a laboratory. You think Putin doesn't have people working on the same projects as Daedalus?'

'I'm sure he has. But it would still be prison.'

'Perhaps. But at least I would be alive.'

Litivenko was quiet for a moment. Isabella watched her face and imagined that she was contemplating what her life might look like if she decided to stay here.

'One mile,' Pope said. 'Make up your mind.'

'What are you offering?'

'The money you wanted is still on the table. Wherever you were going to go, you can still use it to get there. There's no reason for you to hand yourself in to the Russians.'

'Will wanted the money more than I did. And you can't spend it when you're dead.'

'I know one thing: you're going to need it. It's a lot easier to hide with money than without it. You could buy yourself a new identity.'

'Like you said, Mr Pope. I'm not very good at this game.'

Pope didn't answer.

'What about revenge?' Isabella said. It was the first time she had participated in the conversation and it seemed to take Litivenko by surprise. She looked at her. 'You want a reason to do it – how's that? They shot your husband because they were scared about what he was threatening to do to them. You can still damage them. They're still scared. Take the money. Hurt them for what they did.'

'Who did you say you were again? His daughter?'

'I'm not his daughter. But I know what I'm talking about. My father was murdered when I was a little girl and I was taken away from my mother. I'd grown up when she found me again. The people who did that to us were just like the ones who killed your husband. They had money. Power. They thought that meant they could do whatever they wanted. Hurt people. Kill them. Make them disappear. My mother hunted them down. She killed five of them. I killed the sixth when she couldn't.'

Litivenko was staring at her now, slack jawed with surprise. 'Did it make you feel better?'

'Yes. It did. It felt good, because they all had it coming to them. But you don't have to do it because it makes you feel good. You can do it because the people who killed your husband need to know that that has consequences. You can't just roll up and hide.'

Litivenko squeezed her hands together, glanced forward and saw that Pope was looking at her in the mirror. Her eyes locked with Pope's; he didn't show any reaction to what Isabella had said.

'And what do I need to do?'

'Unlock the data,' Pope said.

'I can't,' she said.

'What do you mean?'

'That was what Will did. I'm an embryologist, not a computer scientist. I wouldn't know where to start.'

'There was no failsafe?'

'No.'

Isabella looked at them both: resignation on Litivenko's face and frustration on Pope's. The signage at the side of the road indicated that the exit for Ussuriysk was approaching. Pope saw it, too, and he flicked the indicator and drifted over to where the exit began.

But he didn't turn off. Instead, he switched off the indicator and accelerated again.

'What are you doing?' Litivenko said.

'There's another way.'

PART ELEVEN:
Washington, DC

Chapter Forty-Four

The skies over Washington had promised snow ever since Maia had arrived three days earlier.

She had booked a room at the Ritz-Carlton in Georgetown and had spent the time preparing herself. She ran in Waterfront Park and along the Capital Crescent Trail. The route was built upon the abandoned rail bed of the eleven-mile Georgetown Branch of the B&O Railroad. Maia ran from Georgetown to west Silver Spring and back every day, twenty-two miles that helped her to rediscover her strength and endurance with every session. She took yoga classes in the hotel gym. She bought bags of ice and made herself ice baths in her bathroom every night. Her injuries healed. She felt better than she had for days.

She was returning from her run on the third day when she noticed a chalk mark on the garbage bin that she passed before she turned around at Silver Spring. She stopped, pretending to catch her breath while she ensured that the trail was empty in both directions. When she was sure that it was, she went to the garbage bin and reached inside. There was a small knapsack inside. She opened the toggles, looked inside and saw a large padded envelope. She closed the sack, put it on her back and continued with her run.

Maia returned to the hotel and made her way up to her room.

She opened the knapsack and took out the envelope. It was bulky and reasonably weighty. She sat at the bureau while she opened it and took out the contents. There was a prepaid cell phone with two SIMs, $5,000 in bills of various denominations, a small polymer-framed Beretta Pico .380 ACP and a clear plastic vial filled halfway to the top with a white powder.

There was one final item in the envelope: a Frio cooling wallet. The wallet contained crystals that, when soaked in water, expanded into a gel that then cooled the contents of the wallet for several days. She opened the wallet and took out an injector pen. She lifted up her shirt, held the skin of her chest taut and pressed the pen against it. She selected the dose, pressed the side button and felt the sharp prick as the needle fired into her skin and the dose of citalopram was administered. It would be enough to balance out the dopamine and norepinephrine in her bloodstream and keep her level for a week.

Maia put the pen back into the envelope, meaning to dump it in the hotel garbage later. She switched on the cell phone and held it up so that the retina scan would confirm her identity and unlock the phone. It did. She opened up the 'Notes' application. Maia had been provided with a dossier of information on the target that she had been assigned. There were several photographs, links to websites and news stories, together with an itinerary that anticipated where he could be found.

The target was designated with the codename Seminole.

His name was Jack Coogan.

He was a United States senator.

Maia's orders were to eliminate him tonight.

Maia walked from the hotel to Wisconsin Avenue and purchased the things that she thought she would need for the evening: a flirty dress from Madewell, a leather Le Pliage tote and a pair of red-heeled Louboutins from Steve Madden. The items had cost $2,000, and Maia paid for them in cash.

She returned to the hotel, laid the clothes out on the bed and regarded them. She had no interest in material things. She wasn't interested in fashion. The dress and the shoes would form part of her disguise. They were some of the tools of her trade. She would morph into someone that her target would be pleased to spend time with.

She studied the dossier. The senator's reputation as a ladies' man was well known in the Beltway. There had been multiple affairs, hush money to prevent stories from going public, the suggestion of payments in return for discreet terminations. There was a pattern in the women that the senator favoured: much younger than him, slender and blonde.

She could see why she had been given his file.

She took the vial of white powder from the envelope and put it in the tote.

She checked the time.

Six.

Time to move.

She took out the SIM card, flushed it down the toilet and replaced it with the second card. She undressed and showered, letting the hot water splash over her scalp and skin, sloughing off the dried perspiration that had accreted over the course of the day. She stood in front of the mirror and dried herself. The wound on her shoulder was healing very nicely, just as Aleksandra had said it would. She flexed the muscle, rotating her arm in the socket, and it all felt smooth with just a faint residual stiffness. She was fit enough to be back in the field.

She allowed her mind to drift. Thinking about Aleksandra made her feel wistful. The atmosphere at the facility had been oppressive ever since she had disappeared. Ivanosky had questioned her for hours. That the professor was involved himself was an indication of how seriously the matter was being regarded. The senior man from Manage Risk had shouted and railed at her, saying over and over again that she must have noticed something, that she must have had some idea that Litivenko was planning to leave. Maia had said that she had not. It was the truth. Empathy didn't come easily to her. She hadn't noticed anything.

Still they had interrogated her again and again, and she had come to the realisation that she might not have said anything about Aleksandra even if she had known something was wrong. That had surprised her. It confused her, too. It felt like disloyalty, and she had never felt anything like that before.

She thought about it some more. She knew that she missed Aleksandra. She had been the only person who had cared for her. Prometheus valued her and the staff saw her worth, but there was no affection in any of those relationships. Maia was just an asset to them. Chattel. A tool. Why would anyone feel affection for a tool?

She rarely came into contact with the rest of her cohort and, when she did, there was no connection between them save their peculiar genetics. They had nothing in common. No shared memories. No childhood stories to recount. They were emotionally stunted, never given an opportunity to grow or develop in a way that might be considered normal.

The doctor was the nearest that Maia had to a family.

And she missed her.

She dressed and checked her reflection again. She thought that she looked good. She wasn't vain and it gave her no pleasure, save a satisfaction that she was maximising her chances of bringing herself into range of her target.

The Beretta and cell phone both fit comfortably in the leather tote. She took it, locked the door behind her and started for the elevator.

Chapter Forty-Five

The doorman hailed a taxi for her and she told the driver to take her to 410 First Street. The first flakes of snow started to fall as they headed southeast on Rock Creek and Potomac Parkway. The snow grew heavier, the Lincoln Memorial blurred by the sudden flurries.

'Been promising to do that for days,' the driver said. 'They saying it'll snow all week now.'

They followed Independence Avenue, crossed the water and turned on to Washington Avenue with the solid bulk of the Capitol to the north. Bullfeathers was popular with the staffers who worked in the government buildings nearby. The bar was not particularly impressive, accommodated on the ground floor of a modern three-floor brick building with a subway and a Thai restaurant on one side and the Capitol Hill Office Building on the other. The street was lined with trees, and cars were parked up close to each other on both sides. The driver stopped as near to the bar as he could and Maia paid him.

'You be careful,' he said as she stepped out on to the treacherous asphalt. 'That place is full of snakes.'

A group of men, overcoats warding them from the cold, stood beneath an awning, smoking cigarettes and sharing whatever salacious pieces of gossip that had circulated around the Hill that day. Maia made her way to the door, aware that the men had stopped their conversation to watch her as she approached.

'Evening,' one of them said to her as she went by.

She ignored him, pushed open the door and went into the warmth.

Maia recognised Jack Coogan at once.

The senator was in his mid-forties, handsome in a conventionally wholesome sort of way, with a square jaw, blue eyes and hair that was somewhere between blond and brown. He was dressed in his trademark Italian suit and polished brogues and, as he crossed the room and approached the bar, he flashed a million-megawatt grin at a table of men and women who had turned to acknowledge him.

The file had been thorough. Coogan had been under close surveillance for the past month. A Manage Risk team had been established to run the operation. Half a dozen male and female specialists had been assigned to the job and, by revolving their coverage regularly, they had been able to watch the senator without fear of his security detail making them.

They had quickly identified a weakness in his staff: an intern with a drug problem. She had been only too happy to cooperate in exchange for her cocaine addiction remaining a secret. In return, the intern forwarded Coogan's daily itinerary, allowing them to set up their coverage in advance. She also told them that Coogan visited Bullfeathers every Wednesday, that he often dismissed his security and went alone and that the reason he went alone was because he often picked up women there.

He was alone, as the intelligence had suggested he would be.

He made his way up to the bar.

'What's that?' he said to Maia, pointing at her drink. 'Martini?'

'That's right.'

'Difficult day?'

'You could say that.'

He indicated the empty stool next to her. 'You mind?'

'Not at all.'

He sat down. 'I know what you mean. I've had better days myself.'

'What do you do?'

If her feigned ignorance was a surprise, he pretended not to notice. 'I'm in the Senate.'

'I'm sorry,' she said. 'I didn't recognise you.'

He put out his hand. 'Jack Coogan.'

She took it. 'Sherry McGrath.'

'Nice to meet you, Sherry.' He held her hand a little too long, but Maia didn't attempt to pull away. He glanced down at her almost empty glass. 'You want another one?'

'Sure.'

He summoned the bartender with a peremptory snap of his fingers, the sort of gesture that Maia had seen before from some of the other entitled men that she had been sent to meet. He ordered another martini for her and a vodka tonic for himself.

'What do you do?'

'Law.'

He was looking at her, smiling that same bright smile that was almost his trademark. She wondered how many times he had deployed that smile to charm the women who came across his path.

'You in here on your own tonight?'

'Yes,' she said. 'I was supposed to be on a date, but he stood me up.'

He feigned outrage. 'What? You've got to be kidding me.'

She shrugged.

'Well, forget all about that loser. We can have a good time, right?'

The drinks arrived. He slid hers across the bar and then held up his glass. They touched them together.

'Cheers,' he said, grinning at her again.

Maia was able to stand back and observe the interaction from a professional standpoint. She supposed that the effect of being the focus of his attention might be attractive to some women. It wasn't for her; she had no view on the experience. His personality was larger than life, and there was an undoubted magnetism, but it had no effect on her. It was easy to pretend otherwise, but it was nothing more than an act. She checked off the signs: his eyes on her cleavage, the way he tried to hold her eye, the way he turned to face her on his stool, his legs parted. Tick, tick, tick. She smiled and flirted as she had been trained to do. She was happy for him to think that she was pleased to be with him. It kept him at hand while she waited for her opportunity.

She was prepared to be patient, but she didn't have long to wait.

'I'm just going to the little boys' room,' he said. 'You keep an eye on my drink, okay? I'll be right back.'

'Of course,' she said, mirroring his smile.

She watched as he disappeared across the room and then she looked around: one of the bartenders was staring at the Redskins game on the TV above the bar and the other was serving a customer. There was no one else near her, and she had deliberately taken a seat out of sight of the single CCTV camera next to the TV. She opened her purse and took out the vial of powder that had been left for her at the dead drop. She palmed it, removed the stopper and, checking again that she was unobserved and that the senator was still in the bathroom, she tipped it into his drink.

Maia heard the rap of Coogan's footsteps as he made his way back across the room.

'There's an empty booth out back,' he said, pointing. 'You want to grab it? We could get a bite to eat.'

'Why not,' she said. She stood and smoothed down her dress. She took his glass and handed it to him, quickly glancing into it as she did so. The powder contained flunitrazepam, an intermediate-acting benzodiazepine that was often used to treat severe insomnia. It was colourless and odourless, and it had already dissolved into the vodka.

She collected her clutch, dropped the empty vial inside and followed Coogan to the rear of the room.

Chapter Forty-Six

The senator leaned over to kiss her again almost as soon as the driver had set off. Maia let him. His breath was freighted with the smell of the alcohol that he had been drinking and the rough bristles of his cheeks and chin scraped against her skin.

They had ordered dinner, but they had not stayed for it. The flunitrazepam in Coogan's vodka had started to have an effect within thirty minutes. He had started to slur his speech and had enthusiastically reciprocated when she had leaned over to kiss him. She had suggested that they go somewhere else and he had agreed. He booked an Uber, laid down a fifty to pay for their uneaten food and led her outside.

The snow was falling heavily, the wipers pushing it to the side of the windshield. Coogan put an arm around her and drew her closer to him; she let him do that, too, taking the opportunity to assess him, feeling the muscles in his arms and, as she reached around with her arm, the muscles across his back.

'You're gorgeous,' Coogan slurred.

She pulled away as he started to paw at her dress, his fingers sliding into the gaps between the buttons.

'What's the matter?'

'Not here,' she said with a grin that suggested her reticence would only be temporary.

Maia knew that the senator had a big house on the northwest side of the city. The driver already had the address that Coogan wanted him to deliver them to, so there was no need for Coogan to tell him and no chance for Maia to confirm it. She was not surprised as they headed west on R Street, took Sixteenth Street past Meridian Hill Park and then turned on to Piney Branch Parkway. The dossier had included plenty of detail on the area: Mount Pleasant was to the south and Crestwood to the north, exclusive neighbourhoods to which the commuters who worked in the Capitol returned every night.

They passed through quiet streets, the sounds muffled by the thick snow that was falling all around. The cars parked at the side of the road had lost their shapes, the snow smoothing their lines and anonymising the expensive engineering that lay beneath.

'Just over there,' the senator said, pointing to the magnificent colonial that stood alone behind a set of striking iron gates.

It was a big house. The realty agent's details that had been obtained when Coogan purchased the property six years ago revealed that it had been listed at just under two million dollars. Maia had been able to study the plans. It had four bedrooms, three bathrooms, three entertaining spaces and a large garden to the rear.

'Here, sir?' the driver said.

Coogan looked out through the windows and squinted. 'I . . .' he started to say.

'Thank you,' Maia finished for him. 'Here's fine.'

She opened the door and got out, her heels sinking into the snow. Coogan slid over and she reached down to help him. He was unsteady on his feet and almost tripped as he reached back to slam the door shut.

'How much did I have to drink?' he said, the words tripping over one another.

'Come on,' she said. 'Let's get you inside.'

* * *

The senator collapsed on the sofa as soon as they were inside the house. Maia searched the house quickly and efficiently until she found an insulin pen in the bathroom. She took it and returned to him.

Their research into Coogan had been thorough. They knew that he was a diabetic, and the operational plan took that into account. His file had also included reference to depressive episodes, together with a drink problem that had never been adequately controlled. It would be a simple enough deduction from the available evidence that the senator had returned home and – either accidentally or deliberately – administered an overdose.

She loaded a three-millilitre cartridge of insulin and shook the pen very gently. She screwed on a needle and primed the pen to clear the air. Finally, she dialled in the dose that she wanted to administer: the maximum two hundred and seventy units. She pulled his shirt out of his pants and examined his stomach; she saw the telltale signs of previous injections, small purple contusions around tiny red pinpricks. She removed the cap from the needle and pushed it into a fold of fat just above his belt line.

She pushed down on the plunger. She replaced the empty cartridge with a second, fresh one and injected him again. She did it a third time. She stood and put the pen on the kitchen counter.

She fell back on routine.

She opened the cupboard under the sink, took out a bottle of detergent and a cloth and then made her way through the kitchen and the bedroom and wiped clean all of the surfaces that she might have touched.

She went to Coogan, knelt down, slid her arms beneath his legs and shoulders and then heaved him up. He was much heavier than she was, and although the effort sent a blast of pain through her shoulder, she was able to stagger through into the bedroom and set him down on the bed. She took off his shoes and loosened his tie. His breathing was fast and shallow and his skin felt clammy. The excess of insulin in his bloodstream would cause his body to absorb glucose from his blood. His liver would produce less glucose. These two conditions would work together to create dangerously low glucose levels in his blood. He would slip into a hypoglycaemic coma from which he would never awaken.

Maia left him on the bed and looked around the room. There was a computer on the bureau. She was drawn to it – by force of habit, perhaps – and, with a tissue covering her finger, she tapped the keyboard and woke the screen. Several windows opened: Coogan's email client – one particular email that he had maximised – and several Word documents.

She read the email first.

> LINUS GOSLING
> To: Jack Coogan
> Senator,
> The doctor will arrive at Washington Dulles at
> 11 a.m. She is ready to speak at the hearing.
> Please provide secure pickup. Her safety is
> your responsibility.

She covered the mouse with the tissue and navigated over to the client's 'Sent' folder. She clicked to open it and saw that the last email Coogan had sent earlier that evening was in reply to the message:

> JACK COOGAN
> To: Linus Gosling
> I understand, but the hearing is two weeks
> away. What am I supposed to do with her
> until then?

Maia felt a prickle of dread. She brought the first Word document to the front of the screen and read.

> Aleksandra Litivenko was born on April 26, 1980, in Moscow. Her father is the famous Soviet and Russian biophysicist Trofim Litivenko. In the 1990s, her family moved to Ussuriysk, where she attended middle school. From 1998 to 2003, Litivenko studied in the College of Genetics of the Biology Department of the Moscow State University–Lomonosov. In 2004, she received her PhD in biology from the Moscow State University and, in 2005, she took up a position as Associate Visiting Scientist in the Department of Genetics at the Massachusetts Institute of Technology. She resigned her position in 2006 upon the offer of employment with Daedalus Genetics, Inc., a Delaware-registered corporation developing genetic therapies to fight disease.

Maia stared at the screen. She was confused. Nothing was explicit, but the implication was clear: the doctor referred to in the first email must have been Aleksandra. Why else would Coogan have been studying her biography? The senator was involved with her disappearance in some form or another. What was the hearing that was referred to? Whatever it was, Coogan's involvement with Aleksandra must have been the reason why Maia had been sent to eliminate him. There could be no other reason.

But why had she not been told?

That would have to wait.

She printed the documents and put them in her bag, then covered the handle of the front door with a cloth from the kitchen, opened it and went outside. The snow was falling in a blizzard now and the cold wrapped around her like it was grasping her in an icy fist. The tracks from when they had stumbled out of the taxi had already been filled in. The same would happen to the tracks she left now.

She walked away from the house.

She had an appointment to keep.

Chapter Forty-Seven

Maia hailed a cab and told the driver to take her to the Mall. The man, a dour Arab who hadn't shaved for days and who smelled strongly of hashish, drove them south on Sixteenth Street in silence. Maia recognised the familiar edifices and monuments to power and loss as the city grew taller around them. She saw the Museum of Natural History, leaned forward and told the driver to stop. She paid him and got out.

The car had been warm, and the frigid weather quickly wrapped around her again. She clasped her coat tightly, crossed the empty Madison Drive and moved on to the open expanse of the Mall.

She walked quickly until she reached the carousel in front of the Arts and Industries Building, the blue and yellow canopy above the riderless horses weighed down with snow.

There was a man leaning against the railings. She slowed her pace. The man pushed himself away from the railings and walked across to her. He was wearing a charcoal pea coat, with the top of a navy wool turtleneck visible between the lapels and a woollen beanie. He had a bland and unmemorable face.

It was Curry.

Why was he here?

They continued on, making for the five-hundred-foot obelisk of the Washington Monument.

Curry spoke first. 'Well?'

'It's done.'

'Without issues?'

'I picked him up in the bar and he took me to his place. There was no one there.'

'How?'

'Insulin.'

'What about the camera outside?'

'I destroyed the drive.'

'Well done. Did he say anything?'

'About what?'

'Anything that might be of interest.'

'No,' she said, omitting the documents that she had found. 'Nothing.'

They continued on, past the monument and along the north side of the reflecting pool of the Lincoln Memorial. The water was black and glassy and still, the nearby lights refracted across it.

'Why are you here?' she asked him.

'Our work isn't done.'

'He's dead,' she said. 'Why do you need to be here? Is there another target?'

'That's classified. You know better than to ask me that.'

'Whatever's happening, I want to be involved. I don't like leaving a job unfinished.'

'It *is* finished,' he said firmly. 'You are to return to the safe house tonight and prepare to exfiltrate. You'll take the Northeast Regional train to Richmond. You're booked on a flight to Boston, then to Istanbul, then back to Skopje for the debrief. Here.'

Curry reached into his pocket and took out a paper folder embossed with the logo of Turkish Airlines.

'What aren't you telling me?' she said, even though she was sure that she knew what that was.

'Go to the safe house. Your flight leaves at ten. Make sure you're on it.'

Curry turned, following the path to the north towards Constitution Gardens.

Maia stayed where she was, lit by the glow of an overhead lamp, snow gathering on her shoulders. She felt a prickle of discomfort, a feeling in her stomach that she didn't recognise and couldn't diagnose. Anxiety? She didn't suffer from uncertainty; her life was constrained so that there was no scope for choice, and so no room for doubt.

She watched Curry as he disappeared, absorbed by the curtain of falling snow, and turned to the south.

PART TWELVE:

The Pacific

Chapter Forty-Eight

Pope woke after an unsatisfactory two-hour snooze. They were flying United Business so that they could sleep, but the seat was hard and uncomfortable and he had been wakened several times by various aches and pains.

He listened to the drone of the 777's engines and allowed his mind to drift.

It had been a very long three days.

They had continued north from Ussuriysk until they reached Mikhaylovka. Pope had found a quiet parking lot and had taken the opportunity to change the G-Class for a Lada Samara. The damaged FSB car would have betrayed them eventually, and he had decided that the risk of stealing a second vehicle was less than the risk of proceeding in the same car.

The drive to Vanino had taken thirty-one hours. They only stopped three times: once at a Gazprom Neft filling station in Novostroyka, once at a second station in Dada and then finally at a roadside cafe as they slogged east across Khabarovsk Krai.

It was there that Pope had finally made contact with Atari. The man reported that he had been refused entry to the country because of inconsistencies in his paperwork and had been sent back to China again. Pope explained what he was proposing and, after a moment of disapproval that Pope suspected was because the agenda had tipped away from him, Atari had conceded that it was the best that could be done under the circumstances. He said that he would make the arrangements for their arrival in the United States and that he would be in touch again when it was done.

They had taken the car ferry from Vanino to Kholmsk, on the Russian island of Sakhalin. That voyage had taken nineteen hours, and Pope had managed to sleep a little in the cramped and basic cabin that he had shared with Isabella and Litivenko. There had then followed a two-hour transit across the island to Korsakov and then a five-hour voyage to Hokkaido, Japan's most northerly island. They had taken an internal flight to Tokyo and then transferred to United for the trans-Pacific hop.

He turned over and opened the blind. The view from the porthole window was uniform: a bland carpet of grey and white, breakers rolling over the ocean for as far as he could see. There was no sign of land, and the line where the water met the horizon was blurred and indistinct.

He looked at his watch. It was six. They were due to land in five hours.

Pope had spent the first few hundred miles of their long drive through Russia persuading Litivenko that she should come with them to Washington. She was adamant that the data on the stick was lost to them without it being unencrypted, and Pope believed her when she said that she didn't know how to do it. The data was important, but it would have been second-hand. If Atari and the people he worked with wanted to make an impact at the hearing, then oral testimony from someone deeply involved with Daedalus would be far more powerful and persuasive.

She had dismissed the idea out of hand when he first suggested it, telling him that it was the most foolish thing she had ever heard. He did not give up. She laid out her concerns and then he addressed each of them one after the other. Uppermost in her mind, and with good reason, was her safety. He gave her his word that he would protect her. 'Like my husband?' she had retorted, but Pope had explained, as delicately as he could, that Wheaton's fate had been his own doing. He had chosen the location for the rendezvous because he thought he would be safe in a public place; he had not accounted for the possibility of a sniper and the wide range of firing spots that Chen Yi Square accommodated around its periphery.

She said that the American government would find a reason to detain her as soon as she had given her testimony. Pope agreed that this was a possibility and proposed that they negotiate an agreement whereby that risk was taken off the table. The fact that her evidence would be given in public would be in her favour, too. Until she was ready to spend her money to effect a disappearance, she would be too high profile to detain.

Her final objection was that she had no idea *how* to disappear. Pope said that he would help with that, too. He explained a little of his experience with Group Fifteen and that he had worked with professional 'disappearers' who would be able to make her vanish and then surface her somewhere else with a new identity and no ties to her past. He knew a man by the name of Ed who worked as a violin salesman in New York. Ed had previously worked as a Mossad *sayan*, an agent recruited from within the Jewish diaspora to assist with operations outside Israel. He supplemented his income by putting his old skills to good use. He could provide transportation, new documents, a whole new life. The price for all of that was steep, but Litivenko would be rich. Money would not be a problem for her.

Eventually, she had acceded. Pope was not surprised. The objections were obvious and almost by rote, made until she had accepted the truth of her situation. She had no other options. If she stayed in Russia, the secret service would find her and she would be detained. If she tried to run on her own, her previous employers would find her and kill her.

He could offer a third way; it was not a guarantee, and it was certainly dangerous, but it was all that she had.

⌣

He slept for another hour and was woken by the smell of cooked food and the clatter of a trolley as the crew served breakfast.

He sat up and tapped the button to put his seat back into the upright position.

'Morning.'

Litivenko was in the seat next to him.

'Breakfast,' Pope said. 'You hungry?'

Litivenko put her seat up and folded away her bedding. Pope looked over the aisle to Isabella. She was still curled up beneath her blanket. He would let her sleep.

'Looks like it worked,' Litivenko said.

'That we made it out of Russia?'

'No. Your sales pitch. I'm still not sure this is the best idea.'

The steward arrived with the trolley. They both chose frittata with chicken sausage, a poached egg, banana bread and orange juice.

Pope looked over at the doctor as the steward arranged their food for them. She had dark pouches beneath her eyes and her skin bore a faint pallor. It didn't look as if she had slept at all.

'Enjoy your breakfasts,' the steward said.

Pope took the data stick out of his pocket and put it on the tray. He tapped a finger against it. 'So what's on here?'

'You don't know?'

'I know it's data.'

'You know what about?'

Pope shook his head. 'Not really.'

She looked as if she would welcome the chance to talk. 'What do you know about genetics?' she said.

'Nothing.'

'What did you do before you did this? Are you a military man?'

'Once upon a time,' he said. 'Soldier.'

'I'm a scientist. But I know soldiers. War fighting is a big focus in my work. Daedalus is improving human physiology so that it is better suited for it. Technology is improving at almost exponential rates. Equipment gets more advanced all the time. The one limiting factor that stalls real improvements in efficiencies is human. The operator. The man on the ground. You say you were a soldier – let me ask you a question: if you could change one thing about your own physiology to make yourself a better fighter, what would it be? Speed? Strength?'

'That would help.'

Litivenko encouraged him to continue. 'What about fatigue? Hunger?'

He agreed. 'Tired and hungry soldiers make mistakes.'

Litivenko nodded. 'Correct. I'm an embryologist and a biogeneticist. My area of specialism is ways in which we might extend the boundaries of human performance. Cognition. Physical attributes. Taking men and women beyond the natural limits of physiology. Just think about sleep. Think of the possibilities that would be presented to a soldier who did not need to sleep.'

'Not ever?'

'No, of course not. But not for a few days, perhaps. Let's say this soldier could operate at a high level for seventy-two hours without needing to rest. Think of the benefits that would entail. You could drop a platoon of enhanced soldiers behind the lines and they could operate while the enemy slept. They would be untouchable. And that's not to say that improvements in speed and strength are being ignored. Resilience. The ability to heal wounds faster. They're working on everything. They want to build the metabolically dominant soldier. Sleep. Hunger. Resilience. They're all factors.'

Litivenko paused, looked around and gestured to the passenger on the other side of the aisle. He had a doughnut on a plate next to a cup of coffee. 'You see that doughnut. I'd guess that's about four hundred calories. A Special Forces soldier working for a twelve-hour stretch will burn six to seven thousand calories. He'd need seventeen of those doughnuts just to keep going, maybe thirty of them if we worked him all day. We can't get those calories into him. It's almost impossible. And you know how much a fully loaded pack already weighs.'

'Enough,' Pope acceded.

'He wouldn't be able to carry all the calories that he needs. What if I said we have re-engineered experimental subjects at the cellular level? Do you know what mitochondria are?'

'No.'

'They produce the energy to power cells. We've tweaked them so that they are more efficient. We've made them better at using stored energy. The soldier could consume the calories he might need before deploying. We infiltrate them a little plumper than we normally would. We can remove the need for them to eat anywhere near as much. When they exfiltrate, all that extra fat is gone. And we've doubled the amount of mitochondria available to each cell. We can increase stamina and endurance levels beyond normal human capacity. Our test subjects have been able to run for a hundred yards on a single breath. Walk for miles with packs that normal soldiers wouldn't be able to lift. This isn't science fiction. It's happening now. It's fact. We're beyond monkeys and rats. The technology is stable. It's been successfully tested in human subjects.'

'Male *and* female?'

Litivenko's eyebrows cocked; she detected the interest in Pope's voice. 'Yes. Why do you ask?'

'Before Shanghai, I met someone. A woman. Look at me: I'm a bit over six foot. Fifteen stone. A soldier, like I said. I can look after myself. And this woman, half my size, she kicked my arse.'

'What did she look like?'

Pope remembered easily. 'Slender. Blonde. I think her name was Maia.'

'Are you sure?'

'That's what I was told. Why?'

'I had responsibility for Maia.'

'She was injured,' Pope said. 'Isabella stabbed her.'

'Maia reported back with a stab wound to the shoulder.' Litivenko reached around over her right shoulder and traced a path down to her triceps. 'She had a minor fracture of her leg, too.'

'She jumped out of a third-floor window.'

'So she said.'

'Did you know what her orders were?'

She shook her head. 'They keep the operational details confidential. They have very effective blocks in place. We're not told anything. My job was to study her and tend to her. That was it. The operations are planned and overseen outside of Daedalus. I don't know any more than that.'

They both had cups of black tea on the tray tables in front of them. Pope noticed that Litivenko's hand trembled when she raised her cup to her lips to take a sip.

'What happens when we get to DC?' she asked.

She was travelling on her own passport. Pope knew that was not ideal. That would very likely mean that the people looking for them would be able to locate her. And it took thirteen hours to fly to the eastern seaboard of the United States from Tokyo.

That, he suspected, would be more than time enough for the enemy to have found them.

'We're going to be collected and taken somewhere safe. I'll make the arrangements for you to give your testimony. You don't need to worry. Everything will be fine.'

Pope had promised to keep her safe and he meant to keep that promise.

PART THIRTEEN:

Washington, DC

Chapter Forty-Nine

Maia got up early and sat with a cup of coffee. She hadn't been able to sleep, managing just an hour or two when the clamour of her thoughts eventually quietened for a moment.

She laid the printouts on the floor and sat cross-legged in front of them.

She stared into the coffee and tried to think.

It was hopeless. Her thoughts were slippery and evasive and she couldn't get a firm grip on any of them.

She took out her phone, opened the browser and navigated to the arrivals page of the Dulles Airport website. There were only two flights due from Tokyo today: ANA Flight 2 was due at eight and United Airlines Flight 804 was scheduled to land three hours later.

Maia looked through the printed emails. It said that Aleksandra was due to land at Dulles at 11 a.m.

They were on the United flight.

It was seven in the morning.

Four hours.

She had to hurry.

Maia dressed and went outside.

The safe house was a detached property, small and unloved. It was in a bad state of repair. The windows to the right of the door were covered with sheets of board and the three windows on the first floor looked as if they needed replacing. A large bush had been allowed to grow out of control between the house and the larger semi-detached unit to its left, the branches reaching out and impeding access to the door. The house on the other side of the road was in excellent condition, with lime-green clapboard facings, a neatly clipped lawn and a chain-link fence.

The house was equipped with a car. It was a Chevrolet Cruze, the limited edition Trailer Cruze package with gold-accented alloys and trim. It had evidently been crashed into at some point in its history because the right-side fender was unpainted black while the rest of the body was grey. Maia crunched through the fall of snow to the car, cleared the snow from the window with her arm, opened the door, put her bag inside and slid into the driver's seat. She turned the ignition and got nothing. She turned it again, pumping down on the brake and clutch, and was rewarded with a splutter from the engine. She repeated the procedure and the engine turned over and started.

She switched on the windshield blower and, as it defrosted the glass, she checked the map on her phone. There was a collection of stores on Fortieth Street, half a mile away. The snow had stopped, at least for the moment, but Brooks Street and Benning Road were blanketed beneath piles of it. The centre of the road had been cleared, but the cars on either side were unrecognisable, buried beneath a foot of snow that gathered in deep drifts against the walls of the houses and businesses. Some of the residents were out despite the early hour, digging out their driveways and clearing paths to their doorways.

The stores were marooned in the middle of a large parking lot, next to power lines that fizzed and popped as Maia crossed beneath them. There was a Safeway with a CVS pharmacy, a 7-Eleven and a store identified as Simply Fashion opposite it. Maia opened the door to the pharmacy first. It was warm, the heaters blowing out hot air at full blast, and she loosened her overcoat and started down the aisles with a basket in search of the things that she needed. She picked out a pair of scissors, a pack of disposable razors and a pack of L'Oréal Superior Preference hair dye and dropped them into the basket. She added a bottle of antiseptic, a pack of sterile pads and a roll of zinc oxide tape. She took the basket to the checkout to pay.

She went to the 7-Eleven and bought a bottle of cheap gin and then crossed the parking lot to the clothes store. The owner was just opening up for the day. She made a comment about the weather and Maia responded curtly, in a way that she hoped would foreclose the possibility of further conversation. It did. The owner told Maia to look around and left her to get on with it alone. Maia took a vest, a pair of jeans, a dark turtleneck and a quilted overcoat. The clothes came to just over two hundred dollars; she paid in cash and told the owner that she would like to wear the clothes now. She went into the changing room and changed, stuffing her old clothes into the bag.

She went outside again. There was a dumpster at the rear of the Safeway. She pushed the lid open and dropped her old clothes into it.

She went back to the car.

Maia returned to the house.

She went into the bathroom and stood before the cracked and dusty mirror. She removed her top, took the scissors and started to cut her hair. The long strands fell into the sink and on to the floor, leaving a jagged edge that she tidied up with more care once most of the length had been removed. She cut it back drastically, leaving herself with just a short bob that fell to the nape of her neck. She coated her hairline, ears and neck with Vaseline so that she could more easily remove the dye that would get on to her skin. The packet was marked 'vermillion' and promised a deep red finish. She pulled on the latex gloves that were supplied with the pack, mixed the dye and applied it to her hair, working it in with her gloved fingers. She knew that it would take time. Her hair had been dyed so many times that she could barely remember her natural colour.

The dye needed to be left in for thirty minutes. She took the opportunity to prepare the things that she thought she might need. She had the Beretta Pico purse gun, but that was not going to be enough. She climbed the stairs and, following the directions that she had received in her briefing, she hauled the bed out of the way, pulled up the carpet and located the loose floorboard. She prised her fingers between the boards and pulled the loose one away to reveal a small cache of arms.

There was a Beretta M9 – the 9×19mm Parabellum pistol had long been the primary sidearm of the US armed forces. It was the M9A3 update, with the seventeen-round magazine and the three-slot Picatinny rail. It looked to be reasonably new and, as she checked, she saw that the serial number had been filed off. That made it an illegal weapon, not that Maia had much concern about that. It was a powerful gun, with more than enough stopping power for her needs, but had been unpopular with female soldiers because it was large and weighed over two pounds when it was fully loaded. None of that concerned Maia. She had used the weapon before and liked it.

She reached back into the cache and pulled out a shoulder holster and then several boxes of ammunition. There was a karambit fighting knife with a curved blade; she took it and placed it on the floor next to the pistol. There was a collection of timing devices and detonators. Maia had no use for those and left them in place.

There was also a small box, around the size of a binoculars case. She took it out and opened it. It was freezing cold inside. The box was lined with heat-preserving aluminium foil and the false floor was composed of highly efficient cold gel packs. There was a needle, three barrels, a pen, a small bottle of rubbing alcohol, some swabs and a tourniquet.

Taking blood was a routine that had been drummed into her as far back as she could remember. It was a weekly habit. She was often left in the field for weeks at a time and, when that happened, she'd leave the sample in the temperature-controlled case at a designated dead drop so that it could be collected and analysed and the data added to her file. The habit was strong, and she found herself assembling the equipment without really considering that if she went through with what she had planned, it would be a pointless exercise.

She threaded the needle on to one of the barrels and tightened the tourniquet around her biceps. She palpated a vein, anchored it with her left hand and, with her right, she slid the needle inside and drew off enough blood to fill the barrel. She took the pen, wrote the date on the side of the barrel, put it into the inset and then closed and locked the box.

She took the pistol from yesterday, dropped that into the cache and replaced the board, covering it back over with the carpet and then sliding the bed back to where it had been before.

The dye was ready now. Maia went back to the bathroom, undressed, stepped into the shower and rinsed her hair until the water ran clear. She looked at her reflection. Her hair was a deep, warm red.

She took the make-up and applied it. She only wore make-up when she was on an assignment, and the effect of it always struck her as startling. She painted her lips a deep scarlet and applied mascara to her lashes.

When she was done, she looked completely different from how she had looked just an hour earlier.

There was one more thing that she needed to do. She went into the kitchen and turned on the stove. She took the karambit from its sheath and unfolded the talon blade. The knife had a handle that was carefully designed to fit the hand for both standard and reverse grips. She wrapped the handle in a dishcloth and held the tip of the talon over the burner. She held it there until the metal glowed red and then let it cool. She took the bottle of gin that she had purchased from the store and poured two inches' worth into a clean tumbler. She dipped the blade into the alcohol to be sure. The metal hissed and fizzed.

She reached around with her left hand and quickly found the shallow bump between her C6 and C7 vertebrae. It was an easy place to site the implant: simple to access and usually covered by her hair. Now that it had been cut, the tiny unit would be visible as a pea-sized bump.

Maia took the karambit in her right hand. She lowered her head and, guiding the tip of the blade with the index finger of her left hand, she lined it up just below the protrusion and then pressed down. The blade was sharp, and it slid easily into the skin. She adjusted the angle and pressed down a little more, feeling the blade as it dug down. She felt blood on her skin, a hot dribble down her spine. She pried it up, feeling with the fingers of her left hand as the hard little knot in her neck started to move towards the surface of the skin. She wiggled the blade, slicing around the implant, cutting out a flap that opened just as the implant rose to the surface on a bubble of blood.

She collected the tiny device between thumb and forefinger and placed it on the table in front of her. It was a tiny GPS tracker coated in bioglass. The tracker was powered by an integrated nano-generator that harvested the energy from within the body: heartbeats, blood flow and other almost imperceptible but constant movements. The generator was made from cellulose mixed with polydimethylsiloxane – the silicone found in breast implants – and carbon nanotubes. She looked at it for a long minute. It lay there like an accusation. Removing the chip was a defining moment for her. It was the first time she had deliberately and consciously done something that it was forbidden for her to do.

It was the crossing of a boundary that could not be uncrossed.

She could have laid the blade of the knife against the tracker and crushed it, but that did not serve her purpose. Prometheus would be alerted if the chip stopped transmitting. She wanted it to continue to broadcast where it was. Instead, she wrapped it in a piece of tissue paper and put it in her pocket.

The wound in her neck was not deep, but it was bleeding freely. She took the bottle of antiseptic and poured it over the wound, grimacing from the sharp sting, and then pressed a sterile pad over it. She held the pad in place with two lengths of zinc oxide tape and then dressed, carefully pulling on the turtleneck so that it covered the dressing. She put on her jeans and fitted the woollen beanie over her head.

She emptied out the tote and put the M9, a box of ammunition and the karambit inside.

She put on her new coat, opened the door and stepped back outside into the cold once again.

Union Station was three and a half miles to the west.

Maia took Benning Road across the Anacostia and Kingman Lake, the slate-grey skies growing darker and then, as she turned south on First Street, releasing another dump of snow. She found a space to park the Cruze. She took the pistol and the knife from the leather tote and stowed them in the glove compartment. She collected the bag, opened the door and stepped out.

The great arch of the station's facade was obscured by the shifting curtain of snow. She passed inside and the temperature climbed as the doors closed behind her. She continued towards the ticket office and bought a ticket to Richmond, being sure to pay the sixty-eight dollars on the credit card that she had been given. There was a camera behind the clerk and she looked up, turning to it so that there would be clear evidence that it was she who had purchased the ticket. They would check back along her route when she failed to arrive at the airport for her flight out of the country and she wanted to make it as difficult for them as she could.

Maia went down to the platforms. The 67 Northeast Regional train departed from platform twenty-two. She showed her ticket to the attendant on the gate, climbed aboard and made her way to her allocated coach seat. She was aboard early, and there were only a handful of passengers on the train with her. She took the tracker and, reaching beneath the seat, found the join where two pieces of leather had been stitched together. She forced her fingers between the pieces, finding a little purchase and then pulling back hard enough to open a small rent. She stuffed the tracker inside, pressing it into the upholstery.

She did not know how long the battery would retain a charge outside of her body. It didn't have to manage for long, just enough for the train to head out of the station towards Richmond. That should be all the diversion she needed.

She went back to the car.

Chapter Fifty

The drive from Boston to Washington took them nine hours to complete with a half-hour stop in Trenton. They were in two cars, allowing thirty minutes between each car setting off. Dzhokar was in the first car with Imad. Khasan, Abdul and Hasan followed behind. They split the equipment between the two cars. In the event that one of them was stopped before they could reach their destination, the other would still have a chance of completing the operation.

They shared the driving, changing over when they stopped. Imad had taken the first four hours and had insisted that they listen to recordings of speeches that had been delivered by radical imams from within the caliphate. Dzhokar listened, but quickly found the rhetoric tiring and tuned out. He was glad of the distraction when it was his turn to drive, and even more pleased when Imad took the opportunity to sleep.

The satnav directed them to Bethesda and then instructed him to take exit 45A from I-495, heading west on the Dulles Access Toll Road towards Reston. Dzhokar pulled into a parking area as soon as they passed over the 657 north of McLean. They had agreed to stop here and wait for the others to catch up. He switched off the engine and looked out at the traffic that was coming and going. He heard a roar and looked to the north just in time to see the first jet as it angled down on its glide path to the runway at Dulles. It descended on a gentle slope, crossed over the road at a few hundred feet and then disappeared beyond the steep embankment with a tall chain-link fence that marked the periphery of the terminal.

He looked back and saw the lights of another jet and, beyond that and higher, a second and third.

Maia took the airport Dulles Access Toll Road and passed through Reston and Herndon, the airport facility gradually coming into view. She parked the Cruze in the short-term garage and made her way inside the terminal building.

Ten forty in the morning and the terminal was busy. She went to the information desk and asked where would be the best place to meet a passenger. The man behind the desk told her to go to the arrivals hall and pointed to the entrance.

She found a space at the corner at the northeast side of the hall. She had chosen her vantage point carefully. She could see everything, including the sliding doors through which the incoming passengers arrived. She could see the doors to the west that she had just used. They opened on to the final hall before passengers left the terminal to retrieve their cars or take public transport into the city.

She checked her watch again. The airport displays announced that United Flight 804 had arrived ahead of schedule.

Maia was anxious. She wanted to be in place in plenty of time. She remembered her conversation with Curry last night and the documents that she had taken from Coogan's house. Aleksandra was in terrible danger.

She looked around again. There was nothing out of the ordinary. No obvious threats.

Nothing odd.

Maia felt an emptiness in her stomach.

She was expecting to see Curry. That seemed likely after what he had told her. She had spent half an hour as she drove west worrying about what she would do if she saw him. Would she speak to him? Would she be able to persuade him that he should stand down? No. That was ridiculous. She had quickly concluded that it would have served no purpose save to lose her any element of surprise that she might otherwise have enjoyed.

But she couldn't see him. She would have expected him to adopt a position similar to her own, but he wasn't here. She studied the crowd in the event that he had sought to hide within it, but, unless she had missed him, she had struck out again.

And she still didn't know what she would do if he arrived here.

She reached for the butt of the pistol in the shoulder holster that she wore beneath her jacket. Her fingers danced across the moulded plastic grip, stretched a little further so that she felt the stippled contour of the butt and then the trigger guard and the pliancy of the trigger.

She had made her mind up about one thing, at least.

If they came for Aleksandra, she would defend her.

There would be blood.

They parked in Garage 1.

It was closer to the terminal than the economy parking lot, but they would have had to take a shuttle bus if they had parked farther out, and that would have increased the odds of them being detected before they could reach their target. It was more expensive, of course, but that wasn't something that concerned them. They collected their Pay & Go tickets from the machines, but they had no intention of returning to validate them.

The terminal was accessed by an underground pedestrian walkway. They split into two groups as before, and started out with five minutes between them. Dzhokar and Imad waited while the others went first, and then followed along. There was a moving walkway and they took their places on it.

Dzhokar could see the others at the far end of the walkway stepping off and heading for the elevator that would take them up to the terminal building. Khasan had already scouted the area on two separate occasions. He had explained the layout to them and said that there was a large restroom where they would be able to make their final preparations before heading into the arrivals hall.

Chapter Fifty-One

Passengers emerged through sliding doors into the wide space of the arrivals hall.

'Stay alert,' Pope said quietly to Isabella as they waited to enter. She nodded.

Litivenko turned to face them. 'What are we going to do?'

'We're going to be collected.'

'And then?'

'We'll head into the city. It'll be fine.'

'And then? After the hearing?'

'They'll pay you and you'll be able to go.'

'You'll come with me?'

'What for?'

'I've seen enough so that I don't trust people without proof that they are worthy of it. You did what you said you'd do. I believe you'll protect me.'

Isabella watched as she looked at Pope with wide, entreating eyes and, when he hesitated, Litivenko added, a little desperately, 'I will pay you.'

'I don't need your money. It isn't that. Isabella and I have somewhere we need to go. I don't have time.'

'Then you'll return with me here? At least see that I get here safely?'

'Yes,' Isabella said.

'Yes,' Pope said, too. 'We can do that.'

There were people on either side of the passage just inside the door: some waited with unmasked anticipation, dispensing embraces to arriving relatives and loved ones; taxi drivers held out handwritten signs while checking the messages on their phones. Isabella looked up and saw two ranks of flags that hung down from the ceiling. There were stores and concessions around the edge of the hall, and exits that led to the Metrorail and the Silver Line express buses.

The queue moved slowly until it passed through the door and then, with more space, the passengers were able to disperse more freely. Pope and Litivenko were ahead of her. Pope had his hand on the doctor's elbow, guiding her gently ahead.

Isabella scanned left to right and then back again.

Left to right.

Left to right.

She stopped.

One of the men behind her tutted audibly as he had to divert around her. She barely heard him and did not react.

It was a woman. Isabella saw her standing at the other end of the hall, at two o'clock from her position. She was beneath an overhang, partially obscured by a pillar that supported the floor above her. She looked like any other traveller: jeans, a dark-coloured turtleneck, a padded jacket. A flash of red hair beneath a woollen beanie. She was looking back in her direction, watching the new arrivals as they came into the hall. She was like all the other men and women here waiting to rendezvous with arriving passengers.

She was like them, but not the same.

Isabella recognised her, and her heart skittered.

'Pope,' she said.

He stopped and turned back. 'What is it?'

'The woman over there.'

Pope glanced in the direction that Isabella had indicated.

'Where?'

'Over there. The woman from Italy.'

Pope looked more carefully. 'Are you sure?'

'She's coloured her hair, but it's her.'

The woman had seen them, too, and now she was starting to come their way.

'What is it?' Litivenko asked him.

'Stay close to me,' Pope said.

Isabella tensed. 'What do we do?'

'We'll be safe with these witnesses. But we need to get away from here.'

Litivenko noticed the woman. 'Oh shit,' she said.

'Is it her?' Pope asked.

Isabella was watching. She saw recognition and then confusion on Litivenko's face. 'Yes. It's Maia. They've sent her.'

'Come on.'

'She's come to kill me.'

'Quickly,' Pope urged.

They set off again, hurrying to the left, joining the crowd of people who were heading towards the exit.

Maia changed course and started to jog so that she could cut them off. Pope reached for Litivenko's shoulder and slowed her speed. The doctor stopped. She followed Pope's anxious gaze to the approaching woman.

Maia was just a few feet away from them now.

She blocked the way ahead.

'Doctor,' she said.

'Maia,' Litivenko said, unable to keep the fear from her face. 'What are you doing here?'

'Please. You need to come with me.'

Pope put himself between the two women. 'You're too late,' he said. 'Leave her alone.'

Maia pivoted a little so that she could face him. 'Step out of the way, please.'

'No,' Pope said. 'You want her, you can go through me. And I don't think you'll want to do that here.'

'Step out of the way.'

Pope did not.

Isabella looked left and right, adrenaline pumping around her body so fiercely that her hands trembled. There was something else.

'Pope,' she said.

Maia ignored Pope's warning. 'Aleksandra,' she said, 'you have to listen to me. It's not safe for you here. He can't protect you. I can.'

Maia reached out for Litivenko's arm, but Pope intercepted her and grabbed her wrist. The woman turned fully towards him and tried to break his grip. He held on, although he grunted with the effort. Maia threw a left-handed punch; Pope turned and took it on his shoulder. He grabbed her, wrapping both arms around her torso and hugging her as tightly as he could.

Litivenko started to panic. She backed away from them.

'Pope!' Isabella exclaimed.

She saw two men enter the hall through the door that they had been aiming for. The men were dragging heavy suitcases. They split up. One of them was waiting by the door, standing in their way. The other was making his way to the door through which they had just arrived. He was heading towards them and, as he drew closer, Isabella could see more: he was sweating, a glossy sheen on his forehead; he was wearing a single black glove; and, she saw, he was muttering something under his breath.

'*Pope!*'

The man with the suitcase drew nearer.

Maia freed her right arm and drilled Pope in the face. He fell but managed to hold on to her, dragging her down to the ground with him.

Litivenko saw the blood on Pope's face and fell apart.

She ran.

'No!' Isabella called out.

The man's lips were moving, the same phrase repeated again and again.

Litivenko panicked.

She wasn't aware of what the man with the single glove was about to do.

She ran straight at him.

Isabella started after her.

The man's voice grew louder: a whisper, to a monotone, to a bellow.

'Allahu akbar! Allahu akbar! *Allahu akbar!*'

Chapter Fifty-Two

Isabella saw and heard it all.

The flash of the explosion reflected in the wide windows ahead of her.

The man: there one minute, gone the next.

The boom.

She felt it, a wave of pressure that picked her off her feet and then tossed her away as if she weighed nothing.

She slammed down on to the floor.

Her head crashed off something hard.

She heard the clap of another explosion.

And then another.

Darkness welled at the edges of her vision, swelling, growing.

⌣

She blinked her eyes.

There was a moment of silence, disturbed by the sound of breaking glass, and then the first wails of pain and shock went up.

Isabella checked herself. Her head was sore, but she didn't feel any other pain.

She opened her eyes and found that she was on her back, looking up at the ceiling. Panels had been dislodged, leaving bare patches amid those squares that still remained in place, many of them burned with scorch marks and pocked from the impacts of shrapnel.

She cautiously raised herself on an elbow so that she could look down at her body. Her jacket had been blown almost all the way off, with one sleeve on and the other off, but, save that, everything was intact. There were no signs of injury and, as she pushed herself into a sitting position, she was as confident as she could be that she was unharmed.

There was a column ahead of her. The bomber had stepped behind it as he detonated his device. She had been lucky.

She looked around. It was as if she had been transported to a different place. The hall was unrecognisable from even just ten seconds earlier. The vast windows had been shattered in multiple places, glass sucked into the room and spread out like a carpet of glittering diamond shards. Luggage had been blown open and thrown around the room, the contents spilling out. The men and women and children who had been stood around were scattered like ninepins. Some of them were moving, a few slowly arranging themselves into sitting positions, confusion on their faces. Others lay still. Isabella noticed horrendous injuries.

Blood everywhere.

The man she had seen was gone. He had been turned into a sooty smudge on the wall.

She was looking for Pope and Litivenko when she saw Maia. She was on her hands and knees. She got to her feet and started to walk with a heavy limp, favouring her right leg. She was single-minded; she did not pause and she came on steadily, ignoring the outstretched hands and the cries for help.

She stepped over bodies until she stood over one of the casualties. A woman. She was twenty feet away from Isabella, but close enough for her to recognise the jacket that Litivenko had been wearing.

Maia crouched down over her body.

The sound of alarms was audible from outside the shattered hall: fire and smoke alarms from close by and, in the distance, the sound of sirens.

Maia reached down and touched Litivenko's face.

Then she turned back. Isabella closed her eyes and lay still, playing dead. She opened her eyes a tiny fraction and watched as Maia turned and started away from her, heading to the exit.

Chapter Fifty-Three

P ope.'
He was woozy. The blast had carried him through the air and crashed him against the metal barrier. The back of his head had struck the aluminium and the rest of the impact had punched the air out of his lungs. He blinked his eyes until the room stopped spinning.

'Pope.'

His awareness returned and he blinked and blinked until his vision was a little less blurred. Someone was above him.

'*Pope!*'

It took him a moment to recognise Isabella. He tried to speak, but his throat felt as if it had been sandpapered and all he could manage was a rasping groan.

'Can you hear me?'

He was half on his back and half on his side, his right arm squashed beneath his torso. He could see someone's body a few inches from his face, a blue shirt stained with a widening bloom of blood. He found the energy to roll to his left, freeing his arm. He laid his palm on the floor and tried to push himself upright. He didn't have the strength. The effort sent him plunging into a spiral of dizziness and nausea; he bent over and vomited. Isabella reached her hands beneath his shoulders and helped him to shuffle back until his back was pressed against the barrier.

He blinked his eyes again and looked out. The hall – just a few seconds ago so bright and new – had been rendered unrecognisable. There were fires burning across the floor; flames climbed up the walls, unspooling coils of smoke that blackened the ceiling high overhead.

Some of the bodies on the floor were moving, a few of the men and women getting to their feet and staring dumbfounded at the hellishness into which they had suddenly been plunged. Other bodies lay still. There were three on the floor near to Pope. The blue shirt that he had seen belonged to a Metropolitan Washington Airports Authority policeman, his uniform drenched with blood and his leg missing at the knee; there was a woman, the front of her dress torn away, a shard of metal in her throat; and, just beyond his outstretched leg, there was an elderly man draped incongruously over an upturned luggage trolley.

'Can you hear me?' Isabella said again.

Pope groaned.

'The doctor is dead.'

Her voice sounded distant, as if he were underwater and she was on the surface.

'I'm going after Maia.'

Pope tried to protest, but even the simplest words were beyond him. He mangled them together, making no sense.

Isabella slithered across him. Pope followed her with his eyes. She went to the dead policeman, unclipped the restraining strap on his holster and withdrew his service pistol. She released his handcuffs from their loop on his belt and put them, together with the gun, into a small bag that she found next to the body. Pope felt another wave of lassitude and struggled to keep his eyes open.

'Isabella . . .' he managed, her name little more than a whisper.

'Keep your phone on. I'll call you.'

She passed out of his line of sight. He grimaced from the effort of turning his head and watched as she picked her way across the bodies on the floor, passing through a cascade of falling sparks from a ruptured power line, and then through the open doors at the other end of the room.

Chapter Fifty-Four

Isabella hurried out of the hall.

Maia had a short head start on her, and Isabella worried as she turned out into the corridor beyond that she wouldn't be able to see her. It was eerily empty. Most of the hundreds of passengers who would normally have swilled through this space, heading for the departures lounge or the food court or to meet new arrivals, had fled. One man was on the floor, another man astride him as he pumped rhythmically on his chest, trying to restart a heart that must have stopped from the sudden shock of the explosions. Baggage trolleys had been left, suitcases spilled across the floor.

Isabella looked left and right and then left again; a flash of movement and she saw the figure of the woman as she turned off the corridor.

Isabella ran.

The bag bounced on her shoulder as she picked a path along the corridor, following the route that Maia had taken. Isabella reached the doorway that Maia had passed through. It was a revolving door that opened on to the concourse outside the airport. There was a pedestrian bridge that spanned the Dulles Toll Road and Isabella held back as Maia climbed the steps.

Isabella followed, keeping as far back as she dared.

Maia reached the top and crossed the bridge, climbing down the steps at the other side and hurrying into the parking garage.

Isabella fretted as she quickly descended. If Maia had a car, Isabella was going to find it difficult to follow her. The taxis were on the other side of the bridge, and she doubted that she would be able to find her again if she had to retrace her steps and find one; that was assuming, of course, that the taxis would even be running now.

Maia turned into the garage and made her way to a parked car.

Isabella stopped at the foot of the steps and looked for a way that she could follow. There was a row of motorbikes and scooters immediately inside the garage. She crouched low and hurried inside, staying below the line of the parked cars until she was next to the bikes.

She heard the sound of the car's engine.

The motorbikes were expensive and new; she ignored them in favour of an older TGB 49cc two-stroke moped. She took the cuffs from her bag and used the arm of one of the opened bracelets to pry off the metal ignition cap where the key would usually be inserted. She identified the battery and ignition wires and twisted them together to complete the connection, sending power from the battery to the moped's ignition.

The engine started.

There was a top box at the back of the bike. Isabella forced the lock, took out the helmet and put it on.

The car was moving as Isabella climbed aboard the moped, kicked the stand up and turned the throttle towards her. The moped jerked ahead. Isabella steered into the nearest aisle and followed the car to the exit ramp.

Chapter Fifty-Five

The car headed east and Isabella followed.

They hit traffic at the interchange with I-495 and Isabella allowed herself to pull within ten feet. The car was a Chevrolet Cruze, old and battered. She glimpsed in through the rear window and saw Maia's silhouette, the late-morning sun framing her in the dusty glass.

They drove east, passing through Arlington, crossing the Potomac and then following the Anacostia until they reached Deanwood. The car turned off and followed a new route that brought them on to Brooks Street. It was a quiet residential road on a hill with pleasant trees shielding neat and tidy houses. The snow had been cleared, but the asphalt was topped with a slick surface of ice that made it challenging to ride on. Isabella throttled back and concentrated hard.

They passed Ward Memorial Church, a large modern construction with a tall spire that reached above the telephone poles that ran on either side of the street. They passed a collection of dingy one-floor buildings and two police cruisers that were parked opposite it. Isabella stayed behind, maintaining a steady speed, a van between her and the Chevrolet.

The car pulled over to the right-hand side of the road next to a house marked number 4269. Isabella rode on, passing to the side of the car, not even daring a glance to the right at the woman in the driver's seat. She rode on for fifty yards until the road bent away to the left, and then she pulled over to the side and killed the engine. She flicked down the kickstand and, with her helmet still on, turned to look back to the house. She could still see it, just on the edge of the bend. A flight of stone steps led up from the pavement, offering access to a flagstone path that adjoined an overgrown lawn. Maia passed along the path and paused before a bright red doorway. She unlocked the door and went inside.

Isabella took off the helmet and stowed it in the top box. She collected her bag, put it over her shoulder and headed back on foot. The houses were detached, small wood frame and brick homes sitting on small plots of land. Some of them had been clad in painted clapboard. It was a working-class area, the impression reinforced by the cheap cars that had been parked on either side of the road. Drifts of snow had been pushed to the side of the road.

She reached the Cruze, passing close enough to it so that she could hear the ticking of the engine as it cooled.

Isabella walked back up the hill until she reached the adjacent property. Number 4267 was in the process of being constructed. The timber frame had been erected and there was a collection of materials and a Porta John in the yard. She looked up and down the street, checked the windows of the house that faced the new build and, satisfied that she was not being watched, hopped over the low wall and made her way to the back of the property. The rear yard was small and in a similar state to the front: debris from whatever had been on the plot before competed for space with material for the rebuild, everything covered in thick layers of snow. The yard only reached back for ten metres before it abutted the yard of the house on the street that ran behind Brooks Street.

Isabella pressed herself up against the fence and looked back to number 4269. She could see two windows on the first floor: one was boarded, like the ones in the front, and the other was lit. She crouched down low enough to obscure herself from the street, but still high enough to see over the fence into the neighbouring property.

She saw a woman pass across the open window.

She took her phone out of her pocket and dialled Pope's number. The call rang and rang, but it did not connect and switched over to voicemail. She ended the call and put the phone back into her pocket.

Isabella reached into the bag and wrapped her fingers around the icy-cold butt of the pistol she had taken from the dead cop. The Metropolitan Washington Airports Authority issued its officers with Glock 17s. That was fortunate: Isabella had plenty of experience with that particular nine-millimetre. She drew it out of the bag and quickly chambered a round. She stayed below the line of the fence that divided number 4269 from 4267 until she was close enough to narrow the angle to the first-floor windows so that she wouldn't be visible to anyone who might be looking out. She shoved the gun into the waistband of her jeans, reached up, grabbed the lip of the fence with both hands and hauled herself up. Her feet scrabbled against the wood, the effort dislodging the snow that had rested along the top. She found enough purchase so that she could push herself up and over.

She dropped down, bending her knees as she hit the ground to reduce the sound of her landing as much as she could. The snow muffled the sound. The yard was strewn with detritus: an ancient fridge that had been cast out to rot, an old sofa with tufts of discoloured yellow stuffing poking out of rents in the upholstery that looked as if they might have been carved with a knife.

She followed the line of the house, pressing up against the corner and turning around it, staying flush to the wall. She shuffled along until she was below the open window. She could hear the sound of running water.

There was a door to her left. She reached out and tried the handle. It was open.

She paused. She remembered very well what the woman inside the house was capable of doing. She had handled Pope with dismissive ease in Montepulciano. It would have been difficult for her to have been any more out of her depth than she was already. The sensible course of action would be to observe, to record, to contact Pope and, when he was able, to act in concert with him. Perhaps he would contact Atari for backup. Or perhaps he would contact the authorities and leave it all up to them.

But Isabella thought of her mother and what she would have done. Beatrix would have assessed the situation and reached a different conclusion: she was armed; she had the element of surprise; and, most importantly, the longer she waited, the greater the chance that she would be discovered or the target would leave. It would be almost impossible to conduct extended surveillance in a place like this with just one person. You would need a whole team, enough agents to change in and out so as to minimise the chances that the stake-out was made.

If surveillance was not possible, then there was only one other option available to her.

She would have to take the initiative.

She took the phone out again and tried to reach Pope for a second time. The call rang through to voicemail again. She left a whispered message this time, telling him where she was and that he should come as soon as he was able. She ended the call and put the phone back into her pocket.

She reached back with her right hand, clasped the Glock and brought it out.

And then, with her heart hammering in her chest, she put her left hand on the door handle and turned it.

Chapter Fifty-Six

Maia sat down.

She stared at the wall. She knew that she should not have returned here, but she didn't know what else to do. She was beginning to realise the consequences of what she had done.

She wasn't used to operating outside the carefully calibrated parameters of an operation.

She wasn't used to thinking for herself.

She wasn't used to being alone.

She needed to keep busy while she considered what to do. She removed her clothes, laid them out on the bed and checked them over. There were small splashes of red across the front of the shirt and a half-inch fragment of bone had pierced the denim cuff of her trousers and snagged there. She plucked it out between thumb and forefinger and rubbed the tip of her index finger against it.

She felt strange. It was difficult to describe.

She held up the piece of bone. It was just a physical sensation, the serrated edge of the fragment prickling against her skin. She felt the same way about the bloody patches on her clothes and the stickiness when she touched each of them. Nothing prompted any sort of empathy. She had been trained from an early age to think purely in neutral terms; that neutral and placid state of mind was reinforced by the cocktail of drugs that she took.

She touched the patches of blood and wondered if any of them had come from Aleksandra. Probably. She had been close when the bomb had gone off. She raised her hands to her face and looked at her fingers. The tips were discoloured, as if rusted. She had touched Aleksandra's bloodied face.

She suddenly felt sick. She hurried into the bathroom, bent over the dirty pan of the toilet and threw up. She stayed there for a moment, her hands braced against the porcelain, spitting out acrid phlegm and fighting the wave of vertigo that washed over her.

The dizziness passed, and she rose to her feet. There was a dusty mirror on the wall; she stood before it and checked herself over. She was unmarked. She flexed her muscles, watching the bulge and feeling the power in her biceps and shoulders, and saw a swatch of blood on her neck just above where her collar would have been. She took a handful of toilet paper, moistened it under the tap and then scrubbed the blood away.

The second bout of nausea overtook her so fast she didn't even have a chance to get to the toilet. She bent double and retched, a hot stream of vomit rushing up from her gullet and burning her throat and her tongue, then spattering on to the floor and against the walls.

She crouched down, trying to breathe. She had to bring herself back under control. She had to think.

She took a towel and mopped up the vomit, then reached behind the shower screen and twisted the tap. It was tepid. She would leave it for five minutes to warm up. She decided to go down to the kitchen to get rid of the soiled towel and have a glass of water so that she could wash the taste from her mouth.

Maia descended the stairs and went into the kitchen. She dumped the towel in the bin and ran herself a glass of water.

She turned to go back upstairs again and found that she was not alone.

Isabella Rose was in the hall. She was facing Maia. She had a pistol – Maia recognised it as a Glock 17 – and it was pointed dead at her.

'Don't move.'

Maia had seen the girl at the airport with Pope. She had assumed that she was dead. She would have checked this, but she'd concluded that the odds were very good that both her and Pope had been killed, and she'd not had the luxury of time to confirm that that was true. She could see now that she had made a miscalculation.

Maia was naked and unarmed. Isabella was young and didn't have Maia's advantages, but she evidently knew how to handle the weapon. She had the upper hand. Maia found, to her surprise, that this did not concern her. It was almost a relief to have her freedom of action curtailed, however temporary that might be.

'Put your hands up.'

Maia did as she was told, raising her hands so that they were at the height of her sternum, the palms outward to face her.

'This way. Into the lounge.'

Isabella backed away, the gun kept level with Maia's head. They made their way into the corridor. Isabella stepped back from the open door and waved the gun to indicate that Maia should go inside. She did, and Isabella followed.

'Turn around.'

'What are you going to do?'

'I'm going to cuff you. Turn around.'

Maia did as Isabella asked. The lounge was as unpleasant as the rest of the house. There was a sofa, a table standing on three legs and a wooden chair. The windows were without glass, the apertures covered by boards that had been nailed on to the frames. Isabella told her to go over to the wall. Maia looked for something in which she might be able to watch Isabella's reflection, but there was nothing.

'Kneel down next to the radiator.'

Maia knelt down. The radiator riser led down beneath the floorboards.

'Cuff yourself to it.'

The girl threw out a set of police-issue straight bar cuffs. They slid across the boards and rested against the outside of Maia's lower leg. The metal was cold.

'Do it. I'm not fooling around.'

Maia snapped one of the bracelets around her right wrist and clipped the other to the riser. Isabella looked down at her. She looked frightened. That was reasonable, Maia thought. The riser was made of thin copper pipe, corroded where it joined the radiator. It would have been easy enough for Maia to snap, yet she found that she didn't want to do that. She was content to stay where she was, leaning against the cold metal, looking up at the girl and into the muzzle of the Glock that was aimed at her.

Chapter Fifty-Seven

Isabella sat down in the seat opposite the radiator. She laid her arm on the armrest of the sofa with the pistol clasped in her hand, the weapon trained on the woman. There was enough distance between them; even if the woman was capable of freeing herself, Isabella doubted that she would be able to before Isabella had time enough to shoot her.

But the woman looked quite happy to stay where she was, her back resting against the radiator and her legs curled beneath her. She didn't speak. She didn't try to free herself. She did nothing. Instead, she closed her eyes and her breathing became shallow. She might have been asleep.

Isabella knew that she had taken a risk. So far, it had been justified. But she had acted impetuously, without a plan for what might come next, and that fact became more and more apparent as the first hour bled into the second and then into the third. She was dependent upon Pope, and she had heard nothing from him. She started to worry: perhaps he'd been injured more badly than she'd thought? What if he was detained, or worse? What would she do then?

Isabella took out her phone and checked the time. It was six in the evening. They had been here for six hours.

There was still nothing from Pope.

Where was he?

It was as if the woman could sense her unease. Her eyes flickered open and she gazed at Isabella.

'Is Mr Pope coming?'

'Don't talk to me,' Isabella said defensively.

'You can relax, Isabella. I'm happy to wait.'

'You don't have a choice,' she said, indicating the pistol.

The woman smiled and held up the cuff that shackled her wrist. 'This would be easy enough to snap.'

'Not before I shoot you.'

'You can't shoot me when you're asleep.'

Isabella's confusion must have been obvious.

'You were asleep for twenty minutes.'

'No, I wasn't,' Isabella said.

'There's no shame in it. You must be tired.'

'I didn't sleep.'

Isabella squeezed the pistol a little tighter. Had she fallen asleep? She was tired. There was no point in denying it. She'd travelled thousands of miles during the past twelve days, and the little sleep that she'd got had not been particularly good.

'I'm not trying to make you worry. I'm happy to wait for Mr Pope. I'm not going to hurt you.'

'Like you didn't hurt Aleksandra?'

A frown passed over Maia's face. 'I didn't hurt her.'

'I saw you after the explosions. You went over and checked that she was dead.'

'No. I wanted to help her.'

'You think I'd believe that because I'm young?'

'I was there to protect her,' Maia said. For the first time, there was a little anger buzzing beneath her otherwise impassive voice. 'Mr Pope complicated things. He frightened her. If it'd just been me and her, she would still be alive.'

'*We* frightened her?' Isabella said. 'Are you even listening to yourself?'

Maia exhaled. 'It doesn't matter what you think. I don't blame either of you. I would've done the same. And what's done is done.'

Isabella looked down at her phone again, willing it to ring.

'Was Mr Pope injured?'

'No,' she said. 'I don't think so.'

'Then I'm sure he'll be here.'

Another thirty minutes passed. It was monotonous, but Isabella made a determined effort to stay awake. Maia closed her eyes again, letting her shackled arm hang loose at her side. Isabella looked at her. There was nothing very special about her, yet the memory of what she had watched her do in Montepulciano was still fresh in her mind.

'Wake up, Isabella.'

She opened her eyes, cursing under her breath. She had started to drift off again.

'Talk to me,' Maia said. 'That might help you stay awake.'

Isabella got up and stretched her arms and legs. 'Fine,' she said. 'Since we're talking, I want to ask you a question.'

Maia nodded for her to go ahead.

'When we were in Pope's apartment, you mentioned my mother,' she said. 'You said you were sorry about what happened to her and that she was impressive. What did you mean?'

'I said that because I know who your mother was.'

'How? You met her?'

'No. But I knew who she was. We all did. I knew what she did before she died, too. She was very ill, wasn't she?'

'Yes. She had cancer.'

'Then what she did was impressive.'

'What do you mean – how do you know what she did?'

'Your mother attacked the company that owns me. She killed men and women who worked for the company, and then the man who preceded Michael Pope as Control.'

'No,' Isabella corrected. 'I killed him.'

It was obvious from the surprise that twitched across her face that Maia was unaware of that. 'Really?'

'After what my mother did . . .' Isabella started, then paused until she had recovered her composure. 'After that, he was in hospital, and I shot him. That's what this means.' Isabella unbuttoned her shirt and pulled down the sleeve to reveal the tattoo of a rose that she'd had done in Marrakech. 'My mother had five. One for each of the bastards who killed my father and took me away from her. This one is for the sixth. For Control.'

'He had it coming,' Maia said.

'How do you know anything about us?'

'I was given your mother's file to study. She was causing a lot of concern. They were going to assign me. If it hadn't ended the way it did . . . well, it wasn't necessary for me to be involved. She made sure of that.'

Isabella felt a tight little knot of emotion in her stomach. She tried to wall off her memories of what had happened on that morning and the days that followed it, but her ability to do that had always been weak.

'Do you have any brothers or sisters?'

'No. It's just me and . . .' Isabella trailed off.

'Mr Pope.'

'Yes.' Isabella found the turn that the conversation had taken to be disconcerting. She was saying too much, so she waved a hand to forestall any further talking. 'That's enough.'

Her phone buzzed. She looked down at it.

She recognised the number on the display.

It was Pope.

Chapter Fifty-Eight

P ope handed the driver of the taxi a twenty, told him to keep the change and stepped outside.

He looked over at the house, saw the number – 4269 – and crossed the path to climb the steps into the front garden. Isabella had said that he should go around to the rear. There was a path to the side of the house. Refuse bins had been left there, pushed up against the wall and reeking with the smell of old, rotten food. Pope squeezed by them, pushed through a wild bush that had been allowed to grow unchecked and made his way into the back garden. There was a door into the back of the house. He tried the handle, found that it was unlocked, carefully opened it and went inside.

It was a small house, in poor condition. He was in a room that had been used as a dumping place for the detritus that had not yet graduated to the rear garden. There was an old-fashioned, top-loading washing machine, a tumble dryer crammed into the space next to it, cardboard boxes tossed atop one another and black bin liners that had been gnawed upon by vermin, the clothes inside spilling out on to the floor.

He stopped and listened, concentrating hard, but he couldn't hear anything. He turned the handle of the room's other door and opened it, looking along a small corridor that ended with what he guessed to be the front door of the house. There was a step up from the room to the corridor and he took it, grimacing again from the pressure on his leg, and he slowly made his way down the hall.

There was a door to the left. It was open. Isabella was standing just inside the doorway. She was holding a black pistol in her right hand and was aiming it out of the room straight at him.

'Relax,' Pope said.

She lowered the weapon.

'Are you all right?' he asked.

'I'm fine. You?'

'Cuts and bruises. We got lucky.'

Isabella gestured that he should go inside.

The room must have been used as the lounge at one time, although the days when it would have been pleasant and comfortable were long gone. The furniture was sparse and in poor condition. His attention was drawn to the floor next to the sofa. There was a woman there. She was naked. Her wrist had been cuffed, the other bracelet attached to the riser pipe of the radiator.

Pope went over to the woman on the floor. Maia. There was nothing unusual about her: average height and build, with nothing to suggest she should have been capable of throwing him around the way that she had. Pope could see the lines of the muscles in her chest, the bulges down her arms and legs.

'Hello again, Mr Pope,' she said.

She rolled her shoulders to straighten out the kinks and, as she did so, Pope could see around to the location on her shoulder where Isabella had stabbed her.

There was nothing there.

He felt a shiver of unease.

He could diagnose his foreboding easily enough: it was uncertainty, fear. He had doubted the things that Atari and Litivenko had described to him. It was easy enough to do that, given the outlandishness of their claims, even after witnessing the freakish physical feats that had been carried out by this woman and the man who had pursued them in Shanghai. But here – looking down at the unblemished skin where there should have been a scar, a wound that had healed far more quickly than it had any right to – was a kind of proof that was more visceral and immediate. It suddenly became something real rather than theoretical, much more difficult to dismiss as fantasy.

And it led him inexorably to a second conclusion: that his family was held at the whim of people who had this kind of ugly science at their disposal.

Pope reflexively moved away from her.

'What are you going to do with me?' she said.

'Stay there and be quiet.'

He put his hand on Isabella's shoulder and moved her to the doorway.

'Are you sure you're all right?'

'I'm fine,' she said.

'Has she been any trouble?'

'No. She said she was happy to wait for you. She hasn't tried anything.'

'That doesn't mean we can trust her,' he said, reaching out his hand for the gun.

'What are we going to do?' she said as she handed him the Glock.

'Have you had a chance to look around?'

'I've been down here with her. Didn't want to take any chances.'

'Search the rooms. See if you can find her phone.'

Chapter Fifty-Nine

I sabella returned with a small haul of booty.

She had two Beretta handguns: a small Beretta Pico and an M9. There was a karambit fighting knife, a cell phone, a collection of explosives and detonators and some clothes. Isabella laid everything out on the beaten-up sofa.

'Where did you find those?' Pope asked.

'The M9 and the clothes were on the bed. The explosives and the Pico were under the floorboards. I saw one was loose.'

'Well done,' he said.

'There's this, too.'

Isabella had a sheaf of paper in her other hand. She handed it to Pope and he flicked through the pages. He scanned quickly: there were emails referring to Litivenko and the time she was due to land at Dulles, together with a short biography.

'What does it mean?' Isabella asked.

Pope drew her into the hallway, where they could speak quietly without being overhead. 'She was there today to kill the doctor – this just proves it.'

'She says she wasn't,' Isabella said.

'Really?'

'She says she was there to protect her.'

Pope shook his head. 'She's trying to trick us. She was there to kill her.' He took Isabella by the shoulders and looked down into her face. 'We can't trust anything she says, Isabella. She works for the bad guys. Remember what she did in Italy.'

'I know,' she said.

'You've got to stay sharp. This is an opportunity for us. We just have to work out how to take it.'

'There's one other thing. It was too big to bring with the other stuff. Wait there.'

She climbed the stairs and went into the bedroom. There was a square box with an adjustable webbing shoulder strap and an external display that recorded the temperature inside. She put the strap over her shoulder and took it down to Pope.

'Do you know what this is?' she said.

He examined it. 'Looks like a portable fridge.'

He flicked back the clasps and opened the case. Cold air leaked out. The box was lined with heat-preserving aluminium foil and there was a cold gel pack at the bottom. There were three test tubes inside the inset. He took one out and held it up. The tube contained blood.

He took it into the living room. 'Is this yours?'

Maia nodded. 'I take a sample every week.'

'Why?'

'Because they monitor my blood.'

'They?'

'Daedalus. I take drugs for certain conditions I have. I have a weekly injection. They test the blood to make sure everything is as it should be. There is a balance that needs to be maintained. It can be dangerous if it gets out of control.'

'Dangerous for whom?'

'Mostly for other people, Mr Pope,' she said.

'How do you get the blood to them?'

'A dead drop. I was supposed to leave it there this morning.'

'And you didn't.'

'No. Not this time.'

'Why not?'

'Because I chose not to.'

Pope returned to the portable fridge, slotted the tube back into the inset and closed it. It had given him an idea.

Isabella held up a key fob. 'I found this, too.'

'Do you know which car it's for?'

She nodded. 'It's parked outside.'

'That's good. We need to get out of here. It isn't safe. Grab her clothes – let's get her dressed.'

Pope stood back and aimed the pistol down at Maia as Isabella collected the clothes from the sofa and brought them across the room.

'Give me the phone,' he said.

Isabella did as he asked. He switched it on, navigated to the camera app and snapped a series of photographs of Maia. He made sure that the photographs included a clear shot of her face.

'We're going to leave,' Pope said, making sure to stay out of range. 'Understand?'

Maia nodded.

'I'm going to give you the key for your cuffs. I want you to undo them and then get dressed. If you try anything, I won't think twice: I'll just shoot you. Okay?'

'I understand. Where are we going to go?'

'Just get changed.'

Pope nodded to Isabella. The girl took the key for the bracelets from her pocket and slid it across the floor. Maia took the key and unlocked the cuff.

'Get dressed.'

Pope kept the gun trained on her as she dutifully pulled on her jeans. She leaned forward, and Pope noticed the dressing on the back of her neck.

'What's that?' he asked.

'A cut,' she said. 'It's nothing.'

'Cuff yourself again,' he said. 'Hands in front this time.'

She did as she was told and then, at Pope's instruction, covered her cuffed hands with a throw that she took from the sofa.

Pope went to the window and peered out through a narrow gap between the board and the frame.

'What are you going to do?' Maia asked him.

'You don't need to worry about that.'

'Are you going to offer to exchange me for your family?'

He didn't answer.

'Because if you are, you should be careful. I don't know how valuable I am to them any more.'

He knew there was little to be had by engaging with her, but he couldn't resist. 'Why would you say that?'

'I'm damaged goods.'

'What does that mean?'

'I've disobeyed orders. I know you won't believe me, but I wasn't there to kill the doctor. I wanted to help. They probably know that now. They might prefer it if you shot me. You'd save them a bullet.'

Pope gripped the pistol a little more tightly. 'Shut up, you crazy bitch,' he said. 'If you think I'm going to listen to you, you're nuts.'

'You don't need to worry,' she said. 'I'm not going to struggle. I'm tired. I don't care what you do to me.'

Pope ignored her. He turned to Isabella. 'She's going to ride in front with me until we can find somewhere we won't be overlooked; then she's going in the trunk. You ride in the back with the Pico. Keep it aimed on her. Shoot her if you have to.'

Chapter Sixty

Maia rode in the front of the Cruze with Isabella pressing the little Beretta against her ribs until they were out past Woodland Acres. Pope found a quiet road on the way to Chantilly. He went around to the rear of the car and opened the trunk. He took the gun from Isabella, went back to the front of the car, opened the passenger door and walked Maia to the back. She got into the opened trunk without objection. There was plenty of space for her. She drew her knees up to her chest and stared out at him as he aimed the gun down at her.

'You're very cooperative,' he said.

'I told you. I'm tired. And I don't see any point in resisting. You have the gun.'

Her calmness was disconcerting. Pope slammed the lid of the trunk down and got back into the driver's seat.

Isabella slithered into the front. 'What are we going to do?'

'Maybe we don't need Atari any more. Do you have her phone?'

She handed it to him.

'We have two choices,' he said. 'We could contact Atari and offer to give him Maia if he helps me find my family. That's the easiest of the two options, but I've never really trusted him. He nearly got us killed twice: Shanghai and then today. He has some clever tricks, but I don't think he can keep a secret.'

'So?'

'The second option is we take the initiative.' He nodded his head back towards the trunk. 'You've given us an opportunity. If she is what we think she is, she's very valuable. They're going to want her back again.'

'We swap her?'

Pope nodded.

He knew they had no choice, not really. This was the only course of action open to him. He had to do it. But Isabella didn't.

'You should think about what you want to do now,' he said. 'You don't have to follow me.'

'Why?' she said. 'Because it's dangerous?'

'It will be—'

She cut him off. 'You don't think I'm used to that by now?'

'I know you are—'

'We're in this together. You've said it yourself – I already know too much for me to be safe. I want to see it through.'

Pope didn't argue. He took the cell phone that Isabella had found and scrolled through the calls that had been made and received. There was only one number. It wasn't identified.

He called it.

'*Worldwide Distribution. How can I direct your call?*'

'I'd like to speak to someone about Maia.'

'*Excuse me, sir?*'

'You have an agent. Her name is Maia. I'm with her now – she's in the boot of my car. Put me through to someone who can talk to me about her or I'll call the press instead.'

There was a moment of silence.

'*To whom am I speaking?*'

'Captain Michael Pope.'

'*We'll need proof that you're with her.*'

Pope selected one of the photographs that he had taken of Maia chained to the radiator and sent it.

'Got it?'

There was a pause. Pope thought he could hear another voice, a murmured conversation in the background.

'*Yes,*' the speaker said. '*I've got it.*'

'She was stabbed in the shoulder the last time I saw her. It's amazing how quickly she's healed. Do you think the newspapers would be interested to see what you've done?'

'*You're not in a position to make threats, Captain. Think of your family.*'

'I am thinking of them,' he said. 'It's the only reason I haven't gone to the media already.'

'*What do you want?*'

'I'd like to give her back to you.'

'*That would be helpful, Captain. In exchange for your wife and your daughters?*'

'That's right.'

'*We'll need to talk about it.*'

'I'm not negotiating. This will be the only time we talk.'

There was another pause. Pope watched the traffic rushing by, spray kicking up behind them as the cars and lorries sped through the standing water. He stared at the tail lights until his eyes lost focus and the red became a constant blur.

'*Very well. Where and when?*'

Pope found that his heart was in his mouth. 'One more thing before we get to that,' he said. 'I want Vivian Bloom to be there. He makes the exchange. No one else.'

'*I'm sorry. Who?*'

'Don't waste my time. You know who he is. And it's non-negotiable.'

'*You would risk your family over something like that?*'

'That's the deal. If it's no good for you, just say. My next call will be to the *Post*.'

'*No, that won't be necessary. Mr Bloom will be there. Where would you like to meet?*'

'Bring them to Knoxville in Tennessee. The exchange will be at midnight in two days. I'll call again with the location.'

He ended the call without waiting for a reply. He found that his hand was shaking as he broke the phone open, pulled out the battery and the SIM and dropped them and the phone into the cup holder between the two front seats.

Isabella was looking at him across the cabin. 'What did they say?'

'They said yes.'

'What now?'

'We've got a long drive.'

PART FOURTEEN:

Knoxville

Chapter Sixty-One

Isabella was in charge of navigation.

They followed the interstate, taking I-66 towards Woodstock and then switching on to I-81 for the long, seven-hour drive south to Tennessee. They stopped on two occasions. The second time they stopped, Pope chose a gas station with a large parking lot, a wide empty space where he could park the car and still be confident that Maia would not be able to attract attention if she started to holler from the trunk. He stayed in the car with the gun while Isabella went into the stores for provisions. Once Isabella had returned, and they were on quiet roads again, he pulled over and they both went to the trunk. They each aimed their guns as Pope opened the lid and offered Maia water. He helped her to sit and held the bottle to her lips while she drank.

She said nothing. She was relaxed and cooperative.

The Cruze's tank was three-quarters full, and they had been able to make it all the way down to Blacksburg before they needed to fill up. Pope found a quiet place and Isabella filled the Cruze up with gas as he waited, ready to drive away if Maia tried to pull anything.

Once again, she did not.

They listened to the radio. The top of every hour brought a new development in the story of the Dulles airport attack: the bombers had been positively identified; martyrdom videos had been circulated by channels associated with the Islamic State, with each man pledging allegiance to the caliphate and warning of the commencement of a holy war; the CIA and FBI were confirming that the attack was most likely directed from Syria; and, finally, as they crossed the border into West Virginia, there was an Oval Office statement from the president in which he said that the attack was 'an act of war' and promised that the United States military would retaliate appropriately.

'They're getting what they want,' Pope said. 'London first to get the British on side. That worked. Now this.'

'And Litivenko?'

'You've got to give them credit. They killed two birds with one stone. Nearly three, if you count us.'

'So why was Maia there?'

'To make sure she was dead.'

Isabella stared out of the windshield.

'What is it?' Pope said.

Isabella shrugged. 'So why is she cooperating?'

'She's handcuffed. We're both armed. What's she going to do?'

'It's as if she's resigned to it. She hasn't tried anything, not even when it was just me and her. And I fell asleep.'

Pope reached over and grasped her shoulder. 'Don't let her get into your head. She's dangerous, Isabella. You've seen what she can do. Don't forget it.'

Isabella rested her feet on the dashboard as Pope pulled into the middle lane and overtook a slow-moving convoy of lorries.

'Why are we going to Knoxville?'

'We're meeting a friend there,' Pope said.

'Who?'

'Someone I used to know a long time ago. His name is Chuck. We're going to need help. And this is going to be right up his alley.'

'And then?'

'We'll go south. The Great Smoky Mountains. I know them. I trained up there before. We're going to be outnumbered and out-gunned. We can make the odds a little better if we know the terrain better than they do.'

'You have a plan?'

'I do,' he said.

'Don't think about trying to leave me out of it.'

He snorted. 'Couldn't do that even if I wanted to, could I? There's only two of us, three if you count Chuck. I'm going to need your help.'

Chapter Sixty-Two

They arrived in Knoxville at five in the morning. Pope had called ahead and arranged to meet his friend at the Cracker Barrel Old Country Store, just south of the interstate as it ran the last few miles into the city. The restaurant was in a large, modern building that looked more like a warehouse than a place where you might go to eat, with a parking lot dividing it from the Motel 6 to the west. Pope pulled into the parking lot. It was empty, but he parked the Cruze as far away from the buildings as he could.

It had been a long drive and Isabella was tired. She yawned.

Pope looked over at her and rested his hand on her shoulder. 'I know,' he said. 'Not too much more to do this morning, then we can get some sleep.'

She was about to reply when she saw the lights of another car rake across the side of the building. Pope squinted into the glare.

'Is that him?' she asked.

'I think so.'

The car parked next to theirs. It was an old military vehicle, a four-wheel-drive utility. It had a horizontal slot grille at the front, plenty of ground clearance and the driver was protected by a fold-down roof. The vehicle was in excellent condition, the olive drab paint job glittering in the glow of the lights that towered over the parking lot. Pope and Isabella waited until the grumbling engine was shut off and the driver stepped down.

Isabella looked him over. He was an old man with a thick beard reaching down below his chin. He had thick, bushy white eyebrows and a gap between his two front teeth. He was wearing a padded leather jacket with a patch sewn over the breast. His face broke into a ready grin when he saw Pope.

'Michael Pope, as I live and breathe. I never thought I'd be seeing you again.'

The man reached out his hand and Pope took it. That didn't seem to be enough; the man drew Pope into an embrace and clapped him vigorously on the back.

'Good to see you, Chuck,' Pope said.

'Likewise.'

Pope went over to the jeep and ran his fingers across the grille.

'Is it an original?' Pope asked.

'You recognise it?'

'M151?'

Chuck nodded. 'The quarter-ton. You know your jeeps. This one was used by Creighton Abrams at Long Binh. Came up at auction fifteen years ago. It was one of the ones they couldn't sell, so they quartered it for scrap. I welded it back together, did it up and put it back on the road.'

'She's a beauty,' Pope said.

'But you didn't come all the way down here to admire my wheels, did you?'

'No,' Pope said. 'I appreciate you doing this.'

'What you talking about?'

'Coming out here. You didn't have to.'

'Sure I did. I told you – I ain't never forgotten what you did for me. I owe you, brother. I'm happy I got the opportunity to help.'

'You don't know what I want you to do yet.'

'You want to grab some breakfast and tell me about it?' He nodded to Isabella. 'Who's this one? Your daughter?'

'I'm not his daughter,' Isabella replied tersely.

'Her name is Isabella,' Pope said.

Chuck offered her his hand. She took it. His skin was leathery and dry, his grip firm.

'Nice to meet you, Isabella. My name's Chuck McCluskey. Now, then. I don't know about you two, but I'm so hungry I could eat the north end of a southbound goat. How about y'all?'

Pope smiled, but shook his head. 'Wish I could, but not now.'

'I know a place,' Chuck said. 'Open twenty-four seven, best pancakes this side of paradise.'

'I can't leave the car,' Pope explained. And then, when McCluskey showed his confusion, Pope added, 'Can we go somewhere quiet? Do you still have your place at the airfield?'

'Sure do. Got a couple hangars over there now. It'll be quieter than a mouse pissing on cotton at this time of the morning. We can shut them up good and tight and you can tell me whatever it is you want me to be getting myself into. You want to do it now?'

'No time like the present.'

'Come on, then,' he said, turning to the jeep. 'You can follow me there.'

⌣

Pope got behind the wheel and set off behind the old jeep.

'He's our help?' Isabella said as they pulled away.

'What's the problem?'

'That he's obviously crazy?'

'He's not crazy. He's just eccentric. There's a difference.'

'If you say so,' she said, shaking her head. 'Who is he?'

'An old friend.'

She looked at him and impatiently gestured that he should go on.

'This was a long time ago,' he said, his fingers drumming against the wheel. 'I was in the Group, but it was years before I took over as Control. There was a businessman we had our eye on. The top man in a petrochemical outfit. They were breaching sanctions by buying oil from Iraq. The decision was made that the man had to be removed.'

'Killed,' Isabella said. She had no time for euphemisms. She knew that Pope had been a government assassin. Her mother had held the same position that he'd held. She was inured to surprise, although Pope often seemed to tread carefully whenever the subject came up.

'Fine. You're right. That's what they wanted us to do. He was into winter sports and had a cabin up in Vail. They sent us here to train for the operation. The landscape was similar, the climate was similar, it was a good spot. I came up here with John Milton and a couple of other agents, we put a plan together and then we practised it.'

'How was the old man involved?'

'We planned to go in on foot, but we wanted the option of exfiltrating by helicopter. Chuck used to fly for the 1st Cavalry Division in Vietnam. The way he tells it, he flew six hundred missions without getting shot down. When he got out, he flew for the CIA. He must've been fifty-five when they assigned him to us. We thought they were taking the piss, but they weren't. I've never seen anyone fly helicopters like him.'

'I don't know if you noticed,' Isabella said, 'but he's not fifty-five now. He's a lot older than that.'

'I know,' Pope said. 'But Chuck owes me a favour and we can't just hire a pilot for what we've got to do. Apart from the fact it's way beyond being illegal, no one in their right mind would agree to it. He will. I trust him, he's still flying, and that makes him our best shot. We've got to be creative if we're going to get out of this in one piece.'

McCluskey led them south to a private airfield on the eastern boundary of McGhee Tyson Airport, the domestic hub for the Tennessee area. It was five thirty in the morning when they pulled up at a gate in a high wire-mesh fence. Isabella looked up and saw a sign that announced the Army Aviation Heritage Trust.

'Heritage?' she said.

'Keep an open mind.'

McCluskey drove on to the airfield and parked next to a large steel-framed hangar. He signalled for Pope and Isabella to stay in their car and walked stiffly to the control panel. He unlocked it and then pressed a button so that the hangar door rolled up. He got back into the jeep and drove inside. Pope followed.

The internal lights were off, so the interior was lit by the head-lamps of the jeep and the Chevrolet. Isabella could see five distinct, dark shapes. The beams played across them and she realised that she was looking at a collection of helicopters.

Pope switched off the engine and stepped out. Isabella followed him.

'Jesus,' Pope whistled. 'What have you got here?'

'Hold on.' McCluskey reached the box for the lights and switched them all on. The hangar was bathed in white as banks of lights came on in groups. 'There you go.'

'Look at this,' Pope exclaimed.

Isabella didn't recognise the helicopters, but she could tell that they were of varying age. They were impressive.

'What do you think?' Chuck asked them.

'I think it's amazing,' Pope said. 'Where did you get all these?'

'They come up at auction every now and again. We buy them, restore them, get them into the air again.'

Isabella looked at the helicopters sceptically. 'They still fly?'

'Just one of them at the moment,' McCluskey said. He walked down the row to the farthest chopper from them. He tapped his knuckles against the aluminium fuselage. 'This one.'

Isabella looked at it.

'You recognise that, young lady?'

'No.'

'Huey 624,' Pope said.

'Correct. Call sign's Lucky. I'd guess she's about three times your age. Workhorse of our fleet. Bought brand new by the US Army from Bell Helicopter in sixty-seven, then sent to Vietnam. Did combat service with the 61st Assault Helicopter Company. The company insignia is two dice – six and one, that's the unit designation – and when you add it up, you get lucky seven. That's where she gets her name. She was brought down by ground fire at Ia Drang.'

'Not *that* lucky, then,' Isabella said.

'You got a lip on you, missy, don'tcha?'

McCluskey opened the cockpit door and leaned in to adjust something that Isabella couldn't see. 'We buy historic aircraft like Lucky and get them fixed up so that they can fly again. I got a team of veterans, from Vietnam vets all the way to guys who just got out, and we put them to work preserving the equipment that they used to work on when they were serving. We put them all the way back to their original army specifications, we make sure they're maintained to operational standards, then we get clearance to fly them again. We do air shows and we take old soldiers up, rekindle their memories.' He shut the door. 'Listen to me – I'm going on and on. You didn't come out here to see my helicopters. What can I do for you?'

'You said she was still flying,' Pope said, nodding to the Huey. 'What about you?'

'Well, shit, sure I am. Who else you think flies her?'

'I was hoping you'd say that. Because we're looking for a pilot. That's why we're here.'

'Where do you want to go?'

'That's the thing. I could've hired a commercial pilot if this was straightforward, but it's not. You better come and take a look at this.'

Pope led the way to the back of the Cruze. He drew the pistol.

'What you got in there, partner?' McCluskey said.

Isabella drew her Beretta.

Pope opened the trunk and stood back.

Maia was still curled up, her legs drawn up to her chest. She looked up at them now, blinking into the fierce white light.

McCluskey whistled. 'Right,' he drawled.

Chapter Sixty-Three

Isabella trained the pistol on Maia as Pope and McCluskey lifted her out of the trunk. Maia tentatively put weight on her legs and tried to straighten up; she was cramping, her face reflecting her discomfort. Pope asked if she wanted to go to the bathroom and she said that she did. McCluskey told them it was out back, and Pope told Maia to head towards it, his pistol aimed square between her shoulder blades. Isabella followed.

Pope opened the door to the restroom and stood aside so that Maia could go through.

'On your knees.'

Maia knelt down. Pope aimed the pistol at her torso between her shoulders and waist. She raised her arms so that Isabella could unlock one of the bracelets. Isabella took the key but paused, noticing the small wound on the back of Maia's neck, dead centre, just above her shoulders.

'What happened there?' she asked.

'It doesn't matter,' Maia replied.

'Answer the question,' Pope insisted, brandishing the gun.

'That was where they put my implant,' Maia said.

'What kind of implant?'

'A tracking device.'

'What are you talking about?' Pope said.

'The people I work for like to know where I am. It's the same for all of us. I didn't want them to know where I was, so I removed it.'

'Why would you do something like that?'

'I told you. I found out that Dr Litivenko was flying to Washington and I knew that they would try to kill her. They told me to leave the country. I decided not to do that.'

'Why?' Isabella asked.

'Because Aleksandra was my friend. I was at the airport to help.'

'Don't listen to her,' Pope said. 'She was there to make sure she was dead.'

'No, Mr Pope. That's not true.'

'No more talking,' Pope said. 'Get the cuffs off.'

Isabella turned the key and the bracelet popped open. Maia massaged her wrists.

Pope flicked the gun towards the cubicle. 'In,' he said. 'Don't get ideas. There's nowhere you can go, and we can put rounds through the door if you mess around.'

'You're not listening to me. I told you. I'm not going to do anything.'

Maia was as good as her word. She emerged from the cubicle, knelt on the floor once more and allowed Isabella to cuff her with her hands behind her back. Pope led her back into the hangar. McCluskey was closing the main door.

'Do you have a room where we could leave her?' Pope asked him.

'There's the office,' McCluskey said. 'Ain't no windows in there and we can lock the door, too. No way out without us knowing about it.'

McCluskey pointed to a room at the rear of the hangar. Isabella went over to it. It had steel walls and a steel roof and, when she opened the door, she saw that there was a desk, a filing cabinet and a couple of chairs. There was a phone on the desk; she pulled the cable from the wall and put the unit outside. Maia came through with Pope following behind.

Pope looked around. 'This will be fine,' he said. He nudged Maia between the shoulder blades with the muzzle of the pistol. 'We'll be outside.'

'I'll wait here until you're ready.'

She lowered herself into one of the chairs, her hands still pinned behind her back. Pope closed the door and turned the key in the lock.

McCluskey had boiled a kettle and was making coffee for the three of them. There was a low table and chairs at the front of the space next to a reception desk where visitors could be welcomed. The table had a selection of aviation and military magazines spread across it. Isabella sat down next to Pope and waited for McCluskey to bring over a tray with their drinks.

'You better tell me what's going on.'

Isabella sat and listened as Pope explained what had happened. He gave the broad strokes, leaving much of the detail unsaid. He described the abduction of his family in Montepulciano, but did not relate any of their journey through Syria or the betrayal that had led both him and Isabella to al-Bab. He did not mention Maia's background or that there was any connection between them and the bombing at Dulles. He lied that Maia was an agent working for the Chilean government and that the taking of his family was revenge for a Group Fifteen operation years earlier. He explained that an exchange had been arranged for the following day at midnight.

If McCluskey doubted any of the story, he said nothing.

'Where's the exchange?'

'Clingmans Dome.'

'The observation tower?'

'Just below it.'

'Where we practised before?'

Pope nodded. 'What do you think?'

'Can I still get in and out of there? Sure. There's a big parking lot and it'll be empty this time of year. They close it off for winter – it gets snowed in. Big space like that, I could land with my eyes closed. The only problem might be the weather. If you get a dump of snow up there, you can't see nothing.'

'Is there going to be any?'

'When you thinking of doing this?'

'Tonight.'

'I'd have to check the forecast. They've been saying it's coming.'

'Assuming it isn't – are you in?'

'Land, collect you, get out? Sure. I'm in.'

Chuck put out his hand and Pope clasped it.

'Good man,' Pope said.

'You need anything else?'

'A long gun. You still hunt?'

'Sure do. Got a Winchester Model 70 at home.'

'Could I borrow it?'

'You think things might get hot?'

'They might. And I don't want to go up there unprepared.'

'I can fetch it. Anything else?'

'Is there a decent hunting and fishing shop around here?'

'Sure. There's Gander Mountain and Beikirch's in Knoxville.'

'Good. Could you go over there? I've got a shopping list of stuff I need.'

'I can do that.' The old man gave a nod. 'Snow's gonna make it tough to get up there tonight.'

Pope glanced over at the jeep. 'You don't drive just that, do you? Got anything else?'

'There's a Jeep Cherokee back home.'

Pope looked at him expectantly.

'Shit,' McCluskey said. 'Seriously?'

'I don't like to ask, but unless you've got snow chains for the Chevy...'

'Nah,' the old man said. 'You want to get up there, you'll need a four-by-four. Don't know that chains would cut it, and that piece of shit looks like it's held together by spit and glue. You can borrow the Cherokee.'

'I appreciate it. The weather and the terrain help us. It'll be tough for them and for us. It's a leveller. And we'll get off the mountain quicker than they will.'

'That's where I come in?'

'If you're still up for it?'

'Shit, sounds like fun. You try to stop me.'

Pope told Isabella to get some sleep. There was a sofa in the waiting area and she made herself comfortable on it, then set her alarm for four hours' time so that she could wake to guard Maia while Pope got some sleep of his own. Pope and McCluskey talked, and Isabella drifted away to the sound of their voices. She tried to visualise what might happen later that day, but she was more tired than she realised and she couldn't focus on her thoughts. She was dimly aware of her breathing becoming deeper and that her muscles were relaxing, and then an involuntary jerk as she tripped over the last moments of wakefulness and tumbled into sleep.

PART FIFTEEN:

Great Smoky Mountains

Chapter Sixty-Four

Pope followed the highway through Maryville, Melrose, Walland and Wears Valley. Their destination was another sixty miles from Knoxville, but each mile that passed brought them closer to the prospect of a conclusion. Pope was tense, and it was difficult not to be infected by his anxiety.

They were in Chuck's Jeep Cherokee. It was eight in the evening.

McCluskey had gone out to a hunting store for equipment that afternoon and had returned with appropriate clothes for them: he had bought Isabella an insulated jacket that was, fortunately, almost a perfect fit for her. The boots he had purchased were a little too small, but they were better than the sneakers that she had been wearing and she was glad to swap them.

Maia was cuffed in the trunk space. There was a dog guard between her and the rest of the cabin, and Isabella was facing backwards so that she could cover the woman with the Glock. The precautions had, so far, been unnecessary. Maia sat quietly, staring ahead, as if anticipating what was about to happen.

Pope pulled over to the side of the road, switched off the engine and glanced out of the windshield. The clouds had rolled in as they had made their way higher into the mountains, and now they sealed them off beneath a canopy the colour of slate. The road bent away from them to the left, with a one-lane track cutting off to the right and heading farther up the mountain. It was signposted 'CLINGMANS DOME OBSERVATION DECK', with a second sign beneath that read 'CLOSED FOR WINTER'.

Pope opened the window.

'It's going to snow,' he said.

It was cold, with icy moisture in the air. Isabella heard a crackle of thunder in the distance.

Pope reached into the footwell and brought out the Winchester rifle that Chuck had brought with him when he returned to the hangar that evening. He put the strap over his shoulder and arranged the long gun so that it rested diagonally across his back. He reached back in again and collected the bag with the extra ammunition, the home-made booby trap he had spent the afternoon putting together and the binoculars.

'You remember what we're going to do?' he asked her.

'Yes,' she said.

'It'll be fine. We just need to hold our nerve.'

'I know.'

He nodded. 'Are you nervous?'

'I'm not crazy, Pope. Of course I am.'

'It's all right if you are. It's normal. I'm nervous, too. But this is the best chance we have to bring this to an end.'

Isabella didn't say anything. Pope opened the door and stepped down to the icy road. Isabella climbed across to the driver's seat.

'Don't talk to her,' Pope said. 'Just get her up there. I'll do the rest.'

Isabella leaned forward and turned the ignition. The engine started up.

'The road is slip—'

'I know how to drive,' she said.

'I'm sorry. I know I don't need to worry about you. Force of habit.'

His voice started to choke. It took Isabella by surprise and she didn't know how to react. She wasn't good with emotion; it made her uncomfortable.

'Listen to me,' Pope said. 'We've come a long way together. I'm not very good at this.' He paused and shook his head. 'Look – I'm trying to say I care about you.'

She looked out at Pope standing next to the side of the road. They had been through a lot: London, Switzerland, Turkey, Syria, Italy, and now India, Shanghai, Vladivostok and Washington. She had grown to like him and respect him as a soldier. He was usually so coolly confident; indeed, she realised that she had seldom seen him anything other than composed and calm. He was neither of those things now.

'You, too,' she said.

She put the Jeep into gear and gently pressed down on the accelerator. It edged forward, picking up speed as she pressed down. She glanced back in the mirror: Pope was at the side of the road, watching her go.

The road slowly turned to the left. A trail broke away, cutting sharply left and then climbing steeply. Pope raised his arm, and then, as the trail turned and ascended more steeply, she lost sight of him.

She wondered whether she would ever see him again.

It was growing darker minute by minute and, as she flicked on the headlamps to light the way ahead, the first flakes of snow began to fall. The road curved around the haunches of the mountain, with a steep drop behind a barrier on the left-hand side. Isabella tightened her grip on the wheel.

She felt very alone.

Chapter Sixty-Five

Pope followed the trail as it climbed along the flank of the mountain. It was broad enough for him to proceed quickly for the first few hundred feet, but, as it cut more steeply into the rock, it became more and more treacherous. The surface was composed of loose shale with occasional patches of mud that had been stirred up by the recent downpours that had lashed the mountains.

He had been careful as they had made their way southeast from the airport and he was as confident as he could be that they hadn't been followed. He was even more confident up here. It was pitch-black and the trail was shielded by a dense line of fir trees. That was a relief. There might be others on the mountain, even with the conditions seemingly about to turn, and he didn't want to draw unnecessary attention to himself.

He climbed for thirty minutes, almost slipping on several occasions, just barely maintaining his balance. The trees shouldered up on either side of the track, smothering visibility even farther. He negotiated a tight switchback, gained another twenty feet and then passed out of the treeline.

Snow was falling now. It fell fast and heavy, quickly gathering into windblown drifts.

He stopped and looked around. He had been here before, to this very spot. This was where they had trained for the hit on the man in the

Rockies. Pope remembered the night that he, John Milton and the two other agents that comprised the Group Fifteen hit squad had spent hiking to this lookout spot. He opened his bag and took out the high-powered Armasight night-vision binoculars that Chuck had provided. He put them to his eyes and looked down at the parking area and, beyond that, the visitors' centre. The buildings were unlit and apparently empty. A paved trail continued up from the edge of the parking lot, leading to the final half-mile climb to the summit. The access road stopped here; there was no way to get back down the mountain apart from descending along it again.

There was one vehicle in the parking lot. It was the Cherokee. Pope could make out Isabella in the front seat. He couldn't see Maia.

He lowered the binoculars and looked up into the falling snow. The night was drawing in quickly now, and the thick clouds were covering the moon. Visibility would be at a premium. On the one hand, that was to their benefit. It would be more difficult for the enemy to find him, assuming that they knew to look. On the other hand, it would be more difficult for him to offer cover to Isabella. She would be alone down there, too far away for him to get to her if she needed him. He looked down at the kitbag. He would have to rely upon his ability with the rifle and her persuasiveness. He hoped that both would be enough.

He took the walkie-talkie from the bag. McCluskey had bought him a set of Motorola XT420s from the hunting and fishing store; they had one each.

'Isabella, this is Pope. Can you hear me?'

The squelch of static was quickly replaced by the sound of her voice. '*I can hear you.*'

'Everything look okay?'

'*It's quiet. Didn't see anyone coming up.*'

'I can't see anyone either. Is she all right in the back?'

'*I've got the gun on her now. Nothing to worry about.*'

'Are you ready?'

'*I am.*'

'Stand by. I'll call them.'

341

Chapter Sixty-Six

Vivian Bloom leaned back in the rear seat of the Escalade as they slowly climbed into the mountains. It was a comfortable car, expensive and fully optioned, but he felt every bump and shudder as they rumbled over the road. They were the middle car in a convoy of three vehicles. The car in front of them was also an Escalade. It contained Michael Pope's wife and children and was being driven by one of the men who had been assigned to the task from the Manage Risk detachment based out of the Lodge, Manage Risk's vast training facility just north of Elizabeth City, North Carolina. There was a second man in the car to guard the passengers.

Bloom's car was being driven by a third Manage Risk man, with one of Jamie King's aides-de-camp in the passenger seat. One of the Daedalus assets, the man they referred to as Blaine, was sitting in the back next to Bloom.

The vehicle at the rear of the convoy was a Mercedes-Benz Vito, a light civilian crew van that was equipped to accommodate six people. The van contained a second Daedalus asset – Curry – and another five Manage Risk personnel.

In total, they had eleven men to put against Michael Pope. He didn't count Isabella Rose. It didn't matter how proficient she was, she was a fifteen-year-old girl.

Pope was a dangerous man, and he had successfully vexed them so far, but this was the end of the road for him. Eleven to one. There was reassurance to be found in that ratio. Bloom focused upon it. They had the numbers. They had two assets with them, with presumably a third waiting for them in Pope's custody.

Why, then, did he feel like he wanted to be sick?

The call had been received four hours ago. Pope had insisted that he speak to Bloom. They had expected that, and the call was quickly patched through to him even as they started to run the triangulation algorithms that would allow them to pinpoint the caller's location. Bloom had expected that he might have to keep Pope on the line long enough for the trace to be made, but Pope made all of that irrelevant.

He told him exactly where he was waiting, and invited him to come and make the exchange.

Bloom had been waiting at the Lodge. It was situated within the Great Dismal Swamp, nestled at the centre of hundreds of acres of ranges and testing grounds that were kept away from prying eyes by armed sentries and a sixteen-foot-high wire fence. Pope's location was confirmed as Clingmans Dome, the tallest peak in the Great Smoky Mountains on the border of Tennessee and North Carolina.

Bloom had been taken by private helicopter to an airstrip outside Elizabeth City. Pope's family were already waiting there. The rest of the team assembled. The men were obviously veteran soldiers, arriving with neat kitbags and dressed in black with heavy black boots. Blaine and Curry had arrived together, both men being driven out on to the airstrip, barely saying a word as they took their seats in the waiting area. A Manage Risk Gulfstream waited for them on the taxiway. They boarded and took off, banking sharply to port and plotting a course due west, headed to McGhee Tyson Airport. They landed ninety minutes later, transferred to the convoy and drove east, covering the sixty miles between Knoxville and the mountains in another ninety minutes.

Bloom looked out of the window. The landscape was bleak and desolate, and visibility was drawing in with every minute. The forecast had predicted heavy snow and it was quickly apparent that it was accurate. Deep drifts had already been ploughed to either side of the road, leaving a white path down the middle that was often treacherous. Fat flakes fell down on to them, swept aside by the windshield wipers to gather in plump lines at the edges of the glass.

'What a fucking mess,' he muttered to himself.

Blaine turned to him. 'Are you comfortable with what has been proposed, Mr Bloom?'

'I used to be a field agent,' he said. 'Did you know that?'

The man said nothing. The *man*. What was he thinking? Bloom shrugged at the use of the word, so preposterous in the circumstances.

He continued. 'I was based at Moscow Station during the Cold War. Have you been to Moscow, Blaine?'

'No, Mr Bloom, I have not.'

'Horrible place. Horrible now, of course, but for entirely different reasons. The nouveaux bloody riches rolling around in their obscene petrodollars. When I was there, it was just horrible. Cold. No money. The spirit crushed out of everyone and the bloody KGB everywhere. The world's fucking arsehole, that was what I thought it was. I was there for five years. Hated every day of it.'

The car slipped across a patch of black ice, the rear wheels spinning and the engine whining as the traction control adjusted the power to keep them pointing ahead.

'This reminds me of then. Not the snow, although I suppose that's a part of it. Going to an exchange. I did two of them. Both on the Glienicke Bridge that linked West Berlin with Potsdam. 1985 is the one everyone remembers. Twenty-three American agents swapped for Marian Zacharski and three Soviets. Three years of negotiation, and then everyone drives out to this one place, their chaps are sent out to the middle so they pass our chaps coming the other way. We know they've got snipers. They know we've got snipers. All the time we're worried that they're going to start shooting and they're worried we'll start.'

Blaine watched him as he spoke. 'You know Pope,' he said.

'I suppose I do.'

'What do you think he will do?'

'He'll be careful,' Bloom said, nodding to indicate the lights of the Escalade ahead of them. 'We have his wife and we have his children. We have the advantage on him.'

'Perhaps,' Blaine conceded. 'But he chose to meet here. There's a reason for that. He is an experienced soldier. He will have made a tactical decision that the location suits him.'

'What do you think?'

'I think that this is the only road in and out. He knows we won't allow him to leave. He'll have a plan.'

'And are we confident about our own?'

'Yes, Mr Bloom. Of course. We just need to execute it, and we will. None of them will leave this mountain alive.'

Chapter Sixty-Seven

Isabella turned back to look at the dashboard clock.

It was twenty minutes past four. She had been here for four hours.

'*Isabella,*' Pope radioed. '*They're coming.*'

She saw lights angling up from the road. A car was climbing the access road to the parking lot.

'I see them.'

'*There are two cars and a van behind.*'

'You told them just Bloom.'

'*They were never going to go along with that. It won't make any difference.*'

The cars crested the hill and approached across the parking lot. They were Escalades, big and black and with powerful headlights that swept ahead of them like acquisitive fingers. The cars crunched through the snow, leaving stippled tracks behind them, and pulled up, twenty feet away, one on either side of the Cherokee. They were both angled inwards so that the beams of their headlights hit the Jeep from two sides. Isabella had to blink and look away.

'*Stay in the car,*' Pope instructed.

'Have you got them?'

'*Stay in the car.*'

Bloom waited.

Blaine opened the door first and stepped out, followed by the man in the seat ahead of him. He swivelled in the seat, looking back through the smoked window to see whether he could see the van that had stopped on the slope before they reached the final turn. Blaine had explained that the men inside would fan out and work their way through the trees on either side of the cleared space. They would establish control of the location.

The second Escalade was visible through the window to his right. The lights blazed, but there was no sign of movement from within. Blaine had spoken with the driver over the troop net that all of the men were connected to. Blaine had told the man to hold position until he said otherwise, just as he had told Bloom. They would be cautious.

Bloom looked forward, past the driver and out of the windshield to the Jeep Cherokee that was lit up in the lights of both cars. There were two people inside – one in the front and one right at the back – but the light was bouncing off the glass and it was difficult to make out details.

His door opened. Blaine was there, the handle in his left hand and a pistol in his right.

'Ready, Mr Bloom?'

'Yes.'

'I want you to raise your hands and make your way to a point between them and us. Call for the girl to come out.'

'The girl? Where's Pope?'

'We can't see him. There's someone else in the Jeep. We think it's the girl.'

'And Maia?'

'There's someone in the trunk space. Probably her.'

Bloom's breathing raced; he tried to master it. 'I go out, ask her to come out, too, then . . .'

'Ask to speak to Pope. Everything as we discussed. I'll cover you from here and we have the men in the trees. Pope won't do anything until he has his family.'

'Yes.'

'And listen carefully for my instructions. When I tell you, I want you to drop to the ground and find cover.'

'Yes,' he said, feeling all of his years. 'Find cover. I understand.'

'Now, sir – please, come out. This will soon be over.'

The Mercedes-Benz van had been parked at a right angle to the road, blocking the way back down the mountain. The six men who had travelled inside it dropped down, split into two fire teams and then hurried into the trees at either side of the road.

Curry led the team that headed to the north. They were all armed with M4 carbines, the 5.56×45mm gas-operated assault rifle favoured by the Marine Corps. Curry had fitted an M203 grenade launcher to the barrel of his weapon in the event that they might need additional firepower.

They were dressed all in black; they wore black helmets and their faces had been daubed with black camouflage paint. They wore night-vision goggles on standard assembly rigs that were attached to their helmets, and they had microphones suspended on cantilevered booms. Curry could hear Blaine, all of the other men and the control room back at the Lodge.

Curry picked his way carefully up the slope, moving more slowly than he might otherwise have chosen so that the other two men behind him could keep up. Even at half speed, they found the effort of matching his pace difficult and they started to breathe more heavily.

Curry forced himself to slow.

'Curry to Ops,' he said into his microphone. 'Where's the drone?'

'*Coming on station in T minus twenty minutes.*'

'That's too long.'

'*It's as fast as we can get there.*'

'Is it armed?'

'*Yes, sir. Two Hellfires.*'

'Full IR sweep as soon as it's on station.'

'*Copy that, Curry.*'

Isabella gripped the butt of the Glock a little tighter as the first and second men got out of the Escalade. They stayed near the car, the first man walking slowly around it to reach the other side. The headlamps were too bright, so she couldn't look at the figure for long, but she could see enough to make out that he was male and that he was carrying a pistol in his right hand.

The man with the gun opened the rear passenger door of the Escalade and, after a short moment, a third man stepped out. She tried to make him out, but, again, the light was too bright.

'Pope,' she said into the walkie-talkie. 'Someone else just got out.'

'*It's Bloom,*' he said, a fresh note of steel in his voice.

'The other one?'

'*I can't make him out.*'

'What should I do?'

'*Just as we said. Step out and call over to Bloom that you'll meet him halfway. Then give him the second walkie-talkie so I can speak to him.*'

'What about the man with the gun?'

'*I'm covering him. If he does anything I don't like, I'll drop him.*'

349

Chapter Sixty-Eight

Isabella looked back at Maia. She was still cuffed; she didn't know whether she would be able to get out of the back of the car or not. She showed no inclination to try. Pope had already said that he would fire on her if she made the attempt; perhaps that threat had persuaded her to stay where she was.

Isabella opened the door and stepped out into the cold night air.

She raised her hands and walked forward.

'Where's Vivian Bloom?'

The old man turned to one of the two who had exited the car with him. Words were exchanged; Isabella couldn't hear anything.

'It's me,' the old man said.

'Come over here.'

The old man walked out into the space between the cars. The lights of the vehicles formed a V, meeting at the Jeep. Isabella stepped through them and into the darkness, the beams forming a bright golden barrier behind her.

The old man was close enough for her to see his face now. His eyes were wide. He looked frightened.

'Pope wants to speak to you,' she said, holding up the third of McCluskey's four walkie-talkies.

The snow continued to fall.

She took a step forward, extended her arm and held out the unit. 'Here. Press the button to speak.'

Bloom took it from her a little gingerly, as if it might deliver a shock, and put it to his ear.

He pressed the button on the side of the unit. 'Pope?'

The volume was turned up loud enough so that Isabella could hear Pope's reply: '*Hello, Vivian.*'

'Where are you?'

'*Don't worry. I'm here.*'

'Really? Looks like you sent a girl to do the job for you.'

'*No, I didn't. I don't trust you. And I'm a better shot than she is.*'

'What do you mean?'

'*I can see you, Vivian. I'm looking at you through the sight of my rifle.*'

Isabella watched the old man's face; it looked as if he was about to void his guts.

The walkie-talkie crackled again. '*Are you still there, Vivian?*'

'Yes,' he said, failing miserably to keep the anxiety from his voice.

'*I'm sure you have something similar in mind for us. Snipers. A lot. An ambush. I don't really care. You tried it in Syria, no reason why you wouldn't try it here, too.*'

Bloom looked up into the darkness that cloaked the hills. Isabella knew that it was impossible to see anything.

'*Where are my family?*'

'In the other car,' Bloom said, gesturing behind him.

Isabella heard the sound from above and away to the northwest: a low buzzing, insistent, constant.

Bloom turned to the man behind him. 'What is that?'

The buzzing grew in volume. It became a hum, then a drone, and grew louder and louder.

The other man spoke into a microphone, loud enough for Isabella to hear. 'Blaine to all units. Inbound helicopter. Repeat, helicopter is inbound.'

Chuck McCluskey was concentrating hard. The weather was bad. He remembered what his army instructor had taught him decades ago. Mountain flying was challenging, but you always had to remain in control of the flight. You couldn't let the mountain, the weather or the temptation to compromise do the flying for you. He kept that in mind as he flew into the mouth of a wide pass, staying reasonably low as Pope had instructed.

The snow had eased a little, but, if he had been given a choice in the matter, he would have preferred to stay on the ground tonight. The helicopter could fly through the snow with no problem, but the limited visibility meant that he was reliant on his instruments. Mountainous terrain like this was challenging at the best of times. It was even more so when you could only see the peaks and ridges when you were almost upon them.

McCluskey approached the coordinates that Pope had provided. The snow eased off a little more, and he could see far enough to make out the scene below him. He was descending towards a wide parking lot that had been built on a natural plateau. There was one access road into the lot and then a trail that led up to an observation deck that had been built nearer to the summit of the mountain. There were four vehicles beneath him: one of them, a car, was parked in the centre of the lot, away from the others; there were two big SUVs that had been parked so that they blocked the way to the access road and the descent back down the mountain; the final vehicle was a black crew van, parked behind the two Escalades, slotted across the middle of the road as another block.

He saw people outside the vehicles. There were two men standing in front of the first Escalade. One of the men was old, wrapped up in a thick jacket and with a hat on his head. The other looked to be younger and less encumbered by his clothes. He was armed with a medium-sized automatic rifle. Isabella Rose was standing directly across from them. There were twenty feet between them. They all looked up at the clatter of the Huey's engine.

McCluskey reduced the speed to give himself enough power in reserve should he need to combat downdraught and then slowly started to descend. He didn't want to stay on the ground any longer than he had to. Pope had explained that this was going to be an extraction away from possible hostiles, and it was clear from the rifle that he had not been kidding about that. The longer he stayed on the ground, throwing wet snow up at the helicopter, the greater the chance of something bad happening that would make it difficult to get back into the air. Ice could adhere to flight surfaces and change their aerodynamic properties, making them less efficient at creating lift. Chunks of ice could be thrown off from the rotor blades and get ingested in the engine, creating an engine stall. The chopper was de-iced, with protection on the intakes, main rotor, tail rotor and rear stabiliser, but that only allowed it a few minutes on the ground before it would be unsafe to attempt to take off again.

Pope was going to have to be quick.

⁀

Pope lay still beneath the Mylar blanket that McCluskey had bought for him. He was in the prone position. Both elbows were solidly grounded, with his supporting left elbow directly beneath McCluskey's Winchester rifle. His body was at a slight angle to the gun, with his right leg slightly bent. The fore end of the rifle was supported on his pack; he was able to achieve excellent stability. He had folded the blanket in half so that he was lying on one half at the same time as the other was wrapped over him. He had been in the same position for thirty minutes and, as a result, the blanket had also been covered with an inch of snow. Pope was pleased about that. Between the blanket and the snow, his heat profile was significantly reduced. He had wondered whether Manage Risk would have been able to route a drone overflight at short notice or whether they might have IR night-sights. If they did, this would help hide him for a little longer.

He hoped it would be long enough.

The Huey's engines clattered as it slowed overhead. McCluskey activated a downward-pointing spotlight and slid across the parking lot until he was directly over a wide space away from the three vehicles. The spotlight lit it up, picking out the clouds of snow that were thrown up by the downdraught from the Huey's rotors. The chopper started to descend, a maelstrom of snow thrown up all around it.

Pope put his eye to the sight again and looked through it at Bloom. He put the walkie-talkie to his mouth and opened the channel.

'Are you still there, Vivian?'

Bloom had to shout to make himself heard. '*What are you doing, Pope?*'

'Get my family out and send them to the helicopter. Isabella is going, too. Remember, I'm staying here until this is done. My rifle is trained on you, Vivian. I'm close enough to make this a straightforward shot. I won't miss. You and me are going to stay here until Isabella tells me that she and my family are clear. If anything happens to them, if you try anything to stop them leaving, if you do anything I don't like, I'm going to put a bullet in your head. Now – give the walkie-talkie back to Isabella and do whatever she tells you to do.'

Chapter Sixty-Nine

The helicopter touched down. It stirred up a vortex of snow, wet flakes being flung across the parking lot.

Isabella heard the squelch of static and then Pope's voice. '*Ready?*'

She was frightened, but she tried hard to hide it. 'Yes. Now?'

'*Now,*' he said.

She went around to the back of the Cherokee, gripped the pistol a little tighter and opened the rear door.

Maia was lit by the courtesy light.

'It's time to get out,' Isabella said.

The woman did not demur. She unfolded her legs, brought them over the sill of the loading area and, with Isabella's help, slid over and dropped down to the ground. Isabella told her to walk around the Jeep towards the two Escalades. She started to move. Isabella followed behind her, the pistol quivering a little in her hand.

She looked ahead.

Bloom was still there.

The man who had been standing behind him had gone to the second Escalade.

Isabella led Maia to a spot halfway between their car and the two blacked-out SUVs.

'Stop,' she said.

Maia did as she was told.

'Get on your knees.'

Maia lowered herself down.

The man opened the door of the second Escalade. Three people got out. It was dark, but Isabella could see enough from the glow of the headlamps to make out a woman and two girls.

'Pope?'

She heard the emotion in his voice even through the static of the walkie-talkie. '*It's them. Call out – tell them to go to the helicopter and then get there yourself. Chuck will take off as soon as you're aboard.*' He added, after a pause, '*Thank you, Isabella.*'

'I'll see you afterwards,' she said. 'Thank me then.'

'They're here,' Bloom called out to her over the clamour of the Huey.

'Send them to the helicopter!'

Isabella retreated from Maia, still covering her with her pistol, and started to back towards the helicopter. She turned her head and saw that Pope's wife was shepherding the two girls in the same direction.

That was when she heard the explosion.

The two soldiers were struggling to keep up, so Curry let them get ahead of him. He followed behind as they tracked up through the undergrowth, stumbling through the deep banks of snow. Their boots slipped and slid, the uncertain footing threatening to take them both off their feet. Curry was more careful, crouching down a little to lower his centre of balance and looking where he was putting his boots. They were moving without flashlights, and that made it more difficult. Curry had the advantage on them in that his retinas had many more light-sensitive receptors, meaning that even lower levels of light triggered the cascade of signals that passed through the interneurons and neurons to the optic nerves and then up to his brain. He might have been able to see better than they could, but that didn't mean he was prepared to take unnecessary risks.

Blaine's voice over the troop net was cool and without stress. '*Curry, this is Blaine. What's your situation?*'

'North of your position,' he said as quietly as he could. 'Nothing yet. What about the drone?'

'*Sixteen minutes.*'

'If he's up here, we'll find him. What about Maia?'

'*She's here. We're making the exchange.*'

The two men ran into thicker brush and changed direction, clambering directly up the slope so that they could divert around it.

Curry stopped.

Something was wrong.

He saw it too late: an almost imperceptible filament that had been strung across the first open gap in the undergrowth above the blockage.

'Wait!'

It was fishing line.

A tripwire.

The first man ran straight through it.

There was a depression to Curry's right. He threw himself into it just as the tripwire fired the defensive mine that had been placed on the trunk of a nearby tree. The detonation fired hundreds of steel balls in a fan-shaped arc two metres high and fifty metres wide. Curry heard dozens of individual impacts as the balls thudded into the trunks and branches of the trees on the mountainside. Drifts of snow were dislodged from the branches all around him, landing with soft thuds, and then he heard the moans from the two men who had been ahead of him.

The explosion shook the ground.

Pope had rigged the two booby traps one on either side of him, enclosing him within a protective cordon fifty feet across. He had built his own claymores with the explosives and the detonators that Isabella had found in Maia's safe house, together with the ball bearings and other shrapnel that McCluskey had purchased for him that morning. He had piled everything into large plastic containers and lashed them around the tree trunks with duct tape. The fishing line that triggered them would be very difficult to see with conditions as they were.

It was the mine to his right that had been triggered. The blast had rippled through the air, knocking thick inches of snow from the branches overhead.

He took his binoculars, pressed them to his eyes and scanned the open space beneath him.

The detonation had caused chaos.

He saw Rachel and his kids. They had been walking towards the open door of the Huey, but now they were sprinting.

Isabella was running, too. She had farther to go, but she was faster than they were and she was closing on them quickly.

He heard the sound of a raised voice from the parking lot.

Pope dropped the binoculars and pressed the rubberised eyepiece of the rifle scope to his eye. He sighted Bloom. He had dropped to the ground and was crawling away, heading for the nearest Escalade. Pope centred him within the sight's reticule, slid his finger through the guard, drew in a deep breath and held it. The Huey's downdraught was raising a gyre of snow and it obscured Bloom from him. By the time the cyclone had cleared, he was behind the SUV and in cover.

He looked up. His kids were clambering into the Huey. Rachel was behind, pushing them inside. Isabella was ten feet away.

Come on.

He saw the flash of automatic gunfire, a starburst that bloomed around the muzzle of the rifle aimed by a soldier who had clattered out of the undergrowth on the opposite side of the parking lot.

Get out of there!

The man who had been standing with Bloom – the man who had chased them through the streets of Shanghai – started to run, too.

He headed straight for the Huey.

Chapter Seventy

Curry had landed on his back.

It had been a drop of six feet into the depression, but his fall had been cushioned by the bank of snow at the bottom. He pushed himself to his feet, confirmed that he had avoided injury and then arranged his helmet so that his goggles were correctly aligned over his eyes and the boom held the microphone over his mouth. He scrambled up the rough edges of the cleft until he was at the top again. The snow was falling harder, but as he crept forward, his weapon ready, ghostly green images resolved from the white: he saw body parts, gouts of dark blood that had been spread over the snow and, not far from where he had seen the tripwire, the remains of both soldiers.

He ignored it all.

Pope was close.

Curry lowered himself to a crouch and moved forward. The second man had lost an arm and his leg below the knee. He was as good as dead and, even if Curry had thought he might have been able to evacuate him back down to the others, he wouldn't have done it.

His target was ahead of him. That was his focus.

He heard the sound of the helicopter's engine growing louder and louder, and then the rattle of automatic gunfire.

He stepped over the man's twitching body, his boots leaving bloody prints in the snow. He continued to climb, passing the blackened and broken tree to which the mine must have been attached, the fragments of the trunk standing out at crazy angles, smoke rising through the falling snow, denuded branches scattered all around.

More gunfire. It was coming from the other side of the parking lot, from the second fire team.

Curry slowed, placing his feet carefully, his eyes switching back and forth between the view ahead and the ground. He saw no other tripwires, nor any suggestion that there was anything else that might threaten him. He knew, of course, that the sound of the blast would have warned Pope that he was being approached. He hoped that his focus would be on the exchange in the parking area below, but he was careful enough to avoid moving too quickly and blundering into the business end of a firearm.

McCluskey saw the flash of the explosion against the gloom that clung to the flanks of the mountain. One of Pope's jerry-rigged devices had detonated.

He glanced back into the cabin of the Huey. The door was open and he could see five figures hurrying across the snowy parking lot.

Three of them running together in a group: two children and a woman.

The girl, Isabella, followed a short distance behind them.

A fifth figure brought up the rear. It was a man, and he was devouring Isabella's lead on him.

McCluskey saw the flash of gunfire from the other side of the parking lot and heard the metallic snaps as rounds passed through the thin skin of the Huey's fuselage.

'Pope,' he said into the radio. 'Can you hear me?'

'*Have you got them all?*'

'Nearly.'

'*I'm bugging out. Take—*'

The broadcast was interrupted by a wave of static.

He turned back again and saw that the children and the woman were inside.

Isabella Rose was seconds away.

The man who was chasing her was seconds behind her.

'Strap yourselves in,' he called back into the cabin.

He opened the throttle and the rotor speed increased. He pulled up slowly on the collective, increased the pitch and counteracted the sudden torque by pressing down on the left foot pedal.

Struggling to make himself heard over the sound of the engine, he yelled, 'Is the girl aboard?'

'Yes!' someone shouted.

He kept pulling up, his foot pressed down firmly on the pedal, and the chopper grew light on its skids and slowly lifted off the ground. The downdraught whipped up the fresh snow and McCluskey's visibility was reduced almost to zero once more.

It was a white-out.

He checked his instruments.

They were climbing.

***

The helicopter started to lift. Isabella was on the skid, one hand anchored to a trailing strap on the floor of the cabin and the other gripping the frame of the open door. She looked inside. There was a bench seat facing the door, and the woman who must have been Rachel Pope was sat between two girls: Flora and Clementine Pope. They had fastened the straps, but Rachel had reached out her arms to press her daughters even more firmly against the bench.

'Help!'

Rachel had no idea who she was, but it didn't matter; she reached out a hand to help Isabella inside.

Isabella stretched to take it . . .

. . . when she felt a hand seize her right ankle.

She slipped back, only just managing to hold on to the frame of the door.

She looked down. The man from Shanghai had leapt up just enough so that he was able to grasp the helicopter's skid. He was hanging by his left hand and had used his right to reach up and grab Isabella's leg.

She braced herself against the door frame, but it was no use. The man's grip was fearsome, and as he started to yank, she knew that she wouldn't be able to hold on.

'Help!' she called out desperately.

Rachel Pope reached for her, but her movement was curtailed by the belt. Their fingertips touched for a moment before Isabella was yanked out of the cabin. Her feet fell off the skid and her hands slid down the frame, her fingers wrenched away from it.

She slid down, flinging out her arms at the last moment and grabbing the man's torso. She wrapped both arms around his waist, locking her hands above his stomach. He was still holding on with just one hand; the addition of her weight seemed to make no difference. He fixed his right hand next to the left and grunted with effort as he started to pull them both up.

She jerked her head around and down.

The helicopter was fifteen feet above the ground.

Twenty.

Isabella scrambled up the man's body until she could hook her legs around his waist. She couldn't let him get into the cabin. She let go of his jacket with her right hand and reached up for his face. She stretched up, her muscles burning, trying to claw and scratch his eyes.

The effort was too much. Isabella felt her grip weaken.

They were twenty-five feet above the ground and still climbing.

Isabella clambered up another few inches, enough to reach the man's face. She raked him with her nails, drawing them across his eye and down his cheek.

The helicopter jerked.

She felt blood between her fingers, a warm slickness on her palm.

She felt for his eyes and clawed him again.

He let go.

They fell.

Chapter Seventy-One

Maia was still on her knees.

She watched as Isabella and Blaine tumbled to earth.

The helicopter was a long way up. Twenty or thirty feet. The snow beneath it had been compacted. It wouldn't offer a soft landing.

Blaine was heavier, and he landed first. He took the impact on his back.

Isabella hit a fraction of a second later. Her leg was bent beneath her when she landed; the sound of the crack as it snapped in two was as loud as a gunshot.

The girl bounced once and then lay still.

Maia saw movement to her left. Vivian Bloom had taken advantage of the confusion to move into cover behind the Escalade. He was shielded from Pope by the bulk of the big car.

Bloom pointed at the helicopter. 'Shoot it down!' he screamed.

Three soldiers had emerged from the undergrowth on the other side of the parking lot. They dropped into cover behind the Cherokee, aimed their rifles and unloaded at the Huey. The shots rang off the hull, drawing sparks, but the aircraft continued to rise.

Maia turned back to Isabella. Blaine was on his feet. He looked unhurt. He picked Isabella up. She was still, hanging limply in the crook of his arm.

The helicopter dipped its nose and accelerated away and out of range.

Bloom punched the side of the Escalade. 'Fuck!' he yelled. 'Fuck!'

Maia stayed where she was. She felt strange. She tried to diagnose it, but she could not. She felt a disassociation, as if two parts of her were slowly splitting apart. She closed her eyes. What was it? She felt the throbbing of an incipient migraine. The pain soared up and up until it was intense. She was used to migraines – they were a side effect of her meds – but this was different. It felt as if a vice had been fastened around her temples, and now it was slowly being tightened.

The three soldiers hurried across the parking lot. Blaine arrived, too. His jacket was covered in snow. He dropped Isabella, dumping her to the ground.

'Where's Pope?' Bloom said.

'Curry found where he was hiding. He's not there.'

'So where is he?'

'We're looking.'

'Where's the drone?'

'Still thirteen minutes out. It won't be here in time.'

Maia looked at Isabella. Her left leg was horribly broken. Maia could see the flash of bone where it had pierced the fabric of her trousers. She was face down and unmoving. Was she dead? It had been a steep fall, and the impact had been heavy. She was just a girl. It was possible.

'What do we do now?' Bloom asked.

'We need to leave, sir.'

'The helicopter?'

'It's gone.'

Bloom turned to Maia. 'At least we have her back,' he said.

Maia heard a low moaning.

Blaine heard it, too. He turned to Isabella. 'She's alive,' he said.

Bloom looked old and tired. He rubbed his hand across his face. 'We should take her with us,' he said. 'Maybe Pope cares enough about her to come back. Put her in the car.'

'Yes, sir.'

Maia's head pounded and she felt sick. But she made the effort to raise her head and open her eyes. Blaine crunched through the snow to where Isabella was slowly stirring. He reached down for her again and dragged her up. Her leg jammed down and she shrieked with pain.

Maia felt a throb of adrenaline.

She tried to free her hands. The bar held firm. She closed her eyes again, flexed her shoulders and forced her hands apart. She felt the metal bite into the skin, felt it against the bones in her wrist, but she screwed her eyes shut tighter and increased the pressure.

The cuff around her right wrist popped out of the solid plastic bar that held the pair together. Her hands were free.

Bloom was watching. His mouth fell open.

Adrenaline coursed through Maia's body.

Fight or flight.

The delicious anticipation of violence.

Maia was next to one of the soldiers. The man was cradling his M4 in both hands, the weapon still on the strap. She reached out her leg and swept him to the ground. He fell to his knees. She put her left arm around his body so that her left hand grasped his right shoulder with her right hand around his head. She kept his shoulders firm as she yanked his head around, breaking his neck. His body went limp; she took the strap and yanked the weapon clear as he slumped forward.

'Blaine!' Bloom cried out.

Maia raised the weapon.

⌣⌣

Curry hurried across the slope.

He found the shooting position that Pope had chosen. It was high up, protected from view by a low fringe of scrub and offered a wide view of the parking lot below. The evidence that Pope had been here was all around: a discarded blanket; the imprint from where a body had been prone against the snow.

He heard the sound of footsteps crunching away through the snow. Curry looked down and saw a set of deep prints disappearing into the trees.

Pope was close. He wouldn't be able to hide. Curry would be able to track him easily.

He was about to set off when he heard the sound of a raised voice below him.

'Blaine!'

He went to the trees and looked down.

He saw the two Escalades and the Cherokee.

He saw the body of one of the Manage Risk soldiers on the ground.

He saw Maia. She was standing, an M4 in her hands. She was partially shielded by one of the Escalades.

The girl was on the ground.

Blaine was standing over her.

Maia was aiming the rifle at Blaine.

Curry heard the sound of someone crashing away through the trees to his left.

He couldn't go after Pope. His first priority was to keep Vivian Bloom safe.

He raised his M4 and took aim.

Chapter Seventy-Two

Maia cradled the M4 and aimed it at Blaine's chest.

'The girl goes with me.'

Blaine raised his hands. 'What are you doing? Put the gun down.'

'Put her in the car and stand back. Now, please.'

Bloom backed around until he had the bulk of the car between him and Maia's rifle. 'Have you lost your mind? What's the matter with you? You take orders from *me*. You don't get to choose.'

'I'm not going to do that any longer, Mr Bloom. The girl is coming with me. Blaine – put her in the car or I'll shoot you both.'

Blaine stayed where he was for a moment, an impassive expression on his face. He looked ready to speak, but didn't. Maia knew why: the possibility of insubordination was so alien to him that he couldn't find the words to express himself. She felt the same way. Disobeying orders would not have been something that she would have thought herself capable of doing even a few weeks ago. It was as if she had stepped out of her body.

'Think carefully, Maia,' Blaine said.

'I have.'

'What's happened to you? Did you take your tracker out? We thought it was them.'

'Do it now, please – I won't ask again.'

Blaine faced her squarely. The uncertainty had been replaced by resolution.

'No,' he said.

There was no going back on her decision now that she had made it. She would never be trusted again. There had been others. Young men and women like her whose names began with J, K and L – men and women she had forgotten – who had struggled with their obedience to the programme. They had ignored their medication and tipped into psychosis. Others had shown weakness and failed in the field. They had all disappeared. She knew what happened. They were liquidated, just as surely as the men and women Maia had been sent to liquidate herself.

The same fate would be waiting for Maia as soon as she allowed herself to be returned to the facility for debriefing. They would put her to sleep with no more feeling or regret than if she were a rabid dog that had bitten its owner.

But she surprised herself.

She wanted to live.

And she couldn't turn back.

Blaine walked towards her.

The M4 Maia had taken was in 'Burst' mode. She pulled the trigger and fired a three-shot volley. Her aim was far too good for there to be any possibility that she might miss. The bullets struck Blaine in the centre of the chest, just below the sternum. He stood there for a long moment before, eventually, he took a half step backwards and then fell on to his backside. He put his hand to his chest. Blood bubbled out of his mouth.

The other two soldiers were in the process of raising their own weapons. Maia shot them before they could.

She turned. Bloom had taken the chance to turn and run, hobbling away from her with as much speed as he could muster. But he was old and slow and he was struggling to keep his balance on the slippery surface. His right leg slipped out and he crashed down on to his side with a thud.

She aimed . . .

. . . and saw muzzle flash from the wooded slope. She ducked as a volley of shots peppered the Escalade.

Curry.

Isabella was lying in the lee of the car. Maia crabbed across to her, grabbed her by the shoulders and dragged her farther into cover.

'My leg,' Isabella said.

Maia assessed her quickly. She was deathly pale; the break must have been excruciatingly painful.

'Listen to me,' Maia said. 'I'm going to get you out of here.'

The girl's eyes swam. Before she could speak, she bent over and retched on to the snow.

Another volley of automatic gunfire rained down at them from the slope. Bullets slammed into the bodywork of the Escalade and the rear window exploded with a detonation of fragments.

There was no time to wait. Maia knelt down, scooped the girl up and opened the rear door. She slid her inside as gently as she could, closed the door, opened the driver's-side door and got inside.

The Escalade had been parked with its nose pointing into the parking lot. Maia started the engine, stamped on the accelerator and spun the wheel to full right-hand lock. The wheels slipped and slid on the icy surface, but found enough friction to spin the car around.

She saw the muzzle flash as Curry fired again. The rounds drummed against the side and across the roof of the Escalade, punching open holes in the metal that looked like the petals of a flower.

Maia saw Bloom on the ground, scrambling to get to his feet and falling over again.

She saw Blaine on his side, blood on the snow around his body.

The car spun around through one hundred and eighty degrees and then they were both gone, behind her, the Escalade facing back down the access road.

She straightened the wheel and pressed down on the accelerator, just enough for the tyres to gain grip and for the big car to jerk forward.

The road sloped steeply downwards and the surface was treacherous, but Maia knew that they couldn't afford to tarry. She stamped on the accelerator, fighting with the wheel to correct the slips and slides that threatened to carry the car into the snowy bank on one side of the road or over the edge of the mountain on the other.

The Mercedes-Benz was still parked across the road. It wasn't quite wide enough to block the road completely, and there was a narrow gap between the bank and the rear of the vehicle. Maia drove right at it, the corner of the Escalade slamming into the van. Their momentum was enough to punch the Mercedes-Benz around, and the Escalade raced by as the Mercedes-Benz spun on the icy surface.

Maia glanced back in the mirror. 'Isabella,' she said.

There was nothing.

'Isabella!'

'My leg,' came the faint response.

'Hold on. Keep speaking to me.'

Silence.

Maia looked in the mirror. Isabella had slumped over against the window, her eyes closed.

'Stay with me, Isabella. I'm going to get you out of here.'

PART SIXTEEN:

Commerce

Chapter Seventy-Three

Michael Pope watched the news. The bulletin was dominated by the news that Raqqa had been hit by the most significant bombardment of the campaign to date. Coalition bombers and a barrage of Tomahawk missiles had been in the air and comprehensive damage had been caused to ISIS command and control structures across the territory that they controlled. There were unconfirmed reports that Special Forces soldiers were in theatre in greater numbers and that SAS operatives had been responsible for calling in the strikes. The president had authorised the deployment of marine, infantry and armoured divisions. They would join with the 1st (United Kingdom) Armoured Division, which was already deploying in Turkey.

It was easy to predict what would happen next. There would be a gesture towards diplomacy, but it would be nothing more than window dressing. The Americans and the British would try for a UN resolution, but the Russians and the Chinese would veto it. The US and the UK would build a coalition instead, with the French, maybe. They had skin in the game, after all. Perhaps with a few other European states, as well. Australia. Canada. As soon as they had the assets in place, they would invade.

Bloom and the men and women that he had conspired with would get everything they wanted.

'Turn that down, Michael.'

'Sorry.'

Pope took the remote control and muted the TV.

His wife, Rachel, sat down on the bed next to him.

'How are the girls?' he said.

'Asleep,' she said.

'And?'

'They're frightened.'

'Of course they are,' he said.

'I'm frightened, too.'

'I know. I'm sorry. I had no idea that they would—'

'I know you didn't,' she interrupted, laying a hand on his knee. 'It's not your fault. And you found us again, didn't you?'

She kissed him. Pope closed his eyes and tried to relax.

Chuck had flown Rachel and the girls back to the airfield and then he'd taken them back to his home in Knoxville and put them up there. Pope had intended to be on the Huey himself, but, as events spun out of control, that had proven to be impossible. So he had descended the mountain on foot, following the Appalachian Trail. It had taken him ten hours to reach Cades Cove. He had stolen an RV and driven north to Knoxville.

The reunion with his family had been the happiest moment of his life, but he knew that they did not have the luxury of enjoying it. They had to move. Chuck helped him change the plates on the RV and they set off to the south. They covered two hundred miles in four hours before Pope decided to stop for the night. They had taken two rooms in a Motel 6 off Interstate 85 on the outskirts of Commerce, Georgia.

Rachel stared blankly at the images of war that flashed across the screen.

'What are we going to do?'

'We'll head south and then east.'

'They won't just let us leave?'

'No,' Pope said. 'They won't. But we have this.'

He went over to the bureau and opened the portable fridge that he had taken from Maia. He reached into it and took out one of the vials. He held it up for his wife to see.

'What's that? Blood?'

'It's our insurance,' he said. 'As long as we have it, they'll leave us alone.'

'You can explain what that means later, Michael,' she said. 'I'm too tired to concentrate. Come to bed.'

She undressed and slid beneath the covers. Pope took a shower and, when he joined her, she was asleep.

⌣

Pope couldn't sleep.

He got up, crossed the room and opened the door. The motel was cheap, with rooms on two levels and the building in the shape of an 'L'. His daughters were in the room next door. The RV was parked in the parking lot.

Pope stepped outside into the cool night air. He looked out at the traffic passing by on the interstate. A jet passed overhead, its lights winking through an opening in the cloud.

He went back inside and closed the door.

His wife was sitting up, spectral in the half-light. 'What is it?'

'Sorry,' he said. 'Did I wake you?'

'Is it the girl?'

Isabella.

Rachel was right. Pope hadn't stopped thinking about her. He closed his eyes and all he could see was Isabella tumbling from the helicopter. He had thought that she was safely aboard. The man had somehow managed to vault up high enough to grab the trailing skid, and then they had both fallen. Pope had stayed for as long as he'd dared, but there were men in the woods hunting for him, and his exploding mine had announced where he was. Regardless of all of that, if he had seen any sign that Isabella was alive, he would have stayed.

But he hadn't.

'We were very high, Michael. I don't know . . .'

The words tailed off. Pope knew what she meant.

There was no way Isabella could have survived the fall.

After everything – after Switzerland, after Syria, after Montepulciano and Mumbai and Shanghai and Washington – Isabella was dead.

PART SEVENTEEN:

Epilogue

Chapter Seventy-Four

'Miss Jones?'

Maia recognised the nurse. The woman had given her an update on Isabella's condition after they had finished the operation to reset her leg.

Maia stood.

'How is she?'

'Could you come with me, miss?'

Maia was in the waiting room of Saint Thomas Rutherford Hospital in Murfreesboro, Tennessee. She had been there all night, ever since she had delivered Isabella to the emergency room. The plastic chairs were hard and unforgiving, and she had found it impossible to get comfortable. She could have waited in the car, but that would have meant leaving Isabella, and she wasn't ready to do that. She knew that they might be compromised at any time and, if that happened, she wanted to be ready.

The nurse led the way into the main body of the hospital. Maia looked around as she followed. She was on edge. They passed along a sterile corridor, the soles of her sneakers squeaking on the floor. The hospital was listed as having nearly three hundred beds and had only recently been constructed. The staff had been friendly and helpful when she arrived in the early hours of the morning. She said that Isabella had no insurance, but that hadn't been a problem. They took one look at Isabella's fractured leg and took her inside to be prepped for surgery.

Maia had whiled away the hours she had been waiting by wondering whether she had made the right decision to bring the girl here. She wasn't prone to second-guessing herself, but, as she waited with no update on Isabella's condition, she couldn't help the sickening feeling that she'd made a mistake. Doubt crept in. Would it have been wiser to take one of the other options that were available to her?

Because Maia did have choices.

She could have taken Isabella to the nearest walk-in centre in Maryville or Crossville. She had dismissed the idea. Smaller facilities tended to keep better records, and unusual early-morning admissions were the kinds of thing that would be remembered after the fact. And Maia didn't want their visit to be recorded or remembered.

She had considered a veterinarian. A gun to the head would have forced him or her to provide treatment. But she had discounted that, too. Isabella's leg was bad, and it would require the services of a skilful orthopaedic surgeon to fix, not a vet she would have to threaten into providing treatment.

She decided that her best option was a town or city large enough to accommodate a trauma hospital. She had also considered Chattanooga, Nashville and Atlanta. In the end, she had concluded that Murfreesboro was the best choice. The city was large, but not too large, and Google revealed that it had a selection of suitable facilities. This hospital was well regarded, was specialised in orthopaedics and had an excellent record of treating uninsured patients. All emergency rooms were legally required to treat life-threatening injuries, and a compound fracture was serious enough to qualify.

The nurse led the way into the orthopaedics department.

A doctor in clean scrubs was waiting for them in a consultation room. 'Good morning,' he said.

The nurse retreated. The doctor indicated that Maia should sit. She took the seat on the other side of the desk.

'I'm Dr Marcus,' the man said. 'I operated on your sister.'

'How is she?'

'She's well,' the doctor said. 'That's sort of why I wanted to see you. There's something about it . . . well, there's something that's a little bit unusual and I was hoping you might be able to help me understand it.'

Maia felt a prickle of apprehension. 'Unusual?' she said. 'How?'

'I'm sorry, Miss . . . I'm sorry, I didn't catch your name.'

Maia had found a passport in Isabella's pocket. It had her picture and said that her name was Jones.

'Elizabeth Jones,' she said.

'Well, Elizabeth, it's like I said – it's strange. We reset Isabella's bones within an hour of her being admitted. A lot of soft tissue was lost – too much for us to close the wound with stitches. So we created what we call a local flap. We rotate the muscle tissue from the lower leg to cover the fracture, then we take a patch of skin from the back and graft it on top of the wound. It's standard for bad breaks – I've performed it dozens of times.'

'I don't understand the problem.'

The doctor ran his fingers through his thinning hair. 'It might be easier if I showed you.'

Chapter Seventy-Five

Isabella had been taken to a private room. The doctor peered through the glass panel in the door and then pushed it open. The girl was in bed. She had been changed into hospital-issue pyjamas and was lying on her side. A cannula had been inserted into the back of her hand, a line dripping fluid directly into her vein. Monitors bleeped, and a readout spiked with every beat of her heart.

'Don't worry,' the doctor said. 'We gave her a little sedative. She needs rest.'

'Can I take her home for that?'

'No,' he said. 'I'm afraid that's impossible. She's going to need to stay for observation.'

'How long?'

'A week? Maybe ten days. She was very badly injured, Elizabeth. She was in shock when you brought her in.'

That was out of the question. The last thing she wanted was to stay in one place for too long; a day would have been too long, but a week was impossible. She had plotted a route to Reynosa in Mexico last night, and she planned to leave for the border as soon as she could. The longer they tarried, the greater the chance that the programme would find them. Maia was armed – she had the M4 in the back of the

Escalade and she was carrying Isabella's Beretta shoved down the back of her trousers – but there was only her. They would send Curry and a team of agents. The numbers, and the odds, would be badly against her.

'Miss?'

'Yes,' Maia said, bringing her attention back to the doctor. She needed to react appropriately. 'Whatever you think is best.'

'I'd like to show you something,' the doctor said.

Isabella was lying on her side. The doctor gently pulled down the sheet to reveal her naked back. A large square wound dressing had been taped just above her lumbar region. The doctor very delicately peeled off the tape and pulled the dressing back.

'We did the operation six hours ago,' he explained quietly. 'We took the flap of skin, together with its blood supply, and reattached it to the wounded area. We needed a lot, so used what we call a fasciocutaneous flap. That means we added tissue and deep fascia so we could fill more. There was a lot of blood, as you'd expect, but it clotted remarkably quickly. *Remarkably.* Once the bleeding stops, the body starts to clear out the damaged and dead cells, the bacteria, the pathogens, everything like that. White blood cells head to the wound and literally eat the bad stuff. It usually takes a day or two, but . . .' He stopped. 'Well, look for yourself.'

The man stood back and allowed Maia to bend down for a closer view. A square flap of skin and tissue had been taken out of the flesh, marked by lurid purple lines where the scalpel had made its incisions. Maia was not trained in medicine, but she had been injured enough times to recognise the stages of healing. The flesh was not as livid as it should have been. It looked clean and fresh.

'I would have said that the operation was two or three days ago, not six hours. It's the same with her leg. The flap has already established itself. I've never seen anything like it.'

Isabella exhaled a deep and relaxed breath. Maia stepped back so that the doctor could dress the wound again.

'Has she ever been hurt like this before?' he asked. 'How does she normally heal?'

'No,' Maia said. 'It's the first time. I can't explain it. I guess she's just lucky.'

'I'm going to take some blood,' the man said. 'I'd like to run some tests.'

'We don't have insurance,' she said, hoping that might help.

'Don't worry – the hospital will cover it.' He laughed and added, 'There might be a medical paper in it for me.'

Maia smiled at his attempted joke. 'Would it be all right if I stayed in here with her?'

'Yes,' the man said. 'Of course. That's a good idea. If she wakes up, just press the buzzer for a nurse.'

Chapter Seventy-Six

Maia put the car into gear and pulled out of the hospital parking lot. She had left the Escalade behind and taken a Nissan Murano. The back of the Escalade was covered in Isabella's drying blood and, that apart, it would have been too hot to risk continuing on with it. The Murano was bland and uninteresting and, by the time it was reported missing, she would be out of the state and well on the way to the Mexican border.

Maia glanced back. Isabella was lying across the seats. She was wearing the dressing gown and slippers that Maia had stolen from a locker while she was looking for a wheelchair that she used to get Isabella out of the hospital. Her leg was stretched out. The fracture had been set and then immobilised with an external fixator. The bolts and screws disappeared into Isabella's flesh, the skin around each wound bruised and livid.

Maia saw that the doctor was right. The leg was healing more quickly than should have been possible. The flesh around the bolts and screws was less livid than it ought to have been. Maia knew what that must mean, but she didn't understand how it could be possible.

The girl had stirred when Maia had scooped her out of bed and put her into the chair, but the sedatives in her blood had quickly ushered her back to sleep. Maia knew that Isabella would be in pain when she awoke, and that she would have to find a supply of opiates to relieve her. There would be a pharmacy on the way. Maia would break in and take whatever she needed.

The thought reminded her: she would need more of her own medication, too. She had injected herself two days ago. The dose would keep her stable for four or five days, but things would quickly become critical after that. She would be too dangerous for Isabella to be around unless she was able to address it.

Maia turned back to the road. They were approaching Franklin.

They were coming for her.

She knew they wouldn't rest.

A sign rushed by at the side of the road. There were thirteen hundred miles between them and the border.

Maia pressed down on the accelerator and the car jerked forward.

If the enemy found them, they were dead.

Crossing the border would help, but it wouldn't stop them.

They were going to have to run and keep running.

Author's Note

Building a relationship with my readers is the very best thing about writing. I occasionally send newsletters with details on new releases, special offers and other bits of news relating to the John Milton, Beatrix and Isabella Rose series.

And if you add your details to the mailing list, I'll send you two free books from my bestselling John Milton series. To join the list, just visit www.markjdawson.com.

About the Author

Mark Dawson has worked as a lawyer and now writes full-time. His John Milton series features a disgruntled assassin who aims to make amends for the crimes in his past. The Beatrix Rose series features the headlong fight for justice of a wronged mother – who also happens to be an assassin – against the six names on her kill list. The Isabella Rose series continues the story as Beatrix's daughter finds herself pulled into an international conspiracy. Mark lives in Wiltshire with his family